Rachel, what are you thinking!

Her cheeks burned as she reined in her thoughts. Cale was so off-limits she needed to stop. Now.

Then she made the giant mistake of glancing at Cale's face to see if he'd noticed her fixation. It was too much to ask for him to be sidetracked by something, anything, else—he was looking straight at her and flashed a heart-gripping smile as if to put her at ease.

Such a beautiful, kind man.

Her sister's man.

Rachel looked away quickly as guilt washed through her and threatened to overwhelm her—and maybe make her puke, to boot.

Focus on the meeting. The benefit. Anything but him…

Dear Reader,

Thank you for picking up *A Time for Us!* This story has been brewing in this brain of mine for a long time, and I'm thrilled to finally share it with readers.

At the outset of the story, Fire Lieutenant Cale Jackson and Dr. Rachel Culver don't know each other well, but they've lived through the same recent tragedy—the death of Rachel's twin sister, who was Cale's fiancée.

Rachel and Cale have plenty of heavy stuff to work through, with grief and guilt at the top of the list. Although grief plays a role in bringing these two together, I like to think that their story isn't sad, but hopeful. It's about finding a love that will get them through the rough times and bring them a lifetime of joy. It's about discovering the promise of a future together.

I hope you enjoy Cale and Rachel's story. Feel free to let me know your thoughts on it at amyknupp@amyknupp.com. To learn more about my other books, including the rest of The Texas Firefighters series, please visit my website at www.amyknupp.com.

Happy reading!

Amy Knupp

A Time for Us

AMY KNUPP

ISBN-13: 978-0-373-71855-9

A TIME FOR US

This edition published by arrangement with Harlequin Books S.A.

For questions and comments about the quality of this book, please contact us at CustomerService@Harlequin.com.

Printed in U.S.A.

ABOUT THE AUTHOR

Amy Knupp lives in Wisconsin with her husband, two sons, five cats and two turtles. She graduated from the University of Kansas with degrees in journalism and French and is a die-hard Jayhawks basketball fan. When the right side of her brain gets overworked from writing, she's lucky enough to be able to switch to the left side as a professional copy editor. She's a member of Novelists, Inc., Romance Writers of America, Mad City Romance Writers and Wisconsin Romance Writers. In her spare time, she enjoys reading, playing addictive computer games and coming up with better things to do than clean her house. To learn more about Amy and her stories, visit www.amyknupp.com.

Books by Amy Knupp

HARLEQUIN SUPERROMANCE

1342—UNEXPECTED COMPLICATION
1402—THE BOY NEXT DOOR
1463—DOCTOR IN HER HOUSE
1537—THE SECRET SHE KEPT
1646—PLAYING WITH FIRE*
1652—A LITTLE CONSQUENCE*
1658—FULLY INVOLVED*
1702—BURNING AMBITION*
1748—BECAUSE OF THE LIST
1789—ISLAND HAVEN*
1813—AFTER THE STORM*

*The Texas Firefighters

Other titles by this author available in ebook format.

Acknowledgments

First and foremost, a big thank-you to everyone who has picked up a book by me and read it. Without you, my excitement to write would seriously wane.

A special thanks to those who have written to tell me how much they've enjoyed one of my stories. Your words never fail to motivate me.

Thank you to Dr. Elizabeth Peck, who I've known for too many years to mention, for your patience and responsiveness in answering my medical/hospital/doctor questions for this story.

Thanks once again to Jim Davies for yet more answers to my still more questions about firefighting and emergency medicine.

Thanks to my mom and dad for being supportive of my writing aspirations ever since my second-grade teacher mentioned I had a knack for it. Mom, thanks for always being willing to brainstorm when I'm stumped, and Dad, thanks for being the comma patrol for all those years. Something somewhere must have stuck.

Thanks to my two boys for being amazing kids who have learned to cook and have saved me numerous times from having to stop writing to feed the fam.

Last and definitely not least, thank you, Justin, for being the person you are—understanding, patient, unselfish and the ideal partner in life for me.

CHAPTER ONE

CALE JACKSON SWORE he saw a ghost.

He blinked hard and looked back down the emergency room hallway from outside the big sliding door.

It was Rachel Culver, he realized, and started breathing again. *Doctor* Rachel Culver, it appeared.

Even once he identified her, he couldn't help thinking she was a striking woman. She was the shorter-haired, serious version of the woman he'd loved. It seemed as if he knew Noelle's twin sister better than he did because Noelle had talked about Rachel so much, with the pride, frustration and love only a twin sister could experience.

Once he recovered from his initial shock, he urged himself forward, helping his partner roll their patient from the ambulance into the hospital. Directly toward his once-almost sister-in-law, who was too absorbed in her clipboard to notice him.

Even though Rachel's chin-length hair was shorter than Noelle's had been, it was the same shiny golden color. Rachel's current intense, focused expression had seldom been found on fun-loving Noelle's face, but they'd shared round cheekbones, a narrow nose and those eyes....

Rafe Sandoval, who'd recently been promoted to paramedic captain on San Amaro Island, started briefing the triage nurse on the accident victim, who was currently in stable condition, as they walked. They wheeled him toward the room at the end as directed, then transferred him to the gurney. Cale slipped outside to start on the paperwork.

Rachel remained at the nurse's station, her hair tucked behind her ear, attention focused on the papers in front of her. He walked up to the opposite side of the counter and debated with himself whether to call her by her first name or Dr. Culver. Before he could decide, she looked up.

Cale braced himself for the deep blue-green gaze, but still, it struck him like an electric current when their eyes met. Beautiful eyes so achingly familiar they made something inside him twist into a tight coil.

Rachel did a double take and put a hand to her chest. Her face registered shock for an instant before she was able to mask it, and she lowered her hand. Threw on a too-wide smile.

"Cale," she said in a voice reminiscent of Noelle's but...lower in pitch and volume. More restrained. *Restrained* wasn't a word he'd ever used to describe his fiancée.

Rachel glanced at the emblem on his uniform shirt. "I didn't realize you were an EMT."

"I'm still a lieutenant for the fire department most days. We do medical rotations once a month." He wasn't sure why he had to throw in that he was an officer. As if he needed her to respect him or something. Some E.R. doctors tended to look down on EMTs, and he didn't want that to be an issue between them. "And you finished med school. Congratulations."

"I did. Mostly intact, even. I'm living at home with my mom for a while, though, so some days it seems like I've regressed."

"Same thing happened to me whenever I used to go

home to see my parents on the ranch. And that was only for a few days at a time."

She frowned sympathetically, but Cale suspected that what she was dealing with, living in a home that was so familiar and yet lacking such a key part of her family, went far beyond the awkwardness of staying at his parents' home as an adult. In fact, if he were honest, it was probably pretty damn similar to the soul-deep melancholy that had come over him the one time since Noelle's death that he'd dared to set foot in the condo he'd bought to share with her.

There was an uncomfortable lull between them. He wanted to say something, to reach out to her, to prolong the moment, but no words came. It wasn't the time or place for a conversation of any substance, anyway. They were connected by tragedy and not much else, but he suddenly had the urge to talk about Noelle like he hadn't since her death. With someone who'd known her as well as he had. Better, even.

Their silence dragged on, and the surrounding din of busy people became noticeable. Now that he was close to her, he could see the shadows under her eyes. Like Noelle, she was barely over five feet tall—she didn't seem big enough to handle this position she'd taken on as an E.R. doctor. Until he noticed the determined set of her jaw. At that moment, he was reminded of Noelle's belief in this woman, and he knew she'd do just fine with her new career. More than just fine.

"Will I see you at the meeting tomorrow night?" he asked, searching for some kind of common ground.

"Meeting?"

"Planning meeting for the benefit. Maybe your mom hasn't had time to tell you what she's doing yet."

"Ah," Rachel said, fidgeting with her pen. "The asthma

benefit. I…I can't give that kind of time commitment right now, what with the new job and everything…."

The flash of sadness in her eyes was so fleeting that Cale nearly missed it, and then she attempted to cover it up with another forced, wide grin.

He nodded as if he understood, though he didn't. Sure, finally becoming a full-fledged doctor after all her years of schooling and residencies and who knew what else was a big deal. Huge. But to use that as an excuse to skip out on organizing the fundraiser that would memorialize her twin sister? He wondered if there was more to that than just being busy and adjusting to her career. Noelle had told him repeatedly that Rachel thrived on stress and being over-scheduled, jokingly referring to her as her Wonder Twin.

Rafe's voice carried from the exam room, pulling Cale back to his task. "Guess I better fill out these forms."

She nodded briskly. "I need to check on patients myself."

"It's good to see you, Rachel," he said without even considering her title this time.

"You, too." She again flashed a smile that didn't quite ring true and then hurried off down the hallway…*away* from the exam rooms where her patients were likely waiting for her. On her way, she passed several of her colleagues and other hospital workers, and it struck him: not one of them acknowledged Rachel with a smile or a hello. She may have grown up on the island, but it appeared that she'd been away long enough to be the new girl. Between that and her sister's death, she seemed to be truly forging her way alone. Something in him stirred, most likely that part that couldn't keep from intervening when someone was having a hard time.

RACHEL BARELY GOT the restroom door closed before she puked her guts out into the toilet.

Cale would be married by now. Happily married to my sister. Maybe even with a kid on the way.

And yet she had the nerve to think how good-looking he was. Only for a split second, involuntarily, but still.

Sweat dotted her forehead, and she sank to the cold, sterile floor in front of the toilet. Her head fell back against the tiled wall as her eyes flickered shut.

Coming back to San Amaro Island was turning out to be torture, in multiple ways.

The grant requiring her to work at Southeast Texas General Hospital, the mainland hospital just across the bridge from San Amaro, for three years after finishing her education had seemed like such a good idea at the time. Though her mom, a cardiologist, made good money and had paid for undergrad, she'd insisted that both Rachel and her older brother, Sawyer, pay their own way through med school. Knowing it would take years to pay off her debt even with the grant, Rachel hadn't hesitated. STGH was a reputable small hospital. One where she could begin to make a name for herself in preparation for the day when she could move on to bigger places.

Of course, everything had been different then. Her sister had been very much alive. San Amaro hadn't been full of haunting memories and choking guilt.

Rachel dragged herself up, supporting her tired body on the porcelain sink. Being home didn't have to derail her. She wouldn't let it. There might be moments when reminders of Noelle popped out at her like deadly vipers when she least expected them. Like coming face-to-face with Cale, for instance. But she'd just have to be ready for them. Steel herself and do what she'd always done—focus on her beloved career.

She ran ice-cold water over her hands and splashed it on her face, thankful she hadn't bothered with makeup when she'd come into work hours ago. She fished out a pack of minty gum from the front pocket of her scrubs, unwrapped a stick and shoved it into her mouth. Her reflection caught her attention—she wore death-warmed-over oh-so well.

Out of habit, she pulled her hair back into a ponytail and held it there, staring at her reflection. Noelle had often worn her hair up in a ponytail and if Rachel squinted, it was her sister she saw gazing back at her now.

Some people might think she was twisted, but she looked for her sister in the mirror frequently. Somehow it comforted her. Made her feel as if she weren't so alone. After several seconds, she dropped her hair, cringing at the dark circles under her eyes. Compared to the nurses who she'd guess were about the same age as her, her eyes looked old.

With a deep breath, she smoothed her scrub shirt and walked out of the restroom, trying to look unruffled. In control. Like she could handle whatever came her way. Medically speaking, she could.

As she turned the corner into the hallway that gave her a view of the nurse's station, she hesitated. Sank heavily against the wall. There he was again—Cale.

He leaned his tall frame over the high counter, filling out some of the endless paperwork that was such a tedious part of both of their jobs. His light brown hair had been lightened further by the summer sun until it was almost blond in spots, and he wore it slightly shaggy and decidedly tousled. His face was rounded, with wide cheekbones and a strong chin. Cale was unquestionably attractive, but it was the caring nature so inherent in his intense green eyes that had sucked in Rachel from the moment she'd met him. She distinctly remembered catching her breath that night more than three years ago at the party Noelle had dragged her to. Rachel didn't believe in love at first sight, but her reaction to him was a testament to instant attraction. And then he'd smiled. When Cale smiled, he went from good-looking guy to *hel-lo.*

As she watched him from afar, his killer smile appeared as he gave his attention to someone out of her line of sight. Rachel took a half step forward to satisfy her curiosity.

Gena Mathers. Of course. The cutest, friendliest person in the entire hospital. The E.R. nurse everyone seemed to like—Rachel included. Gena had welcomed Rachel her first day on the job, while the other nurses had kept her at a distance.

Gena laughed at something Cale said. Rachel wasn't close enough to hear their words over the constant bustle, but she suspected they were flirting. Gena moved from the far counter to the spot where Rachel had stood earlier, near Cale. He'd apparently finished his reports and was preparing to leave. Before he walked away, back to the ambulance, he touched her upper arm and smiled as he spoke again.

A familiar emptiness gnawed at Rachel and she tried to ignore it. But she couldn't deny it—it bothered her that Cale was talking to, maybe even flirting with, Gena.

Was it that he was getting over her sister, moving on with his life? Or was it because he wasn't flirting with *Rachel?*

She forced the thought out of her mind. It was totally wrong. Her feelings for Cale were wrong, both in the past and now.

CHAPTER TWO

CALE WAS STARTING to feel like a stalker by the time Rachel walked out of the hospital the next morning. He'd been sitting there in the early morning sunshine for over an hour, staring at the exit that most of the hospital personnel used, so as not to miss her.

Once again, when she came into sight, he was momentarily shocked by her looks, so similar to Noelle from a distance. As soon as the logic part of his brain kicked in, he recovered and automatically began to inventory the sisters' physical differences. Rachel walked with a whole lot less sway in her hips. Her hair was obviously a different length, and her mannerisms were more precise and economic, whereas Noelle had seemed to flow through life more.

Rachel's shoulders drooped with fatigue. Her blue scrubs were wrinkled, as if she'd camped out in them for several days. For all he knew, she had. Though she was significantly late leaving after her shift, he'd bet she hadn't been chatting it up with colleagues or messing around. Noelle had told him on many occasions what a workaholic her sister was. He got the impression that, on some level, she'd admired Rachel because of it—it wasn't a trait the sisters had shared. He'd liked Noelle's easygoing way. Rachel, at times, put out a vibe of being untouchable, and if he hadn't previously known her outside of the hospital, hadn't seen beyond her all-business shell to the less secure woman beneath, he wasn't sure he'd have the nerve to stake her out now.

He kept his eyes on her as she approached, and when she spotted him, there was a barely discernible instant of hesitation. He wondered if she held something against him specifically, or if that was just more of her don't-bug-me persona. Was it that he reminded her of her sister? Wasn't staying in the house where Noelle had lived a bigger reminder? He didn't care for the idea that he might make her sad.

"Hi," he said as she angled closer, squinting into the already hot June sun. He'd left his sunglasses in his Sport Trac, not planning to be here for this long.

"You're out and about early." She shifted her practical, expensive-looking leather bag from one shoulder to the other.

"Went off duty at seven. Kind of figured you did, too."

"Technically, yes. I wanted to look up some information for a patient." She went on to mention a condition he'd heard of in passing but knew nothing about, seeming to become more comfortable the longer she talked shop.

Cale nodded and tried not to feel dumb. She stopped midsentence, met his eyes briefly, then lowered her gaze.

"Sorry," she said. "Guess I'm preoccupied. So what are you doing here?"

"Waiting for you."

Was that panic or surprise on her face?

"Why?"

He smiled to try to put her at ease, wishing she'd smile back. "Nothing bad. Thought I'd offer to buy you breakfast." He pointed toward the round-the-clock breakfast joint across the street that was usually full of off-duty or on-break medical personnel. Noting her hesitancy, though, he was beginning to lose confidence in his idea.

She stiffened and shielded her eyes from the sun with one hand, managing to hide from him, as well. “I’ve been up for almost twenty-four hours. That’s probably nothing to you, but I’m beat.”

He was painfully familiar with the overtired sensation after a long, drama-filled shift. “You still have to eat, though, right?”

“I hadn’t thought about it, actually.” She placed her hand on her abdomen quickly and looked embarrassed. “That would be my stomach telling me differently.”

“I make you uncomfortable.”

She shook her head and stammered. “It’s just—”

“That’s not my intention at all. We were almost family, Rachel. That doesn’t have to change because Noelle isn’t here.” Damn the lump in his throat.

She was obviously debating with herself as she pegged him with reserved, gulf-blue eyes, and he found himself holding his breath, caring too much about her response. Finally, she nodded. “I could use something more substantial than corn flakes.”

They headed across the parking lot in the direction of the Egg-omaniac.

“Busy night?” he asked.

“That’s one word for it. What about you?”

“Busy enough to keep us up more than we slept. How’d the cardiac-arrest woman we brought in fare?”

“She’s holding her own. We had an elderly man later who wasn’t as lucky.”

“I’m sorry.”

She nodded. “It’s hard to get used to.”

“Tell me about it. Don’t think you ever do completely.” He held up two fingers to the hostess when they walked into the restaurant. “Was it your first one?”

“No. I lost a few patients as a resident. Goes along

with emergency medicine, but then, you probably know that. This was the first one I didn't beat myself up about, though."

"Somehow that doesn't surprise me about you," he said as they followed the hostess to a booth against the far wall. When she whipped her head around to him, he said, "That's not an insult, necessarily."

"You don't really know me." She spoke as they sat on opposite sides of an orange laminate table that had scratches all over it. A couple of nearby tables had single occupants dressed in scrubs, and a noisy group over in the large corner booth was undoubtedly a gaggle of nurses who'd finished the overnight shift, as well.

"Not directly, I guess. Only through Noelle. She talked about you a lot so I feel like I know you better."

"What are you ordering?" she asked abruptly as the hostess placed menus in front of them. She fidgeted with the menu, bending the corner back and forth.

Okay, so she doesn't want to discuss her sister, apparently.

Cale opened the menu and located his usual. "Pecan waffles. Maple syrup. Side of bacon, not crispy."

"If I remember right, it's hard to beat Egg-omaniac's waffles," she said, closing her menu and setting it aside.

The waitress appeared with a pitcher of ice water then took their order.

As they waited for their food, she questioned him about the alarms he'd been on last night, again seeming more at ease with shop talk than small talk. She managed to keep the focus away from herself, he noticed. That only served to pique his curiosity.

"So what else do you do besides work?" he asked when she'd paused to take a drink of water.

"Uh..." She frowned as she set her glass down. "I have

no idea. It's been years since I had free time. I think I lost all my hobbies."

"What'd you do in, say, high school for fun?"

"Study." Her lips, the lightest color of pink and all natural, flirted with a sheepish grin. Finally. "That kind of sounds pathetic, doesn't it? Someday I'll figure out what I like to do in my spare time. As soon as I find some spare time."

He didn't really believe that she'd try. Didn't think she believed herself.

"So tell me why I'm really here," Rachel said, back to her serious self.

Cale refilled both their glasses with water from the pitcher. Took a drink. Removed his silverware from the wrapped-up napkin. He shrugged. "You just seemed kind of alone. I don't know. Noelle would want us to be friends."

"There's no way for you to know that." She stared at her water glass as she said it, speaking so quietly that Cale could barely hear her.

"I know it bothered her that you and I weren't closer. That we didn't have many occasions to get better acquainted."

Rachel's eyes closed in unmistakable pain, making it clear his desire to talk about her twin was going to go unheeded for now.

In an attempt to lighten the mood, he said, "I seem to remember you're a self-proclaimed…what was it? 'Chronic introvert in frequent need of a social rescue.' Let's just say *that's* why I asked you to breakfast."

Her head jerked up, and surprise shone in her eyes as she stared at him. "You remember that?"

RACHEL FELT STRANGELY exposed. Though she could recite almost the entire conversation she'd had with Cale the night she'd met him—which was maybe an hour and a half before Noelle had met him—she'd figured Cale had long ago forgotten it. That was the way it had always been—guys tended to forget all about Rachel as soon as Noelle came along. Her sister had always been one of the most beloved girls around, and Rachel had accepted that—most of the time. When it had come to a few specific guys over the years, it had been tougher to swallow.

She'd been home for a visit three years ago, and Noelle had insisted on taking her to a friend's party, dragging her away from a week's worth of reading that had to be squeezed into the long weekend. Rachel had known succumbing to her sister's pleas for more "sister time" had been a mistake the second they had walked in the door of the ritzy house on the bay. The open-layout main floor had been packed with people—loud, over-happy, in-varying-stages-of-drunkenness people, none of whom Rachel had known. An hour or so into the evening, when Noelle had rushed over to a recently engaged acquaintance to check out her ring, Rachel had escaped out the back door for fresh air.

She'd gone out on a deck that stretched over the dark, calm water, the uncharacteristic early spring chilliness probably to blame—or thank, if you asked Rachel—for the fact that it was completely deserted. She'd just started to relax when the door behind her opened, allowing the raucous noise to hit her before it shut. Huddled in a shadowed corner, she crossed her fingers that whoever it was wouldn't notice her.

He had.

Cale had talked to her. Made her smile. Made her suddenly glad she'd come to the party after all. And he hadn't tried to use a single line on her. Hadn't flirted. He'd been…real. Something Rachel didn't run into every day. The egos of some male med students had always repelled her. Cale's obvious differences were refreshing.

They'd spent a good half hour or more outside talking, just the two of them. Cale had sympathized that she didn't know anyone else at the party, and once he'd found out she was a med student, he'd taken her inside and tracked down a woman he knew who was also studying to become a doctor and had introduced them.

Hence, the rescuer. Her knight.

Later on, when Rachel was chatting with the other med student, she'd watched from across the room the moment Cale had spotted Noelle and had immediately introduced himself to her, no doubt making a comment about the sisters' identical twin-ness. For some reason, Rachel hadn't mentioned it when she and Cale had spoken.

It had hit her then, as she watched the two of them interact, that there was a reason Cale hadn't flirted with her. She wasn't the type of girl whom guys flirted with. Not like Noelle was.

The waitress chose that moment to set their Belgian waffles in front of them, forcing Rachel to snap out of the trip down memory lane.

"You don't need to rescue me anymore," she said as she selected the blueberry syrup and poured it over her plate. "I can take care of myself."

"Some people need to be rescued from themselves." He'd jabbed his first bite of waffle but paused with it hovering over his plate, dripping maple syrup, to send her a penetrating gaze.

"Me?"

"No." He straightened and popped the food into his mouth. "Course not. Just a general comment."

When she continued to stare at him, trying to discern

whether it really was a general comment or an accusation, he shook his head.

"Really, Rachel. Didn't mean anything by it. The capable, competent Dr. Rachel Culver absolutely, positively doesn't need to be rescued from herself." He grinned and she found it hard to be annoyed. "As far as I know. I reserve the right to amend that statement at any time."

She couldn't help laughing quietly, in spite of her fatigue, in spite of not wanting to let herself have a good time, as she shook her head.

"So the benefit..." Cale said, switching gears so fast her head spun.

"That again," Rachel muttered, renewing her focus on her food.

"I'm surprised your mom hasn't roped you in yet." He smiled and looked sympathetic as he said it, but there was sincerity behind the words.

"Yeah. She tried. She's..." Rachel shook her head, unsure what, exactly, she wanted to say. Unsure why she'd started saying anything about her mom.

"She's what? Probably happy as hell to have you back."

Rachel shook her head, staring off at nothing as she thought of the uncharacteristic distance between her and her mom these days. *Happy* was not the word she'd choose. It was as if her mom had lost her focus on the important things or something. "She's changed. Noelle's dea—" She shook her head again, unable, or maybe unwilling, to say the words. "My mom is just different now."

Cale studied her too hard as he continued to wolf down his breakfast. "It's tough, all the way around. Some days, I wake up, and I don't immediately think about it. About Noelle and what happened. And then, *wham,* it hits me, and for a minute, it's like it's new again." He swallowed. Grasped his glass without taking a drink. "Going to these meetings for your mom's benefit has made Noelle top of mind, and that's not easy. I get that, Rachel. Like you wouldn't believe."

Rachel was about to remind him that she was too overwhelmed with her job when he stuck his palm out toward her and nodded. "I know. New job and all that. You don't have to defend yourself to me."

"I'm not being defensive," she said, swirling her waffle through a puddle of syrup.

"I know." He flashed her another smile. "It's cool. The event itself is going to be pretty amazing. Has your mom told you about it? That we got Tim Bowman?"

"She did mention that." Several times in her attempts to sway Rachel.

Tim Bowman was the local boy turned rock star. He was a few years younger than Rachel, but San Amaro was a small place so she'd known of him vaguely before he'd hit it big. She had to admit it was a genius idea for a fundraiser.

As Cale continued on about all the details, Rachel only heard a fraction of what he said. She was too busy reassuring herself to concentrate on the conversation.

She'd only been in her job for a week. She'd taken on an extra shift already and planned to take as many more as she could get approved for. Her goal had always been to position herself well so that at the end of her three years at STGH, her résumé and her reputation would stand out. That was a tall order, but she specialized in tall orders. Always had.

She was legitimately too busy to become involved in a huge volunteer event. Even if it was to memorialize her twin sister.

She'd support it by going, but that was all she could give right now.

As she pushed away her half-eaten breakfast, she forced herself to tune back into what Cale was saying. When he'd finished everything on his plate—and hers, after she'd offered it—she threw enough cash on the table to cover both their meals and a tip. And then she wasted no time getting out of there, away from Cale's penetrating eyes.

CHAPTER THREE

RACHEL HAD BEEN back on San Amaro Island for just over a week, and already she was getting tired of waking up with Yoda staring her in the face instead of in her own bed. Especially considering the way-too-realistic figurine, and the headboard of the captain-style bed it was perched on, belonged to her thirty-six-year-old surgeon brother, Sawyer. Granted, he hadn't lived here in their mom's house since he'd gone off to college, but would it be so hard to pack away the decor? At least the pieces with eyeballs? Her mom hadn't touched the bedroom Rachel and Noelle had shared, but that was different. Rachel wasn't about to tackle that project, either. Which was why she started each day with the Wise Green One staring her in the face.

The next thing she became aware of was an aroma teasing her nostrils. Food. Really good-smelling food. Her stomach rumbled automatically and she registered that it was empty. The Belgian waffle from this morning, with Cale, was history. How the heck long had she been sleeping? She drowsily checked her watch then sprang upright. Double-checking the digital clock on the headboard shelf, just inches from Yoda himself, she verified it was after 6:00 p.m. She'd collapsed in bed at 9:47 a.m. and had been asleep moments later. Eight hours straight of sleep? She wasn't even sure she'd moved at all during that time.

Unheard of. And, in her mind, unforgivable. Who had time to lie around all day?

She had reading she wanted to catch up on, and she needed to check in to see how one of her patients from last night had fared. But first…food.

Who the heck was cooking? Nowadays in the Culver house, waking up to a home-cooked meal was like waking up on a different planet. Noelle had been the cook in the family—the only one. Rachel's sister had taught herself the skill when they were twelve, probably out of self-preservation. Prior to that, fried chicken from a box and bright orange mac and cheese had been status quo. Since Noelle's death, as far as Rachel knew, the kitchen had been rarely used.

She ignored the pang in her chest at the thought of her sister, the feeling that she should be able to walk down the stairs to the kitchen and see her twin slaving over the stove as she hummed an off-key tune.

She frowned when she did, in fact, enter the kitchen to find her mother clearing the counter of what appeared to be a full meal—some kind of pork chop dish with onion slices on top, broccoli with cheese sauce and a potato casserole.

"You're up," Jackie Culver said with a smile. "I didn't want to wake you."

"I meant to be up hours ago. What's going on here?" Rachel indicated the kitchen with a sweeping gesture.

"I've kept some warm for you, sweetie." Her mom opened the microwave and took out a plate of food.

"Where'd it come from?"

"What do you mean where did it come from?"

"It's… You don't cook."

Her mom laughed as she scooped the remaining broccoli into a storage bowl. "I learned. I try to cook three or four nights a week. It's just been an unusual week since you got home and this was my first opportunity."

"And you let me sleep through it." There was no accusation in Rachel's voice, just an observation. She was kicking herself for not setting her alarm, frankly, but not because she was worried about missing any meals.

"You apparently needed it. You worked a double shift?"

Rachel nodded and sat down at the table, salivating at the plate of food her mom set in front of her. She popped a piece of cheesy broccoli in her mouth. Her mom sat across from her. Perplexed, she stared at her mom as she chewed.

"Do I have food on my face?" Jackie asked, touching her fingers to the corners of her mouth.

"Drop of cheese beneath your collar," Rachel said. "How long did this take, Mom?"

Her mom shrugged. "Less than an hour. The meat had to simmer for quite a while, otherwise it would have been faster. It was no big deal."

"That means you had to be home from work…before five?" Rachel couldn't keep the scandalized tone out of her voice.

"My four-thirty canceled. There was no reason to hang around."

Rachel narrowed her eyes at her mom and jabbed a bite of pork.

"You like it?" Jackie continued.

"It's…fantastic." The quality of the food was so not the issue here. "You never mentioned you'd taken up cooking."

Her mom had never so much as shown an interest in food or the preparation of it, beyond fueling her driven body so that she could work some more.

"You've barely been home since you moved back," her mom said.

"Before that."

Jackie chuckled, crossing her arms over her chest. "You haven't exactly talked to me a lot, Rach."

"You know how crazy busy I've been, finishing my residency, getting ready to move back…"

"I know. I hope…" Her mom shook her head and left the sentence dangling. "I worry about you is all."

Rachel laughed incredulously. "Mom. *What* are you worried about? I made it through med school. Top of my class. I've got the job I've always wanted." Or a variation thereof. "This is what it's all about. You know that! I've made it."

Her mom knew it because Rachel had followed in her mom's footsteps almost exactly, with the exception that her mother's specialty of choice was cardiology instead of emergency medicine. Medicine was in the Culver blood. And though Sawyer was different in a lot of ways, both Rachel and her mother were type A, driven, almost obsessive about their careers of choice. It was something Rachel had always admired in her mother, something that made them closer, this similarity.

Except…her mom was *worrying* about her? Was that an effect that losing Noelle had had on her?

Warily, she affirmed, "I'm good, Mom. Are…you?"

Another similarity they had was the dislike of getting too personal with conversation. Neither was touchy-feely, neither was prone to emotional outbursts other than the random overtired temper tantrum here and there. It made Rachel uncomfortable to ask such a prying question.

"I'm doing really well, Rach." Her mom's voice sounded happy, but…two years ago, leaving the office a half an hour before it even closed would have been unheard of for Dr. Jackie Culver.

"Okay, then," Rachel said skeptically. "I'm glad. Just a little freaked out by your new hobby."

"Do you like what you're eating or not?" Her mom gestured smugly to her half-empty plate.

"I'm completely impressed, as I said." Rachel couldn't imagine the hours it must have taken for her mom to become comfortable in the kitchen when, previously, toasting Pop-Tarts had been her specialty.

Her mother stood. "Okay, then. Less questioning, more eating. I need to get going."

It took Rachel a few seconds to remember what day it was and where her mom must be going. The meeting. To plan her sister's memorial benefit.

The food she'd wolfed down so far settled like a rock in her gut, and her instinct was to push the plate away. That, however, would make her mom suspicious. More than suspicious.

She waited for another round of how-great-this-is-going-to-be-you-should-join to begin. Her chest tightened and she felt unreasonably hot all of a sudden. She should have tried to get an extra shift tonight. *Every* Wednesday. That would stop the badgering, the pleading, the guilt….

Well, no. Nothing would ever stop the guilt. Any of it.

Instead of trying yet again to get Rachel to go with her to the meeting, Jackie merely ran a dishrag over the counter, rinsed her hands and put her remaining lemonade in the refrigerator to save for later. She headed toward the kitchen doorway, no doubt to freshen up in the master bath before she left, as she always did. Rachel was almost home free when her mother stopped. Turned to her.

"Rachel—"

"I'm not going, Mom."

They stared at each other, and she could see in her mom's eyes she wanted to say so many things, wanted to run all the arguments past Rachel again, wanted to draw her into her crusade. Then her mom surprised her with a smile and a loosening of her shoulders.

"I was just going to tell you to save some food for your brother. I promised him leftovers for lunch tomorrow. He's coming over to clean out the garage on his day off."

Rachel breathed.

"I'm not going to push you anymore. About the benefit. I understand it's hard for you to face right now. It'll get easier, sweetie."

Then her mom did something unheard of. She strode over to her daughter, brushed Rachel's hair behind her ear, leaned down and kissed the top of her forehead.

The quiet understanding was more than Rachel could stand. She fought the tears that threatened with every fiber of her being, forced them back, sucked in oxygen to equalize herself. Her mom pulled away, finally, and Rachel felt her staring at her. Assessing.

Dammit. She couldn't meet her gaze, not without giving away too much. Not without letting on that her mom might have hit the nail on its head.

HER MOM HAD LEFT the house ten minutes ago, and still, Rachel, who hadn't moved from her place at the kitchen table, couldn't get a full breath.

In spite of her very acceptable stated reasons for not participating in the planning of the asthma benefit, both Cale and her mom had jumped to the same conclusion. They both believed she couldn't handle the task emotionally. They both believed that, in spite of the fact she'd just started a brand-new job—heck, her new *career* that she'd been working toward for years—in spite of the long hours, the double shifts and the learning curve of how this emergency department functioned, in spite of it all, they'd both basically accused her of not being able to face up to the task of memorializing her twin sister.

Maybe if they'd left it unspoken, it would have been easier to let it go. She could have allowed them to think what they would and gone on with her busy life. But they'd said it out loud, both of them, separately. That didn't sit well with her.

Shaking her head in frustration, she pushed up out of her chair with more force than necessary. She took her empty plate to the counter, dumping the pork bone in the trash on the way, rinsed the dish and silverware and put it all in the dishwasher. Ignoring the nagging voice in her head, she scrubbed at the countertop her mother had cleaned less than thirty minutes ago, going after a stain that had been there since she and Noelle had painted their bedroom in honor of their sixteenth birthday. The stain had faded, but it was still clearly the electric green from Noelle's side of the room.

Her jaw ached from the tight set of her teeth, and she consciously loosened it. She closed her eyes and tried to reason with herself.

In spite of eight hours of deadlike sleep, she still felt as though she was running on empty. It pained her to acknowledge that her job was kicking her ass this first week. Didn't matter if that was normal or expected by other people—she wasn't other people.

Beyond her fatigue, she no doubt looked like hell. She strode into the hall powder room, checked the mirror and verified. Yep. Her blond hair was tangled from sleep, the usual precise, off-center part looking more as if someone had thrown up a shovelful of hay and let it fall every which way. Her eyes…ugh. She widened them, tried to fake them into looking alive, but the weariness in her bones was reflected back at her from blue eyes that looked like neither hers nor her sister's. The eyes of a stranger.

Her clothes—an old pair of cutoff denim shorts and a faded SeaWorld T-shirt her mom had brought back from a conference aeons ago—weren't appropriate for leaving the house, let alone for going to a meeting of any kind. Come to think of it, she had no idea what *would* be appropriate. She spent 90 percent of her time wearing scrubs and tennis shoes. She could restart a human heart, but when it came to fashion, she was about as savvy as a four-year-old boy.

She stood there arguing with her reflection for an eternity, and then, recalling one more time how Cale and her mother had been so infuriatingly understanding, she went in search of a less-faded T-shirt, ran a brush through her hair and stormed out of the house.

RACHEL HAD THOUGHT the worst part of the meeting would be walking in and sitting down, especially since, by the time she'd worked up the courage to go, she was late.

She'd been grossly mistaken.

Not wanting to jolt everyone in the library meeting room by looking so obviously identical to the girl they were memorializing, she'd pulled out an old ball cap—a White Sox cap, no less, which her Cubs-fan sister would never have deigned to touch—that she'd long ago stuffed in the glove compartment of her Honda. She'd kept her discount store-special sunglasses on, as well. Disguise master she wasn't, apparently. When she'd walked into the room of fifteen people sitting around a long conference table, she'd taken a seat along the wall, behind the row of chairs at the table, so as not to interrupt. But there had been whispers and looks anyway. Confusion, surprise, sympathy. A couple of people—one of whom was Cale—had shot her quick, welcoming smiles, and then she'd pointed her eyes at her mom, who was speaking, in an attempt to block everybody else out.

Her grand entrance, however, wasn't the worst part. The worst part was that, as she sat there, minding her own business and trying to focus on the discussion…she felt Noelle there. Not in a spooky, ghostlike way. It was hard to put into words, but just the knowledge of why they were all gathered in that stuffy room, volunteering their time—to create a memorial for Noelle and maybe help make it so someone else could avoid her fate—made Rachel shiver. Noelle was just…there. In her thoughts, in her consciousness. And that caused a lump the size of a baseball to lodge in her throat. A throbbing began in her temples, and Rachel spent a painful fifteen minutes blinking and fighting not to tear up. When the woman in front of her shifted in her seat a little, allowing Rachel a view of a folder on the table, she felt as if a wrecking ball had collided with her gut.

On the folder, someone—apparently Trina Jankovich, one of Noelle's close friends and the person the folder sat in front of—had taped a full-color photo of Noelle, tanned and happy. It was a candid and looked to have been taken at a party or a bar. Noelle's long, blond hair had been curled at the ends, she wore expertly applied, smoky shadow around her eyes and her smile was 100 percent natural, not forced at all. In short, Noelle looked gorgeous and so full of life. It was one of the best pictures Rachel had ever seen of her twin, and that was saying something because Noelle was as photogenic as an adorable baby panda bear.

The tears that had been threatening like a tropical storm finally hit. The lump in her throat expanded and seemed to seal out any oxygen from getting to her lungs. With a covert swipe at her eyes, Rachel checked to see if anyone was looking at her. A fruitless attempt because she couldn't see through the stinking tears, anyway.

She gathered her notebook from her lap, bowed her head and got the hell out of the room before it could shrink in on her and swallow her up.

CALE HAD BEEN surprised to see Rachel walk in to the meeting room after the way she'd paled when he'd brought up the subject. He'd been strangely happy she'd made it—until he'd noticed she once again looked as if she might pass out.

Her plan to sit on the outskirts of the group and remain as anonymous as possible had only partly worked. Distancing herself from the group had been a start, but if she thought the hat and glasses threw anyone off of her identity for even a second, she was mistaken. It just happened to be a sympathetic crowd. He'd bet everyone there had wanted to allow Rachel her privacy—a fact that was proven by how they all went out of their way to not stare or whisper. Everyone but him. He'd found it difficult to stop watching her—maybe because, in spite of the half-assed disguise, she was so similar to Noelle in looks, if not manner.

Throughout the forty-five or so minutes she'd been there, Cale had kept an eye on her, gauging her reactions to what was said, watching her fight to keep it together. When her mom had stuck her on the publicity committee with him, Eddie and Cale's sister, Mariah, she'd pulled her hat a little farther down over her eyes and barely nodded her acknowledgment. As the meeting had proceeded, Rachel had become further removed and more emotional, her gaze turning downward. When she'd finally retreated, he hadn't been too surprised. Just concerned.

He'd noticed her purse soon after she'd hauled ass out of the room. From his place at the far end of the table, he could see the plain black leather bag on the floor next to the chair she'd been sitting in. Instead of taking off after her, he'd counted on handing it to Rachel's mother after the meeting and letting her take it home to Rachel. The older Dr. Culver, however, had ended up being called away to the hospital less than five minutes after Rachel had taken off and had left Erin, who served as her right-hand woman, to finish up the last few minutes of the meeting.

As everyone began packing up their supplies and chatter rose around the table, Cale jumped up and grabbed the purse without a second thought. He knew the Culver home well. It was no big deal to drop it off on his way home. By the time he got there, surely Rachel would have regained her composure.

He had no desire to intrude on her when she was so overwhelmed by sadness, and hopefully getting out of the meeting had done the trick for her. Even though he inherently understood her sadness—or maybe *because* he understood it so well—he wasn't a fan of trying to comfort an upset woman. Former almost-sister-in-law or not.

CHAPTER FOUR

CALE ALMOST MISSED Rachel on his way out the back door of the library. If it hadn't been for the sudden slosh of water against the embankment—an uncharacteristic sound on the relatively placid bay side at night—he would have walked right on by.

When he automatically glanced out at the water to see if he could spot the boat responsible for the ripple, her blond hair blowing in the slight breeze caught his eye, even though she was camped out on one of two Adirondack chairs deep in the shadows. There was no hiding that hair short of absolute darkness.

Being intentionally noisy so he didn't give her cardiac arrest, he followed the short path toward the chairs, which sat a few feet from the man-made shore. In daylight, the area, lined by flower beds and native plants, made a peaceful place to sit and read a book or watch the fishing and pleasure boats come in after a day on the gulf. It was one of several spots scattered along the bay on the city property that also held the library. All the others were deserted now that the library was closed and the sun had gone down.

"Not much to see out here at this hour, is there?" he said as he approached.

In spite of his heavy steps, Rachel's shoulders jerked when he spoke. Cale lowered himself into the chair next to her, but she didn't spare him a glance.

"You might be surprised." Rachel's voice was ragged around the edges, alerting him that she was still emotional.

It was too late to escape now. Besides, he wasn't that much of a coward. And there was that part of him that felt compelled to ease her troubles somehow. Especially if he could do that just by sitting with her.

A wave, invisible in the dark, splashed the shore again. "Fishing boat go through?" he asked.

"Yacht. Headed for the marina."

As Cale's eyes adjusted to the darkness, he was able to make out the serene surface of the bay. He watched for action of any kind—a fish jumping, a kayaker—but nothing broke the smooth, glasslike surface for as far as he could see. "So what are you watching?"

She turned her head halfway toward him but didn't make eye contact. "Just…this." With her arm, she gestured toward the entire expanse of water in front of them. "It's so…tranquil. Beautiful. I forgot how much I love the bay."

Cale grinned and leaned forward, her purse still grasped in his left hand. "Noelle used to say how opposite you two were. She'd be bored out of her skull sitting here staring at nothing, wouldn't she?"

"She could watch the waves on the other side of the island for hours, like a movie marathon," Rachel said quietly, a wistful smile in her voice. "She claimed to love the drama. So fitting for her."

"And you crave the peace," Cale said.

Apparently uncomfortable with the personal turn, she stiffened her shoulders.

"Why aren't you on your way home?" Rachel asked, the wistfulness gone completely.

"I brought you this." He held her purse out between them.

Rachel frowned, as if upset she hadn't even realized it was missing yet, and took it from him. "Thanks."

"Your mom got called in right after you left, otherwise I would have had her take it home."

"I saw her hurry past to the parking lot. I hope everything's okay with her patients."

"She didn't say, but if I had to guess…"

Rachel nodded. "Probably not, if she got called in."

"The publicity committee—of which you're now one fourth—is supposed to meet Sunday afternoon at two to go over our next step."

"I'll have to miss it. I'm working a double." There was no regret in her voice.

"Another double?"

"They schedule me for night shifts exclusively—I'm guessing because I'm the newbie. Most nights, there's not much action. I could probably squeeze in a nap here and there if I were the type. If I don't take extra shifts, my brain is going to rot away from lack of action and I'll forget everything I learned in med school."

"If you work yourself to exhaustion, your brain won't work right, anyway."

She didn't respond, and the noises of the night began to filter into Cale's brain in the quiet. There was a slosh of water just south of them, probably a fish beneath the dock at the Lug Nut Bar. A frog had taken up residence somewhere nearby, singing his heart out, looking for a girlfriend or whatever it was amphibians did when the lights went out. Then he noticed Rachel's index finger rhythmically scraping over the wooden arm of the chair repeatedly. It was a nervous action, one she might not even have been aware of, but after several seconds of it, it seemed to cut into the night's tranquillity. Cale reached out and put his hand gently over hers to end the sound.

Rachel stopped her finger at the first contact. Even more telling was that she didn't move any other muscle, didn't so much as look at him. Tension came off her in waves.

"I know that was hard," Cale said, nodding his head vaguely to the building behind them. He noticed the roughness in his own voice. "Sitting through that..."

"It wasn't hard. It was...fine."

"The meeting was fine," he repeated, stunned at the blatant untruth. "Then why did you leave early?"

Several seconds ticked past before she replied. "I needed air."

"It gets easier, Rachel. Takes a couple of meetings, but eventually it gets better."

He waited for her to say something, but the frog was the only one to make a noise.

He tried again, unsure why he was pushing the matter. "You *will* get to the point where you're no longer sitting there, shell-shocked, thinking how fundamentally wrong it is to be planning a memorial *anything* for a woman who was so alive. So damn full of life."

"Right. Sure." Rachel pulled her hand from under his and didn't even bother to try to sound convinced.

"The meetings turn into something to do," he continued. "A list of somethings that need to be accomplished, so you won't always be thinking so hard about the reality, the enormity of what that concert on the beach really signifies."

She bolted out of her chair—as much as bolting out of an Adirondack was possible—and took four steps to the edge of the shore. Arms crossed, her back to him, she searched across the bay for who knew what. Obviously, he'd pushed too far, rattled on to put her at ease too much, but when you got down to it, he'd barely said anything of substance, barely scratched the surface.

It struck him as odd—concerning, even—that she was so resistant to any talk of her sister. Almost as if she wore a hard shell over her skin so that everything he said just bounced off. Almost.

"It's late," Rachel said tightly. "I'm gonna go home." With a self-conscious glance at him, she took off up the path toward the parking lot. "Thanks for bringing me my purse," she added over her shoulder.

Cale opened his mouth to say something, but no words came out. He didn't know what to say to this woman who was so clearly in need of…something. She was messed up, and that was putting it mildly.

It didn't concern him. Wasn't his problem. And yet… Noelle would have wanted him to do whatever he could to ease her twin's transition to life back in San Amaro. He was fairly certain Rachel had no one to talk to, no real friends now that her sister was gone. She seemed to need someone. And maybe it was the part inside of him that made him a rescuer, but, Noelle's wish or not, he wanted to somehow help Rachel cope.

RACHEL FOCUSED ALL HER energy on even, unhurried steps all the way to the car. Cale hadn't gotten to her. The meeting hadn't gotten to her. Nothing could get to her unless she allowed it to.

Yeah, she couldn't even convince herself of that this time.

She got in the car and pulled the door shut, ensuring her touch was gentle in an effort not to slam it. Sucking in a slow, measured breath, she put the keys in the ignition and started the engine. She calmly pulled the gear stick into Reverse and got the hell out of the well-lit library parking lot and away from Cale.

For the duration of the drive home, she worked to compose herself. The lump in her throat grew so big as she tried to block out everything Cale had said that it caused her pulse to pound in her temples. She could no longer breathe, couldn't swallow. God…she couldn't stand this.

She lowered her window and the cool wind that rushed at her helped a little. When she finally was able to inhale again, it was a shaky, shallow breath. As she exhaled, she pounded her fist on the steering wheel.

She was not going to succumb to tears. Not. Going. To. Cry.

In the year and a half since that awful night, she'd not lost it yet. Had not had a single crying jag—and she wasn't about to give in now. Because Rachel was pretty damn certain that if she weakened for an instant and let the first tear fall, she would never, ever be able to stop.

CHAPTER FIVE

RACHEL'S HEAD WAS still spinning Saturday morning from her mother's frantic departure—to play eighteen holes of golf, of all things—when her brother, Sawyer, sauntered through the back door.

"Another day off?" she asked from her perch on the kitchen counter, where she was eating a gourmet ham and three-cheese omelet her mom had whipped up. "I wanna be a surgeon when I grow up."

"You wouldn't be tall enough to reach the operating table, shorty." Sawyer winked and tossed his keys on the table. He opened the refrigerator to hunt down some food. The way he ate, he should have weighed four hundred pounds.

"I came to finish up the garage from hell. Only made it about halfway through the other day. What's up with you? Just get off work?" he asked, eyeing her scrubs.

"No. These have just permanently melded with my skin, so I don't need to worry about changing clothes anymore."

He nodded knowingly. "How was the night in the E.R.? Busy?"

"Extraordinarily slow until about five a.m. Now I'm so keyed up I don't know if I'll be able to sleep."

"Good thing you can run on no sleep, just like Mom. Where'd she run off to, anyway? I saw her tearing around the corner in her car."

Rachel jabbed a bite of omelet with her fork and shook her head. "The woman I used to know as my mother was on her way to play golf."

Sawyer emerged from his refrigerator search with a fat carrot. As he noisily crunched a bite off, Rachel couldn't help laughing to herself at the boyish image he presented. No one would ever guess he was a brilliant surgeon who could pretty much write his ticket to anywhere if he only wanted to. His ash-brown hair reached almost down to his collar in back and he was wearing a baseball cap backward on his head. She couldn't remember the last time she'd seen him without a healthy goatee, shaggy enough it was clear he hadn't just forgotten to shave for a couple of days, but not dense enough to call a beard.

"Is Tatiana Goodwin playing with her?" he asked.

"Who's that?"

"Mom's archenemy on the course. She pretty much always beats Mom, and Mom's on the perpetual warpath."

"I don't know the first thing about it," Rachel said. "I kind of got stuck on the fact that Mom is getting all recreational. Golf? Really?"

"It's a good sport."

"The mom I remember doesn't play sports. She doesn't play at all. It's like living with an alien."

He laughed as he finished the carrot and went back to the fridge.

"You think I'm kidding," Rachel said, twisting forty-five degrees so her legs dangled off the counter. "It's like she's a different person, Sawyer. Makes me wonder if she's got a brain tumor or something. Has she had a checkup lately?"

"A little med school and a lot of imagination are a bad combo." He shook his head as if she was crazy. "Mom is healthy. How can you look at her and think otherwise?"

"It's not so much the way she looks. She's leaving the office early. Playing golf on her days off. *Golf,* Sawyer. That's not just a fifteen-minute pastime between patients. It's a game where people actually age significantly between the first and last holes."

Sawyer laughed again. "Glad to see you haven't lost your sense of drama."

"I'm not the dramatic one—" She froze and the silence in the kitchen practically buzzed with the truth her statement pointed to.

Rachel had never been the drama queen. *That was Noelle.*

Before too many uncomfortable seconds ticked by, Rachel hopped down from the counter and rinsed her plate off in the sink. "It's not just the golf and the leaving-the-office-early things. She's cooking, too. Real food. Gourmet omelets. Three-course meals."

Sawyer narrowed his eyes at her for a second, just long enough to let her know he'd noticed her panicked change of subject. "What's wrong with cooking? From what I've seen, she's gotten pretty damn good. Almost good enough to make me want to move home again."

"You can't. Your bed is taken."

"I figured. What's the big deal about Mom, Rach? She's doing okay."

"It's just that she's…not Mom anymore." She put her plate in the dishwasher, closed it and busied herself running her finger over the ancient paint stain on the countertop. "It's all been since Noelle…" Again, she broke off, shaking her head. "It messed her up."

"It messed all of us up. How could it not?" Sawyer said, his voice going gravelly with sadness. "But Mom's doing okay, Rachel. Really. She's…learning how to live, I think she called it. Finally. It's a relief to see, believe me. She was bad enough before, working killer hours. After Noelle died, Mom was putting in so many hours at the hospital and her office she didn't even sleep in her own bed half the time."

"That's the mom I know, though. That's who she is… or always was. She loved her career."

"She buried herself in her career to avoid thinking about things. Facing them." Sawyer peeled back the top of a container of yogurt. "Kind of like someone else I know," he said gently.

"Hello, brand-new career here." Rachel started her spiel practically on automatic pilot.

"I don't just mean now. But it is harder to avoid the big ugly truth of what happened when you're here on the island. Damn hard to avoid it living in this house."

Amen to that. She wanted nothing more than to block out thoughts of losing her twin sister, her best friend, her other half. But every day when Rachel got out of bed from the relative safeness of the Yoda haven, she was accosted the second she exited her brother's bedroom—by *the door.* The closed door of the bedroom she and Noelle had shared. The room where Noelle had been living on that night…

"I'm not trying to avoid anything," she fibbed, knowing he spoke of much more than a stupid six-panel wooden door. "I'm just…trying to cope the best way I know how."

Sawyer tugged affectionately at several strands of hair near her shoulder, something he'd done to both her and Noelle since they'd been toddlers. "You and Mom are alike in so many ways. Always have been."

"Yeah, well, she lost me with golf."

"Who knows. Maybe in six months, you'll be teeing up, too."

"I'll trust you to commit me to a nice, white padded room if so."

Sawyer didn't bother to grin at her admittedly lame attempt at humor. Instead, he went all serious on her. "I can't begin to imagine what it's like for you, being her twin. It was hard enough as the big brother who couldn't protect her." He paused, swallowed hard, and Rachel could see his pain, there in his eyes. "But I do know this. You're a strong person, just like Mom. You'll get through this okay. As soon as you let yourself stop avoiding and allow the healing to begin, you're going to be fine, Rach."

His words made a wave of nausea swell inside of her, but she tried to ignore the nasty feeling. "Sawyer?" she said, tilting her head and attempting a grin. "You make a much better surgeon than shrink."

"Sucks when your big brother has mad wisdom powers, doesn't it?"

His irresistible grin was all that kept her from throwing a sharp object at him.

Sawyer tossed the now-empty yogurt container in the trash and headed for the back door. "I'm off to fight the evils of the Culver garage."

Which meant Rachel was once again left alone in the house. It was a big house, but thanks to her brother's little speech, she could barely get a full breath of air. Even though that closed door was up a flight of stairs and down a hallway, she could feel it from here, taunting her. Challenging her. Calling to her to face up to what lay behind it.

Luckily for her, she'd found a new-to-her website filled with case studies on seizures that she was itching to read. Without going up the stairs, she threw some sandals on, grabbed her laptop and left to study…anywhere but here.

Cale set down the four hot pizza boxes in the center of the crowded patio table and collapsed into the last empty striped-cushion chair on his parents' new balcony overlooking the Gulf of Mexico. His younger sister, mom and dad were flanked by Clay Marlow, Evan Drake and Dylan Long, Cale's firefighter buddies who'd spent the past two days helping with his parents' move.

"It's official," Cale said to his mom and dad. "Your first meal in your new home. Welcome to San Amaro Island."

"I'll drink to that." Evan held up his bottle of beer, and those who had drinks clinked their bottles and glasses to his. "Hope you love it here on the beach."

"What's not to love?" Mariah, Cale's sister and roommate, said, glancing out at the waves and the sand that stretched almost up to the condo building. From the sixth floor, they could see for miles out into the gulf on a clear day like today.

"It's a big change from the ranch," Ted Jackson said in his brusque way as he pulled his wheelchair closer to the table, his eyes on the food.

Ronnie, Cale's mother, stood and leaned her short, round frame over the table to begin serving. She might be hundreds of miles from what she knew as home, but this table was technically hers, and she wasn't one to allow anyone else to take charge of a meal under her roof. The role of ranch wife was ingrained in her as much as her love of the horse figurines that had filled six medium-size moving boxes and weighed as much as a submarine. "We'll get used to it eventually, I'm sure. Who wants veggie deluxe?"

"Is there any meat on that at all, ma'am?" Clay asked suspiciously.

"Might as well just pass it my way." Mariah reached for the box of vegetarian pizza with a smug grin.

"That's not real pizza," her dad informed her. "Need some beef on there or you won't get full."

Clay and Evan voiced their agreement.

"I'm not picky," Dylan said to Mariah with a hungry look Cale wasn't sure was directed solely at the food. "Don't go assuming that's all yours."

"Could it be? A man with some self-control?" Mariah said. "We don't have those in our family." She took two slices of her sacred, meat-free pie and handed the box to Dylan as her dad grumbled at her.

"I didn't say a thing about self-control." Dylan served himself. "Just thought I could get a slice of veggie faster, while those three dolts hem and haw over what flavor of cholesterol they want first." He nodded toward his friends.

Cale's mom doled out two giant slices at a time to the guys—one of the many reasons Cale knew she was the best mom in the world. Her pineapple upside-down cake recipe was another.

"Who needs more to drink?" Ronnie asked before sitting down to her own plate.

"I've got it, Mom. Relax," Cale said. He took requests and went inside and loaded up on bottles for those who needed them.

"I don't know how we would have done this move without you kids," Ronnie was saying when Cale came back outside. "We're so very thankful…." She raised her glass of ice water to her lips in an attempt to hide her emotions.

Cale squeezed her shoulder supportively as he retook his seat next to her. His mom put up a brave front, but he knew how hard the past few months had been on her, what with his dad's tractor accident and subsequent health deterioration, having to close down the farming-implement store that'd been in the Jackson family for three generations, and now relocating to the island, where Cale and Mariah could help them out more easily.

When Cale had first suggested the move, his mom had protested as loudly as his dad had. Neither of them had ever lived outside of the twenty-mile radius from the farm store. They'd lived on the same ranch for the forty-some years they'd been married. But as the months had dragged on and she'd become responsible for more and more as her husband got worse instead of better, she'd had to face reality. Had to admit she couldn't do it all anymore, couldn't handle the ranch, pared down though it'd become, and couldn't keep telling her husband and children she was okay when she wasn't. She'd needed support, both physically and emotionally. It'd taken Cale almost a year, but he'd finally convinced them to purchase this condo.

"It was nothing, Mrs. J.," Evan said. "Moving you in was the easy part. Looks like Cale's going to stay busy with all the handyman projects you mentioned."

The place was mostly handicap accessible, but there were a couple changes Ted insisted on, like a lower counter in the bathroom and a wider doorway to one of the spare bedrooms he planned to use as a den. Plus there was the list of updates Cale's mom had made before she would agree to put an offer on the place. Cale had promised to do the work himself, even though his mom and dad were sufficiently flush after selling the implement business and the ranch and could have easily paid a professional to do the work. His mom refused to have a bunch of "strange workers" in her home, and Cale was determined to do whatever he could to make their transition easier.

"Yeah, are you sure you can handle everything yourself?" Mariah asked him, pegging him with a meaningful look.

"Looking forward to it. You know I like to do projects." As soon as he said the words, he wished he could take them back and change the subject. He realized his sister was thinking about his own condo—the one he hadn't managed to get back to remodeling since Noelle's death.

"I wasn't aware of that, no," his sister said, keeping her tone light. That didn't prevent the heavy feeling of dread that settled over him.

"Are you still working on your condo?" his mom asked, managing to sound slightly outraged with a side of scolding. "I assumed that was finished long ago, Cale."

"I've…" A rock lodged itself in the bottom of Cale's gut. "I had to take a break from it when Noelle died."

Sympathetic looks from Clay and Evan made him sit up straighter. "As soon as I get done here, it's probably time—okay, past time—for me to get back to it. It's been so long that I don't really remember everything I have left to do." Time and a mental block had taken care of that for him. All he knew was that the last time he'd gone there, he'd left, well, a mess, to put it mildly.

"How can you live in a place and not remember what needs to be done, son?" Ted nodded toward the box of hamburger pizza and waited for his daughter to push it his way.

"He's been living with me," Mariah said. "I needed the help on the rent, and he needed to get away. Believe it or not, we do pretty well as roommates."

Cale sent her a look of thanks for making it sound like no big deal.

"You pay rent at your sister's and a mortgage on your place?" his dad asked in disbelief.

"Just a little rent." And it'd been worth every damn penny. After Noelle's death, just walking into the beach condo they'd planned to share as soon as they were married had been like a knife to his chest.

"It works, Dad," Mariah said.

"I'm glad you two can get along. There were days when you were little that I wondered," their mom said.

Bunking with Mariah had worked—too well. It'd been the easy way out for him, he realized now. Cale mentally kicked himself for taking her hospitality for granted. He'd overstayed his welcome, no matter how gracious his sister acted.

He felt as though he'd been through hell, but more importantly, he'd made it "back." After spending more than a year grieving Noelle and wondering when he would be able to return to some semblance of normalcy, he'd made a lot of progress and started moving toward getting his life on track. He'd made an effort to be more social, to go out with the guys from the station when they invited him, to stop hiding out in his private quarters at the station all the time. He'd even been set up on a couple of dates, although he had no intention whatsoever of getting further involved with either of the women he'd gone out with. Or any woman, for that matter. It'd be years before he could even think about that—if ever. But the dates had been a major step for him.

And yet, with all the positive action he'd taken in an attempt to settle into his life without Noelle, he'd ignored one of the biggest aspects.

His first obligation was to get his parents' projects

done as he'd promised, but then…maybe it was high time to face the memories he'd been avoiding and get to work on his own home.

CHAPTER SIX

RACHEL CONSIDERED HERSELF a lot of things—and not all of them were good things—but a coward was not on the list of traits she'd ever claimed willingly.

Early Sunday afternoon, after her mom had fluttered off to a dolphin cruise with her sudden group of friends, Rachel stood outside *the door.* The closed door to her childhood bedroom. Noelle's bedroom. She grasped the knob but then dropped her unsteady hand as if she'd been burned.

Damn her brother for pointing out her preference for avoidance. Though he hadn't mentioned her untouched bedroom out loud, this intricately grained, six-panel plank of oak had become like a living, breathing enemy for Rachel. One she could mostly ignore as long as no one accused her of being scared of it.

She wasn't going to be scared of it anymore. It was just a room, a hundred and fifty square feet of stuff. Things. Items that she'd assigned too much importance to. The room only had as much significance as she gave it. Noelle was *not* in that room.

With a frustrated grunt at herself, she straightened and stepped back up to the door. She inhaled deeply and held the air inside her lungs.

Just a slab of wood leading to a room.

She twisted the knob and pushed the door open with so much force it bounced off the wall and back at her.

She smacked the door back to the wall, funneling all her freaked-out anticipation into it.

As she took in the room and its contents, she felt as if she had all the air knocked out of her.

Nothing had been touched.

The twin bed to the left—Noelle's—had the hot-pink-and-purple polka-dotted sheets strewn about and the pillow cattywampus, as if Noelle had just crawled out of it twenty minutes ago. The heel of one beaded flip-flop stuck out from under her bed, and her countless makeup containers littered the dainty vanity table along the wall that Noelle had long ago outgrown but had continued to use.

Rachel's half of the room was neat, as always, her bed made and a reading lamp and digital alarm clock the only items on top of her nightstand. Everything in the two-toned room—on both sides—had a thick layer of dust covering it.

It was amazing how their two lives and their sisterhood were so accurately summed up and displayed in this one room. The room was an L shape, and three walls, those on Noelle's side, were painted electric green, but the color was barely visible with all the wall hangings—a couple of movie posters starring one of Noelle's celebrity crushes, a wildly colorful print of a Brazil street during Carnival, a two-years-out-of-date beefcake calendar of male dancers given to Noelle by her friend Trina and a bulletin board full of candids of Noelle and her friends from over the years.

Rachel's three walls were a light, mellow, coral color interrupted only by a single item on two of them—a print of one of Monet's lily-pad scenes done in muted colors and a photo Rachel herself had taken of the glasslike bay at dawn. A window took up much of the third wall.

She and Noelle had separated the space with an invisible diagonal line down the center, from one corner to the other. The door was on one of Noelle's walls, and Rachel remembered the time they'd been arguing about who knew what and Noelle had informed her the door was off-limits since it was in her part of the room. Rachel had just as stubbornly declared the single window to be her property and had made a point of lowering the blinds and closing the windows to lock out the incessant island breeze—exactly the opposite of the way her sister had liked it. The standoff had lasted until Rachel had needed to go to the bathroom and had threatened to pee just over the line on Noelle's side. And she would have, too, because all was fair and reasonable when it came to an argument between the twins. And yet, neither one of them had ever petitioned to move to the extra bedroom that had always served as their mother's home office because, when you got down to it, in spite of all their differences, they were a unit. They were "the twins."

Rachel fought to swallow, then she slowly backed out of the room and gently closed the door.

She'd been right about one thing—her sister was not in the room. But that victory was hollow, because what was there was something even harder to face…it was the leftovers of a life that should still be going strong. A freeze-frame view into Noelle's existence on that awful day. Rachel wondered if her sister would have left things differently had she known it would be the last time she was walking out of the room. Would she have straightened her shoes? Made her bed? Lined up the makeup neatly?

Squeezing her eyes tightly closed, Rachel struggled against the tsunami-force wall of emotions trying to level her. She shook her head and repeated to herself that she wasn't letting it in. Not today. Not for as long as she could hold it at bay.

When she was able to breathe evenly, without the telltale shakiness, she walked away, down the stairs, out the back door. Though she was wearing shorts and a T-shirt, she did a shallow dive into the family pool, which was seldom used but painstakingly maintained by a weekly pool boy, and swam underwater to the opposite end. When she surfaced, her back to the house, she hitched her elbows on the side of the pool and forced her mind back into the present moment.

Opening that door and peering into the bedroom from a distance was all Rachel could handle for now. That was going to have to be enough for today.

IF RACHEL HAD been the one to die and Noelle had lived instead, Noelle would have handled things so much differently. So much better. Noelle would never have failed her sister so completely.

Those were the words Rachel repeated to herself as she stood on the seashell welcome mat outside Cale and Mariah's apartment waiting for someone to open the door.

There were multiple voices from within, becoming louder, and then the knob turned. Mariah Jackson, a willowy redhead whom Rachel had met only a couple of times before, looked momentarily shocked at the sight of Rachel. She caught herself quickly, though, and smiled. "Hi, Rachel."

There was no mistaking the surprise in her voice.

Before Rachel could respond with anything besides a hello, Cale came barreling into the entryway.

"Hey, Rachel. What are you doing here?"

"She's here for the meeting, you twit," Mariah said.

"Did I get the time wrong?" Rachel asked in a rush of anxiety.

"No, no, come on in. Eddie, our third...*fourth* member, is in the other room. We just got started. It's good to see you. Other than the meeting, it's been a long time...."

Since the funeral, Rachel silently filled in.

"I thought you had to work today," Cale said as the three of them walked through the living room into the open dining area.

"I thought I did, too, but apparently the schedule god is determined that I stick with the slowest, most mind-numbing shifts. He nixed the extra shift and gave me a lecture about overdoing it. I suspect my brother paid him to do it."

"Really?" Mariah said, her voice sounding scandalized.

"I doubt it, but I wouldn't put it past him."

"Isn't brotherly love just...fabulous?" Mariah said drily. "Rachel, this is Eddie Vandermeyer, our fearless leader and the only one of the three of us who really has any clue about publicity. Eddie, Rachel is—"

"Noelle's sister," he said as he stood and shook her hand. "Honored to meet you, Rachel."

"Nice to meet you," Rachel said, a little flustered over his use of the word *honored.* It was little stuff like that that made her really squirm at the idea of working on any part of this fundraising project.

Noelle would do it for you in a heartbeat—with a genuine smile on her face.

The thought reminded Rachel to force a smile of her own. "Sorry I'm late. It took me a while to sort through my mom's notes to find out where you guys were meeting."

"Help yourself to a drink from the fridge," Mariah

said. "We were just talking about ticket sales. It's been two weeks since we announced the event and it looks like the initial rush to purchase is over. We've sold just under five thousand tickets. Not bad considering the population of the island, but we have the capacity for more than double that."

Rachel went to the refrigerator and took out a bottle of iced coffee, listening to the others discuss ideas to broaden awareness of the event beyond San Amaro. Eddie was a marketing consultant, and apparently was involved with Mariah somehow, judging by the way the two kept touching. He had a boatload of ideas, making Rachel wonder why her mom had thought this committee needed another member. Or maybe the fact that they *didn't* really need an engaging, idea-filled member was exactly why her mother had stuck her here.

"Did you find out if we can set up a booth at the Thursday free concerts?" Cale asked Mariah as Rachel wandered back to the dining room.

Mariah flipped the page in her planner and perused it. "I'm supposed to get the final word tomorrow but it looks like it'll be approved. If so, I'll be there this week with flyers and tickets."

Opening her bottle, Rachel took the fourth chair at the table and told herself this was just another meeting. Just another project. Nothing personal. Nothing to make her feel as if she was about to be presented to the firing squad. "What can I do to help?" she forced herself to ask.

"I like this girl," Eddie said, eagerly tapping on his electronic tablet. "Let's see…we've got a few flyers up but we need to get more posted. Anywhere. Everywhere you can get the okay. Mariah, hand her a stack. Then there's the radio shows. I've got dates with all the morning shows in the area, but I could always stand to have someone come with me."

"Flyers sound good," Rachel said without hesitation. There was an expectant silence as they seemed to wait for her to say more. "I'm not really your radio girl. Consider me the socially challenged of the group."

She held her breath, but her reasoning was apparently accepted by Eddie, as he nodded once and checked his notes again. Mariah, on the other hand, continued to watch Rachel, making her fidget with her bottle cap.

"I can go with you on the days I'm not working," Cale said to Eddie. As was his way, he smoothed things over for Rachel, compensating for her insecurities. Just like he had that first night she'd met him and she'd been nervous about the party full of strangers. She'd liked that about him from the first moment. "Just email me the schedule."

"You know what would be great…?" Mariah said, still looking at Rachel, her mind obviously going full speed. Some kind of premonition hit Rachel a split second before Cale's sister continued. "What if you were to say a few words at the actual concert?"

"Me?" Rachel said, a dozen alarms screaming in her head.

"Kind of a mini memorial speech. A couple lines about your sister, like whether Noelle would have enjoyed the concert or the beautiful night, or whatever would be appropriate. Something personal, as her twin sister. That would have an impact on a lot of people."

Iced coffee and sugar churned in Rachel's stomach and threatened to come back up.

"Mariah," Cale said sharply, protectively. "It's Rachel's first meeting. Why don't we try not to scare her away." He said it with a half grin, but there was no mistaking that he was genuinely worried. And while there was a corner of Rachel's mind, or maybe her heart, that reveled in his innocent protectiveness, the rest of her—every fiber—saw the truth in his eyes. He didn't think she could handle it. The meeting, the concert, any of it. She'd seen the same expression in Sawyer's eyes on more than one occasion, and she hated it.

But they were right—no matter how much she was loath to admit it.

The silent doubt of others may have pushed her to go to that first planning meeting last week, but there was nothing in the universe that could get her to stand up in front of thousands of people and speak about her sister.

"Just a suggestion," Mariah said, filling the silence. "A genius idea if I do say so myself, but Cale's right. No pressure."

Again, a heavy expectance hung in the room—they were waiting for her to respond. Rachel made the mistake, as she placed the lid back on her bottle and slid it away from her nervously, of meeting Cale's gaze. Of seeing his sympathy. That set off her defenses like nothing else could, and she mentally recoiled from even pondering the possibilities.

"I…I don't think so." She shook her head emphatically one time. "I just don't think I could do it. Not without losing it and embarrassing myself completely."

"It would be so amazing," Mariah gushed, as if she hadn't heard Rachel's answer. "It'd be hard but we'd be there with you. Behind you all the way." She reached across the table and grabbed Rachel's wrist lightly. Over-enthusiastically.

"She said no, Mariah." Cale leaned forward, steel in his voice.

"Okay, okay." Mariah released Rachel's arm and sagged into her chair like a chastised puppy. "Got it, big brother.

You can relax." To Rachel, she said with an embarrassed half grin, "Sorry. I get carried away sometimes."

"Sometimes?" Cale said. "Like a shark sometimes goes after a drop of blood?"

"It's okay," Rachel said quickly, hoping to prevent an ongoing battle between them. She just wanted the subject dropped completely.

Thankfully, Eddie seemed to grasp her intentions and moved on to discussing TV appearances and other godawful things. Cale and Mariah were easily swayed into changing the subject, but Rachel was unable to pay attention to much of anything. She'd hit overload at the mere thought of Mariah's suggestion.

On the bright side, she checked her watch and realized her work shift started in less than five hours. She could get away with going to the hospital an hour early or so, under the pretense of getting ready for her shift. With any luck, maybe the emergency room would be hopping tonight—it was a full moon, after all—and she could enjoy a good twelve or thirteen hours of escape from the nagging thoughts that she was somehow failing her sister.

CHAPTER SEVEN

EMERGENCY MEDICINE WAS a live, ongoing demonstration of the saying "You win some, you lose some," Rachel thought as she got into her car after her shift ended Tuesday morning.

She had become well acquainted with that reality as a resident and had received all kinds of advice on how to handle losing patients. Generally speaking, she was able to swallow a patient's death more easily if she was secure in the fact that she'd done everything possible and had made no mistakes in her treatments. She knew she wasn't God. The kids were the hardest to take, though. Even if she'd done every procedure called for and administered treatments that nine times out of ten would work, she couldn't walk away from a child who'd lost his or her fight without feeling as if she'd had a reminder from the universe that "fair" had nothing to do with anything.

The seven-month-old girl who'd suffered a venomous bite had been particularly hard to take last night. Didn't matter that too much time had passed before her parents had brought the baby in, or that the treatments Rachel had given the baby had only a slim chance to succeed. After calling that beautiful girl's death a few hours ago, Rachel couldn't reason her way out of the anger or the sadness that had weighed her down ever since.

She started the car but couldn't bring herself to put it into Reverse to go home. These days, home offered no comfort, a fact that was especially true when Rachel found herself there by herself. It was too quiet. She was too sensitive to the fact she hadn't so much as looked at *the door* since she'd opened it on Sunday morning.

Knowing her mother would already be at work, Rachel finally pulled out of the hospital lot, drove the short distance to the bridge, crossed to the island and drove right on past the turn that would have led her home.

Just the sight of the old, increasingly lopsided, formerly bright yellow boathouse had Rachel sitting up straighter and breathing more easily. Why hadn't she managed to come here since she'd moved back to San Amaro?

There were a handful of other cars in the gravel lot but not a person in view as she made her way to the door of the boathouse. Taking solace in the hand-painted Come On In sign that was almost as old as she was, Rachel felt her burden lighten as she opened the screen door.

"Holy moly, look what the beautiful day dragged in. My eyes must be failin' me."

Rachel couldn't help smiling at the sound of that familiar gravelly voice, even though she wasn't able to make out the man sitting in the deep shadows yet. "Buck!" she said, moving toward him as her eyes began to adjust to the low light.

"Rachel Culver, I have half a mind to kick you outta here. Saw in the newspaper you were back in town bein' a doctor at long last. Guess you have better things to do than tend to your boat or visit an ornery old man."

"Oh, stop it," Rachel said, grinning from ear to ear. "I'm here now, ornery old man." She waited for him to gain his feet, holding her hand out to steady him.

"Not only are you about five years past due, but you're late. It's almost eight a.m. Sun's been up for hours."

"I just got done with a shift at the hospital. I came straight here."

"Eight a.m. will have to work just fine, then."

Buck grasped both of her hands and studied her, working his jaw as he did. Rachel took the opportunity to size him up, as well, drinking in the sight of him. He'd aged more, but then, he had to be in his mid-nineties by now. Other than being a little more stooped over and having a few extra sun-roughened wrinkles, he looked the same as always. His faded yellow T-shirt said Buck's Boat Rentals, and his skinny, knobby-kneed legs jutted out from baggy, wrinkle-free khaki shorts. He wore his usual sports sandals and life-loving, sunken-in grin.

At last, he nodded his approval at what he saw, so Rachel did the same. "Looking good, Buck Winfrey. Life must be treating you right."

"Can't complain. Got a full boathouse and my whittlin' keeps me busy." He nodded to the cluttered end table next to where he'd been sitting. Now that Rachel could see in the lower light, she spotted a piece of wood and some tools. "You here to get out on the bay?"

"I am," Rachel said eagerly, glancing down the rows of boats for a glimpse of her blue-and-green kayak. "It's been way too long."

"Come on, then," Buck said, leading the way to her storage space at the opposite end of the third row.

"How's Bob?" Rachel asked, eyeing the shadowed corner where the two sides met the ceiling. The darker spot wasn't recognizable, but she knew it was the resident bat.

"Happy as can be. Bugs are keeping that ol' bat well fed this year. Won't be long before he's too fat to fly."

"That wouldn't necessarily be a bad thing, in my opinion," she said, casting one more nervous glance toward the corner.

Rachel helped Buck free her kayak from its rack, surprised as always by his strength, which was so incongruent with his bony, slightly hunched body. "I got this," he said. "You gonna wear those doctor clothes out on the water?"

She hadn't even stopped to think about her lack of a swimsuit or suitable kayaking clothes. Her scrubs were comfortable but…

"I got somethin' for ya." Buck motioned with his head toward the door she'd come in through. Rachel followed him and helped him lower the kayak to the dirt floor, leaning it against the wall by the door.

Buck walked over to the wall behind the open door and started digging through a large, open cardboard box. "Here we go." He faced her with a victorious glimmer in his eyes. "Think this'll work? Ladies' medium. Might be a little big on the likes of you, but I didn't order anything smaller. Would've if I'd known you were gonna show up."

He held up a yellow tank with Buck's Boat Rentals on the chest.

"Looks perfect to me. Thanks, Buck. I'll change into that and roll up my pants. It'll do."

"A Buck's shirt will more'n do, young lady. I don't give them out for free to just anybody! Them are twelve-dollar shirts."

"Well, then, I'll pay you twelve dollars when I get my purse out of the car."

"No, you will not. It's a gift, just for you, Miss Rachel. Now, you get changed and then we'll get you on the water."

There was no arguing with Buck. Never had been. Rachel took the shirt and tried not to show any reluctance whatsoever to go in the tiny restroom Buck had installed in the boathouse corner years ago. It was no bigger than the bathroom on an airplane, with barely enough room to turn around, let alone lift her elbows to change her shirt. And the cleanliness factor, or lack thereof... Rachel closed her eyes, breathed through her mouth and put the tank on as fast as humanly possible. She burst out of the tiny space and struck what she thought, in her fashion-moron way, might be a modeling pose before Buck could tell she was gasping for fresh air.

"That's some damn good advertising," he said. "Be better with some of them puny little shorts to show off your legs, but we can work with the doctor pants."

"Nobody will be seeing me in 'puny little shorts' any-time soon." Rachel bent over to roll up her scrubs.

While she'd been in the restroom, Buck had retrieved her two-sided paddle—she was impressed he could put his hands on it so quickly since she'd been away so long—and was holding it up like an oversize walking cane.

"You ready yet?" Buck said good-naturedly.

She straightened and eyed her beloved boat. "Like you wouldn't believe."

"Need help?"

"I've got this," Rachel said as she picked up her kayak and headed for the dock.

She set the boat into the water and climbed in, scoring no points for grace, but she didn't care. The second she was floating, she felt some of her tension leave her body as if a pressure-release button had been pushed. Buck handed her the familiar, orange-tipped paddle and she pushed off the dock with a wave.

With every dip of the paddle, Rachel relaxed more. The bay was shallow here and clear enough to see to the sandy bottom. She watched for fish, just as she always had, as she began a calming, rhythmic pace with the paddle, from one side to the other. A gull screeched from the shore behind her. In the distance, she could hear the captain's voice over the intercom on a tourist boat as it set out on one of its daily fishing excursions. The gentle splash of her paddle hitting the water with each stroke mesmerized her. Took her further from her cares and worries. By the time she made it to the middle of the bay, the professional fishermen had left shore hours before and the dolphin tours were not yet under way. She was gloriously alone in her favorite place in the world.

With her back to the bridge that spanned the bay, Rachel stilled. Breathed in. Closed her eyes briefly in gratitude for the peacefulness around her as it seeped into her bones.

Noelle had never gotten it. She'd kayaked with Rachel plenty of times but swore it was dull on the bay. Whitewater kayaking would have been much more her style, though Rachel was pretty sure her sister had never gotten the opportunity to try it. Rachel had tried countless times to explain how being alone in a single-person boat out in the middle of the bay was soothing and restorative to her.

"There's nothing to do but think out there," Noelle had said more than once. "It's like the water magnifies your problems and that's all that exists. There's nothing to distract you from whatever's eating away at you. It could drive a girl to drink."

Noelle had never understood Rachel's explanations. For Rachel, the solitude and the closeness of the water had the opposite effect—they took her away. They allowed her to set all her other thoughts aside, to be drawn out of her own problems into the quiet drama of nature. She could sit for hours watching for fish, looking for bubbles in the water, stirring the water with her paddle without a care as to where she drifted. The gentle sounds the water made against the boat soothed her, cleared her mind. Noelle had loved the wildness of the gulf side of the island, the turmoil and the nonstop commotion of the waves smashing continually on the beach. Her favorite place to be whenever she'd been upset was in the middle of the crashing waves. Rachel grew agitated if she watched the never-ending waves for too long.

She dipped her fingers into the tepid water, closed her eyes and raised her chin so the sun could beat down on her and color her skin. Several feet away, a fish splashed, forming ripples on the otherwise placid surface. She cleared her mind and just…was.

It was much later—an hour? Two?—when she noticed her shoulders were pink and the boat traffic from the marina out to the gulf was picking up. As she gazed south to the other side of the bridge, she spotted two competing dolphin tours heading out south toward where the bay and the gulf intersected. A growl from her stomach reminded her she hadn't eaten since an early dinner before her shift last night. Reluctantly, she dipped her paddle in to turn the boat toward the shore.

She'd be back much more frequently, now that she remembered the therapeutic value of passing the hours in the kayak. Though paddling back to the dock was the last thing she wanted to do, at least now she felt as though she could handle life and whatever it threw at her.

CHAPTER EIGHT

"HEY, STRANGER," Sawyer Culver called out as Cale made his way from the street to the Culver garage late Tuesday morning. "Haven't seen you for several months. What's the occasion, man?"

"Just your lucky day," Cale said. Sawyer set down a large, obviously heavy cardboard box on top of another at the edge of the garage and held out his hand for Cale to shake. "Looks like you're having a blast here."

Sawyer, who wore a sweaty T-shirt and old gym shorts, wiped his forehead and gave Cale a look that said otherwise. He shook his head. "My mom hasn't cleaned out the garage for years. I still don't know what the hell I was thinking when I offered to do it."

There were a dozen or so boxes stacked on the driveway and a couple in the back of Sawyer's pickup.

"Somebody moving out?" Cale asked, immediately thinking of Rachel.

Sawyer shook his head. "Making a Goodwill run. They'll either be thrilled when they see me pull up or sorry as hell."

Cale frowned and swallowed hard. "Is this some of Noelle's stuff?"

"Naw." Sawyer shook his head, his mouth open as if he were searching for words. "No one has even started to go through her belongings yet."

Blinking in confusion, Cale tilted his head in question.

"Crazy, isn't it?" Sawyer said.

"It's been…a long time." Long enough that it seemed as if someone would sort through her things and at least pack them away even if they couldn't bear to get rid of them yet.

"Don't I know it." Sawyer lifted another box from the ground up into the back of the truck. "I'd do it, but you know as well as I do that I'd do it all wrong. My mom refuses to take care of it herself because she thinks Rachel should be in on it since they were so close. Rachel… well… First off, she's been at school until recently."

"And second?" Cale asked, curious to learn more about his fiancée's twin sister.

"Second, she's been the queen of avoidance lately, at least when it comes to anything relating to Noelle."

"Gotta be hard to lose a twin."

"Hell yeah. Probably as hard as losing a fiancée." Sawyer paused and gave him a sympathetic look. Cale turned away, gazed up the street at nothing in particular. He'd worked through two tons of baggage and grief, but that didn't mean he liked talking about it.

"I think that's why we don't push her. But she's not…" Sawyer shook his head. "Who knows. Rachel has to handle things her own way, I guess. I worry about her constantly. Curse of the big brother."

"I hear you." He couldn't imagine having to watch Mariah go through something so tough. "Is she here? I actually stopped by to see her."

"Rachel?" Sawyer eyed him curiously for a moment. "She hasn't come home from work yet, as far as I know." He glanced at his watch. "I have no idea where the hell she is. She should be here anytime. Should've been here a couple of hours ago."

"She's dedicated to her job."

Sawyer scoffed. "That's one word for it. She won't listen to me about that, either, though."

"Stubbornness seems to be something the Culver twins had in common."

"Hell, Cale. The stories I could tell you about those two..." Sawyer became quiet as if the subject were getting to him. He lifted the closest box and headed for the back of the truck again.

Cale had no words to offer. He knew it was best not to say more about Noelle unless Sawyer wanted to pursue the conversation. He walked over to one of the boxes, pointed to it and asked, "This one going, too?"

Sawyer merely nodded and said, "Thanks, man."

They were just about done loading all the sealed boxes into the truck when Rachel pulled up beside it in her ancient Honda Accord.

Cale couldn't deny that his heart sped up in an inappropriate way as he watched her make her way toward the garage. Must have been an ingrained reaction and some part of his brain hadn't figured out this was Rachel instead of Noelle yet.

Rachel looked more tousled than he'd ever seen her. More like Noelle, he couldn't help noticing. Her hair was windblown, her cheeks and shoulders lightly sunburned, and her wrinkled clothes were damp in places. Obviously she hadn't come straight from work.

"Where have you been, wild girl?" Sawyer asked.

When Rachel spotted Cale in the shadows of the garage, she faltered, slowing her steps but then covering the reaction quickly. She turned and searched out his Sport Trac, parked across the street.

Instead of answering the question, Rachel narrowed her eyes, took in the load of boxes in the truck and faced Sawyer. "Are you moving back home or something?"

"Sorry to disappoint, but no. This stuff is on its way out."

"Hi," she said, finally acknowledging Cale.

"Hey. I was guessing overtime but the outfit says otherwise."

"I took my kayak out after work."

"You fried," Sawyer said.

She glanced down at her shoulders. "Mildly pink is all. The trip wasn't planned. I didn't take any sunscreen. Buck gave me the shirt."

"And you forgot a brush, too." Her brother yanked lightly, affectionately, at the tangled strands next to her face.

"Kayak hair looks good on you," Cale said, grinning. "Definitely a different side of the multifaceted Dr. Rachel Culver."

"Are you two best buddies now or something?" she asked, ignoring Cale's comments and heading toward the back stairs to the house.

"Naw, we can't stand each other," Sawyer said. "He's here to see you."

Again, Cale could swear he saw her falter. "Got a few minutes?"

"If you don't mind my eating lunch."

"Give him a beer, Rach. I owe him for helping me."

"We don't have any beer, but there might be some tea or lemonade." She spoke over her shoulder as they went up the steps.

Cale couldn't help watching her ascend from the back—what guy wouldn't? Her rolled-up scrubs were baggy and did their best to hide any curves, but the sunlight shone just so through the back windows of the garage, giving him a hint of the outline of her thighs and hips. She'd tucked in the too-big tank, which highlighted the narrowness of her waist. Her shoulders and arms were sculpted and firm, making him wonder when she had time to work out.

"Your arms and shoulders are different from Noelle's," he said without thinking.

Rachel reached the top of the stairs, opened the kitchen door and stared at him, clearly not thrilled with his observation.

"Yours are more muscular," he continued, hoping that the compliment would smooth over the fact that he had no place comparing anything about the two sisters, let alone parts of their bodies. It seemed an insignificant victory that he'd avoided blurting out his observation that Rachel's hips didn't swing as much as her sister's. Nor that he found the lack of sway…intriguing.

Obviously, Cale had been alone for too damn long if he was starting to notice his fiancée's sister's body.

"My arms were always stronger," Rachel said matter-of-factly, as if they were discussing the color of the pansies in the whiskey barrel in the backyard by the pool. "I started kayaking when I was ten." She set down her work bag and her folded scrub shirt then opened the refrigerator. "Good God, a quiche?" She picked up a round pan and sniffed. "The woman made a quiche. On a Tuesday. My mother has lost her mind."

"I guess there could be worse repercussions than a quiche."

"Want some?" she asked as she pulled back the plastic wrap and investigated. She took down a saucer and served herself a slice.

"No, thanks. I went to breakfast with a couple of the guys after we got off work. Bad habit."

Rachel stuck the plate in the microwave and started it. "You worked last night? Were you guys busy?"

"Yesterday was nuts. It seems the new batch of weekly tourists is hell-bent on destruction. We had a car fire, a teenager who fell from a second-story hotel balcony and a Dumpster fire within a five-hour time span."

"Must have been leftover full-moon stuff," she said wistfully. "The E.R. was hopping Sunday night but last night was long. I actually got some research reading done between patients." She opened the fridge again. "Sun-brewed tea—probably pomegranate, knowing my mom—milk, or diet cola?"

"I can help myself to water." Cale went to the cupboard with glasses before she did and helped himself.

"I forgot you know your way around our house."

He'd spent as much time here as he had at his own place. "It's been a while. Rachel..."

The microwave beeped and she took out her food. "Yeah?" she said without looking at him, instead digging for a fork from the drawer and then jabbing a corner of her wedge of quiche.

He was about to speak when she put the bite in her mouth and yelled. "Damn! I cooked it too long." She fanned the air in front of her mouth as if that would cool the piping-hot bite on her tongue. Cale slid his glass of water to her, and she took a drink and gave him a grateful look.

"Thanks. Can you hold that thought and give me two minutes to change my clothes while my food cools?"

"Go right ahead."

"Make yourself comfortable," she said as she rushed from the room.

Cale took a swallow of water and looked around at the familiar kitchen. It *had* been a while since he'd been here. Since the day of Noelle's funeral, now that he thought about it. The Culvers had had people over after the service for a meal made up from the dozens of dishes friends, neighbors and even Noelle's mom's patients had brought with them. Nothing had changed since then, as far as he could tell.

He wandered toward the living room, glancing up the stairs as he passed by them to see if Rachel was on her way down yet. All three doors in the hallway were closed.

He was drawn to the bank of grade-school photos on the stairwell wall. He'd gone by these pictures countless times in the past, but he stopped and studied the ones of Noelle and Rachel again. He knew which sister was which in every single photo because he'd been fascinated with the subject soon after he and Noelle had started dating and she'd made a point of quizzing him for fun. But now he looked more closely, searching for differences between them.

Up through second grade, the girls looked as if they could be the same person dressed in different-colored, similar clothes. Their hair was the same length, styled the same. From third grade on, though, it was evident they'd started showing their opposite personalities in earnest. Rachel's hair was always the shorter of the two and neater, as well. Her clothes were more conservative, in less vivid, less noticeable colors. Noelle's smile was bright and natural in every last photo. Rachel looked as if someone had been holding a gun to her head off camera and threatening her if she didn't smile.

One of the doors in the hall opened—Sawyer's bedroom door, Cale noticed in his peripheral vision. Not Rachel's room. He frowned and recalled his earlier conversation with Sawyer.

"I hated those things," Rachel said, gesturing at the photos as she came to the top of the steps. "I could never figure out how to smile on cue and make it look real. Obviously." She shuddered with exaggeration as she studied her fifth-grade mug shot.

"My hair was always, without fail, a mess in grade school," Cale said.

"Guys' hair is supposed to be a mess. Try having everyone and their grandpa compare your picture to that of your perfectly photogenic twin sister's. As you can see," she said as she gestured to the row of photos with a sweep of her hand, "Noelle's turned out twenty times better than mine did every single year. I used to kind of hate her for that...until report cards came out and I trumped her every time. Of course, she claimed to not care about grades."

Rachel whisked by him, down the stairs and back into the kitchen, leaving no question she was on a mission for food. That was the thing about Rachel, he was noticing—she always had a purpose. Noelle had been more of an in-the-moment kind of girl.

He silently reprimanded himself to stop comparing the twins. There was no comparison. Rachel was Rachel, a very competent, serious brainiac. Noelle was the woman he had loved and made plans to spend the rest of his life with. They just happened to look a lot alike, and he needed to get over that.

By the time he joined her in the kitchen, Rachel was standing with her back to the counter, leaning against it, digging in to her lunch. She'd changed into jeans that hit just below her knees and a faded, black University of Iowa med school T-shirt. It appeared that she'd brushed her hair, but her cheeks and nose still had that pink afterglow from the sun.

"You came out of Sawyer's room," Cale said, approaching her.

"Yep."

"Is that your room now?"

"It's the room I'm using."

Sawyer had said she was an expert at avoidance. Cale could guess why she wasn't using the room she'd shared with her sister, but he wondered how long this family could go on just stepping around the fact that Noelle was no longer with them. Rachel obviously wasn't up for a discussion about it now, though, judging by the stiffness of her shoulders and forced concentration on her food. He saw her sneak a sideways look at him when he settled against the counter a couple of feet away.

After she finished the bite in her mouth, she spoke. "You never said why you're here, but I'm guessing it's not to watch me eat some really freaking good quiche."

He held back a smile at her veiled defensiveness. "I wanted to apologize for Mariah being so...*overzealous* the other day at the meeting."

"Overzealous?"

"With her grand ideas and enthusiasm."

She frowned and finished another bite. "You came all the way over here for that?"

"'All the way' being a mile and a half or so, yes, I did. And to make sure you don't feel pressured to speak at the benefit."

Her lids lowered for a moment, just long enough that he noticed, and then she set aside her half-eaten quiche.

"It's okay. I can't blame her for trying. Objectively, I can see how it would seem like a cool thing to do."

He could practically see her swallowing back...emotion? Anger? Grief? It was gone too quickly for him to tell.

"Rachel—"

"What?" she snapped.

"Pretend she never mentioned it. The concert will be

successful without you giving a speech." He looked at her as she stared at the floor, and an urge came over him to brush her hair back from her face, to hug her. Reassure her. He ignored the urge.

"There's no way I could keep my composure...."

"I understand," he said gently. He could tell she was beating herself up for something he never would have asked her in the first place had it been up to him. Not this early, anyway.

"I wish I could manage," Rachel said, crossing her arms and still staring downward. "For Noelle. If our places were reversed..."

The regret in her voice was real, making her sound younger than she was. She seemed so alone at that moment, and again, Cale considered pulling her into his arms and trying to make all the pain go away—for both of them. He settled for brushing against her arm and covering her fingers with his hand. "Don't. It's okay."

She met his eyes. Looked as if she were about to say something and then swallowed and shook her head. "Never mind." It was clear that she was fighting to keep her composure.

"Hey, Rach," he said, turning to face her. "I know we don't know each other that well when you get down to it, but what I don't understand is why you shut me out. Why we can't, I don't know, be there for each other. Be friends or something." He nudged under her chin with his knuckle, forcing her to meet his gaze. "I lost her, too," he whispered.

She stared into his eyes with her turquoise ones for maybe three full seconds and then lowered her lids again. Clenched her jaw tightly in a battle against, he would bet, losing it completely.

Because he could feel the lump in his own throat

swelling, he ignored all the arguments in his head, pulled her close without another word and wrapped his arms tightly around her, unsure whom he was trying harder to comfort—her or himself.

God, moments like this still knocked him on his ass out of nowhere. He ignored the dampness of his eyes and fought to get through the next minute or two. He breathed in Rachel's scent of coconut and soap. Registered every one of her breaths, as her rib cage expanded repeatedly against his arms and chest. And when she raised her arms and wound them around his middle, he put all his awareness into the feel of her touch on his back.

Minutes ticked by and Cale gradually leveled out, contented himself with the woman in his arms who was very much alive, instead of haunting himself with her sister… who wasn't.

As his wave of killer emotions subsided, it felt awkward to be holding on to Noelle's sister so tightly, for so long. They seemed to become self-conscious at the same time, and he stepped back a few inches as they both dropped their arms, him to his sides, hers back in front of her chest.

"Your sister didn't mean to make me feel bad, I know. Her idea would be good…for someone else. She seems like a nice person."

"She means well," Cale said.

"I'm okay. Really." She flashed a forced grin. "Thank you, though."

She didn't say exactly what she was thanking him for. Didn't say anything else, but in that moment, as he looked down at her, he saw so much more than she knew. He saw her backbone and her deep, deep love for her sister and, yes, a good dose of stubbornness. A mix he couldn't help but admire. A mix that, it turned out, he couldn't get out of his mind for the rest of the day.

CHAPTER NINE

IT WAS DARK when Rachel opened her eyes.

She blinked several times, trying to grasp where she was and what time it was. With a turn of her head, the outline of Yoda against the glow of the digital clock came into view. Ah, yes, home sweet Yoda. But…9:07? At night?

After Cale had left, she'd tidied up the kitchen, caught up on email and then finally crashed in the early afternoon. She wished she could say she'd slept soundly but that would have been a lie.

She'd tossed, turned, dreamed and woken up wanting. Rinse and repeat a dozen or so times. No matter how agitated she'd been when she woke up, no matter how many times she'd told her brain to move on to something besides Cale Jackson, every time she'd drifted off again, there he was. Calming her, comforting her, touching her, making her want more. The dreams had been delicious, but waking up to the reality of being alone every few minutes…not so delightful.

A light tapping sounded on the bedroom door.

"Yeah?" She cleared her throat and the grogginess from her voice as the door was eased open, letting in the bright light from the hallway. Rachel closed her eyes against it.

"Are you okay, sweetie?" her mom asked from the doorway.

Embarrassed that she'd wasted the entire day, Rachel sat up. "Yeah. Fine. Fabulous."

"I'm sorry to wake you up, but I was worried. It's not like you to sleep the whole day away."

"You didn't wake me up. I took my kayak out after work so I didn't go to sleep until late. I meant to be up for dinner, though. What'd I miss?"

"I made some spinach and ricotta manicotti. You lucked out—even half the recipe makes enough for several meals…well, unless your brother's home. There's some in the fridge."

"I'm becoming addicted to your gourmet leftovers. The quiche was excellent."

"Glad you liked it. I'm no expert, but I'll give you cooking lessons anytime."

The prospect had absolutely no appeal. "Why would I want to do that when there's another dish of something awesome in the refrigerator every time I open it? Plus there's the time thing…"

"Just offering. I'm heading to bed. Hospital rounds come early and I've got a tennis match tomorrow after work."

"I'll be at work by the time you get home tomorrow evening, then," Rachel said. When she looked at her mom again, she did a double take at the doorway beyond and her heart felt as though it had crashed to a halt. "Mom? Why is that door open?"

Her mom glanced at the door to Rachel and Noelle's room. To her credit, she didn't play stupid.

"I just thought, after all this time, it was time to open it," her mom said curtly. "The air in there is stale, and it's become this void in our house. One of these days we need to do something about it."

"Have at it," Rachel said, glad the lights were still off so she could hide her scowl.

"I thought it would be best if you went through the room yourself, sweetie. Half of it's yours, and the other half… I figured you have the right to any of your sister's things that have special meaning to you."

Knowing she risked protesting too much and unwilling to draw her mom's attention to her inability to even step in the room, Rachel remained quiet. Counted the seconds and waited for her mom to leave. She could feel the open door, the room and everything in it, taunting her. Disquieting her.

"Well, good night," her mom finally said after an uncomfortable pause.

"Close my door, please, would you? I'm going to change and get out of here for a while," Rachel said, unsure of what her plans were beyond fresh air and escape. "Night, Mom."

Her mom pulled the door shut, leaving the room in full, blessed darkness again. Feeling as if she'd been struck by a wrecking ball, Rachel lay back down on the bed, rolling on her stomach and blocking out the sight of the open door across the hall from her mind's eye.

Closing her eyes, she coached herself to think calming, happier thoughts. Like Cale. His muscular arms around her. His words…

What I don't understand is why you shut me out. Why we can't, I don't know, be there for each other. Be friends or something.

She hadn't intentionally shut him out—it just seemed to be her way. She wasn't a social goddess like Noelle and never would be. When the sadness started stabbing at her, she didn't want anyone to witness it, so she did whatever she had to to close herself off. But Cale was right. They'd suffered the same tragedy, were battling with similar losses. Rachel's age-old feelings for him aside, they should be able to be some kind of support for each other. She was no expert at "friends," but for Cale, she would figure it out. There was no one she wanted to see right now more than him.

Tossing off her slept-in capris and T-shirt, she located a clean pair of khaki shorts and a striped shirt. Once she'd thrown them on and brushed the tangles out of her hair, she set off to find her mom's benefit binder with the master list of volunteers and phone numbers and her own cell phone.

Rachel had never been the type of girl to call a guy she wasn't seeing regularly, let alone invite him out for ice cream. Apparently she was turning over a new leaf.

SHE STOOD OUTSIDE the door of Lambert's Ice Cream Shoppe waiting for Cale to get there, trying to ignore the doubts that poked at her over whether he would indeed show. Studying the colorful menu board through the floor-to-ceiling windows, she tried to decide what she was in the mood for. Butter rum…caramel pecan…rocky road…triple dip? Only if she wanted to look like a cow.

When she spotted Cale getting out of the impossible-to-miss, bright orange Sport Trac, her mood improved tenfold and she insisted to herself it was just because he hadn't left her standing there alone, feeling like a loser. She had trouble believing her lie when he reached her, put his hand at her waist and flashed a smile at her in greeting, sending her heart racing. As he looked down at her, smiling that amazing smile, he pierced her with those vivid green eyes she wanted to drown in.

Rachel shut down the little voice in her head that suggested she shouldn't be thinking those thoughts about him, that the only possible thing between them was a friendship that didn't include a racing heart or butterflies of excitement. Just for this moment, for tonight, she needed to feel good for a change, and looking at Cale, having ice cream with him, and not overthinking the situation, accomplished that.

"You weren't waiting too long, were you?" he asked.

"Just long enough to decide my flavors."

"And those are?" He opened the door and held it for her, still touching her with his other hand as he ushered her inside.

"Double dip. Rocky road and marshmallow dream. I had trouble choosing between marshmallow and toasted almond but the extra sugar power wins."

"Well done," Cale said as they stepped into the line to wait their turn. "Very…complementary. They'll blend well."

"Exactly. Unlike my sister's clashing ice cream tastes."

"Bubble gum, mint chocolate chip—"

"And orange sherbet," she finished. "I have no idea how she could stand it but that was her standby since we were three feet tall."

Cale smiled sadly. "Sometimes I suspected she didn't even like the combination that much, but she took so much flak from everyone that she kept ordering it out of stubbornness."

"That'd be our Noelle," Rachel said and they both sobered. "What are you getting?"

"Strawberry cheesecake and vanilla."

She nodded her approval. "Another good mix. Clearly we're both ice cream blending experts."

When they received their sugar cones packed with oversize dips of creamy perfection, Rachel insisted on treating. That made it less of a date, in her mind. "I dragged you out."

"Yeah, horrible of you," Cale said. "You bought breakfast, too. You're making me look bad. Next time, it's on me—no arguments."

They turned around to find a place to sit in the small, overcrowded seating area.

"It's loud and bright in here. Want to go outside?" Cale suggested.

In reply, Rachel headed for the door. Once they were outside, the noise level diminished several decibels, and she breathed out. The three outdoor tables were occupied, so Cale nodded toward the beach, which was about twenty feet away. "Can you stand the chaos of the waves on the beach for a few minutes?" he joked.

"The ice cream will soothe my nerves, or at least occupy my attention."

They walked down the half flight of stairs to the sand and headed north, parallel to the waterline. When they reached the concrete seawall that protected one of the older motel properties, Cale gestured to it. "It's quieter here and there's a wall to lean against. That okay?"

"Perfect."

Rachel slid her back down the rough wall and sat on the cool, dry sand. Cale sat next to her, maybe an inch away, close enough that she could feel the heat coming off his body. The sensation, combined with his faint, masculine scent, was responsible for the goose bumps up her arms and left her with a slightly heady feeling.

"Thanks for meeting me tonight," Rachel said between licks of marshmallow. "I needed to get out of the house like you wouldn't believe."

"Issues with your mom?"

"Not really. She was heading to bed." She debated

mentioning the whole bedroom issue and decided if anyone would understand, Cale would. "When I woke up this evening, I discovered my well-meaning mother has decided to open *the door.*" She emphasized the last two words to convey their significance.

"Which door?" Cale asked, crunching his first bite of cone already.

"The door to our bedroom. Mine and Noelle's."

"Ah," he said, understanding registering in his tone. "It was closed this morning when I was there, right?"

"It's been closed since I've been home. Since…probably since the night Noelle died." Her throat threatened to close up as the memories of that night tried to force their way in. When she could breathe, she added, "That probably sounds twisted, I guess."

Cale chuckled quietly. "Not so much. I get it."

"I'd hoped my mom would have gone through everything long ago, before I moved back home. I couldn't believe it when I discovered she hadn't touched a single thing."

"Probably just as hard for her, don't you think?"

"I have no idea, to be honest. I don't even recognize the person she's become, but that's a whole different story."

Neither of them spoke for a couple of minutes as they worked on their cones. The waves roared on, but Rachel hardly noticed them for once.

"It's just a room," she finally said emphatically.

"It's her room. Full of her stuff." Cale's simple understanding sent a shot of warmth through her. Made it easier to say more.

"The other day, I worked up the courage to open the door and tried to go in." She licked her ice cream several times and attempted to focus on the richness of the cocoa flavor, the crunchiness of the nuts.

"How'd that go?"

"I couldn't do it. But I looked inside for a few minutes. Saw all her stuff just where she'd left it. That's… progress." She scoffed at herself. "Like I said, twisted."

"Twisted," Cale repeated. "Bet I can outtwist you any day."

"Yeah?" she asked, catching an ice cream drip on her cone before it landed in her lap. "How's that?"

He took his time answering, taking several bites of cone first. When his cone was half-gone, he tilted his head back, groaned and shook his head. "You have a room you've been avoiding. I have a whole condominium."

"You live with your sister, right?"

He shoved the rest of the cone in his mouth and finished it. "Yep. That's the twisted part. I have a condo of my own—Noelle helped me pick it out for our future together. A condo right on the beach, that a lot of people would kill for, and I live with my sister in her dinky two-bedroom apartment in the middle of town."

As Rachel tried to absorb that, a drop of cold ice cream hit her leg. She licked from the bottom to the top of the cone to prevent more drips and dabbed at her leg with her finger.

"I remember Noelle talking about condos. The one you bought is on the first floor, right? Opens right out to the sand?"

She didn't really need to ask. She remembered it as if it'd been last week, not two years ago. Noelle had foregone email and text messages—their usual means of communication—and had called Rachel the day Cale had made an offer on the condo. She'd been so excited she could hardly get the news out. She'd always wanted to live right on the beach. Rachel had been thrilled for her sister, honestly. And yet, at the same time, the announcement had been almost as painful as the night Noelle had called to share the news of her engagement. When Cale had bought the condo, he and Noelle had not yet gotten around to setting a wedding date, allowing Rachel to continue to play the denial game. But buying a home, even if Noelle's name hadn't been on the mortgage—that had hit Rachel hard, and she'd had to work to bury yet another bout of disappointment. In the end, she had, because she truly wanted her sister to be happy as much as she wanted her own happiness.

"It is," Cale answered. "Up north of here. It's a small, older building near Miller Street. I lucked into a fixer-upper unit on the first floor, with sand six feet from our door. Noelle swore she was going to sleep on the patio once she moved in—which we planned for after we got married." His voice became gravelly with sadness and, without thinking, Rachel reached out and touched his thigh just above his knee where his shorts ended. She relished the texture of his light-colored hair and the warmth of his skin beneath her fingers.

He was quiet for a bit, and neither of them moved, except for Rachel's continued attempt to consume her ice cream before she wore it.

"The unit I bought has so much potential," he finally continued, "but it needs a lot of work. I fully intended to do it myself. Even started some of it. And then..."

She didn't need to ask what the *and then* was.

Rachel quickly finished her ice cream and licked her fingers clean. The combination of the sea breeze and the ice cream made her shiver, so she scooted toward him, closing the small distance between them.

"What are you going to do?" she asked.

He seemed lost in his thoughts as he started running his fingers up and down the back of her hand, still resting on his leg. "I'm going to get back to it. As soon as I finish some projects for my parents."

"Good for you."

The movement of his fingers on her hand was mesmerizing. The innocent motion awoke a hunger in her, a yearning she hadn't felt for…ages. If ever. Not just a physical wanting, but more. She wanted to ease his sadness. Wanted him to ease hers. The strength of her need to become closer to him, emotionally and otherwise, at that moment, was overpowering. She closed her eyes and waited for the intensity to die down before she embarrassed herself.

"Have you been in your condo since she died?" Rachel asked in a voice barely above a whisper, unsure if he could hear her over the continuous roar of the waves.

He sucked in the sea air, his chest expanding up against her side. "Once." The word was hoarse, croaklike. "About a month afterward. It was still too fresh. Awful. All I could think about as I looked at the partially stripped-out kitchen was the way she'd stood in that room and talked so animatedly about the project. Her excitement about every little decision we had yet to make, because according to her, planning it all out in advance would be too much of a chore. It'd ruin the 'journey.'"

"She was a seat-of-the-pants girl all the way," Rachel said with a bittersweet smile.

Cale ceased tracing her fingers and took her hand in his instead.

"Let me guess," he said. "You're a planner, one hundred percent."

"I try to be. Noelle, God love her, used to make me

nuts with her inability to even plan the next day in advance."

"There were downsides," he agreed. "Like planning a trip or, say, a wedding. I sometimes wondered if she was going to show up one day with some crazy idea of getting married that weekend or something."

"You never knew with her. When we were seniors in high school, she convinced me to drop everything one weekend and drive to Houston with her to power-shop. No hotel reservations, no idea where we'd end up. She loved it. It freaked me out."

Cale laughed quietly, a deep rumble in his chest. "At times it was challenging, but I did love her spontaneity and playfulness."

"Yeah," Rachel said, trying not to think about how much she herself didn't even begin to embody those traits. Instead, she let herself recall the Houston shopping trip in more detail, which had turned out to be one of the best weekends the two sisters had ever spent together. They'd gotten makeovers at one of the department-store makeup counters, had gone to dinner at a fancy, high-priced restaurant as they'd tried to act older than they were. Once they had found a hotel—a four-star one because Noelle had insisted they deserved to splurge—the fun had continued. Noelle, being daring, flirty Noelle, had introduced herself to a couple of brothers they'd run into in the lobby, and the four of them had gone swimming and then sat in the hot tub for the rest of the evening. It had led to Rachel's first kiss, something that never would have happened without her sister's spirit of adventure. "God, I miss her."

Cale squeezed her hand and put his other arm around her, pulling her closer to his side. The movement jolted her from her reverie, in a good way. She normally didn't let herself think back on specific memories of Noelle very often. It was too damn painful.

She looked up at him with a vague smile of gratitude. His gaze met hers, so close she could see the lighter flecks in his eyes, and she was suddenly unable to drag her eyes away. Instead, she was drawn in deeper, lured into glancing at his lips, and that was all it took for her to forget who she was and who he was. She lifted her head and pressed her lips to his.

CHAPTER TEN

CALE SHOULD HAVE been shocked at Rachel's bold move. Maybe he was, for an instant, but that was quickly swept aside by a wave of heat that rushed through him at the feel of Rachel's soft, sweet-tasting lips on his.

Holy shit, the girl was more assertive than he ever would have imagined. There was nothing tentative about her kiss—she slid her hand around to the back of his neck and pulled him closer, not that he was trying to get away. He was taken by her way of going after what she wanted full-throttle.

The sexy little sound she made struck him deep and low, got his blood pumping to parts that hadn't had any action in a damn long time. Her tropical, coconut scent surrounded him as he ran his fingers through her hair. At the touch of her tongue to his, his need ratcheted higher, and he wished her body was closer to his, wanted to press his into hers and fit their bodies together. As soon as he had the thought, he felt her leg sliding over his lap, her torso turning toward his, breasts pressing into his chest, arms winding around his neck. He ran his hands over her greedily, learning her curves, exploring the softness of her skin by sliding his fingers beneath her shirt.

Rachel's fervor was a turn-on in itself and, again, surprising, given the lack of self-confidence he knew she harbored in situations outside of her job. Once again, so opposite of her sister. Noelle had been plenty passionate in bed, but she'd always been a shy, hesitant kisser and rarely one to make the first move.

Abruptly, he pulled away, turned his head, closing his eyes and swearing to himself. Rachel nipped the corner of his lips lightly then eased back enough to peg him with a questioning look.

Cale shook his head minutely. "This is too weird."

When he opened his eyes, he caught the look on Rachel's face—embarrassment, just for a moment, and then regret. She swallowed as her lids lowered, and then she quickly climbed off him and stood, leaving him sitting on the ground alone. "Yeah." She glanced around at the waves, then up the beach and down it at the various groups of people in the distance, as she took a step back from him. "I…I'm gonna go." She dared a look down at him, where he still sat, stunned at himself.

He knew he should say something. Tell her…what? Something. At the very least, he should walk her back to her car, not that there was any safety concern, but just to be a gentleman. Before he could force something out or make himself move, though, she nodded once and walked back the way they'd come from.

Cale let her go, too caught up in the maelstrom inside him as his heart rate gradually slowed.

How in the name of God could he kiss his fiancée's twin sister? What the hell was wrong with him?

RACHEL KNEW THE CHANCES of Buck being at the boathouse at 11:32 p.m. were next to nothing, but she drove there anyway. If she could only get out on the bay, paddle all the way to the middle, where nothing could get at her, no thoughts, no guilt, no humiliation…

The gravel lot was deserted as expected, but she pulled in and parked right next to the dark, closed-up boathouse, stubbornly ignoring reality. She only vaguely felt like a criminal when she rattled the door against its padlock to make sure it was indeed locked. She knocked. Just in case…

There was, of course, no reply. There was no sound whatsoever. Barring her disappointment, the silence of the area in general was a welcome respite after the nonstop hammering of the waves on the shore at the other side of the island.

God, she just needed to breathe.

The placid, mirrorlike water beckoned to her, even though all she could see of it from that distance was a dark void. She could see the lights of the mainland reflecting on the far side, though, and as she walked closer, the calm surface of the water came into focus just feet away. Without hesitating, she walked out onto the old, wooden dock.

Down the way about three quarters of a mile, she could see the bright security lights shining at the marina. To the north, all was dark, with the exception of a couple of restaurants and a few houses scattered in the distance, including the one where she'd met Cale. Where Noelle had met Cale.

Rachel got down on her belly and stretched out on the dock with her head propped on her arms at the very edge. The water was high—only a few inches of space separated the wood planks from it. It was as close to being in her kayak as she could get for now, and being facedown above the water made her feel as if she was floating in the air. Unfortunately, that wasn't enough to take her away from what had just transpired.

Pressing her face into her arms, she wished with all she was worth that she could hide. She squeezed her eyes tightly shut, unable to protect herself from the guilt that closed in on her from every direction, making it impossible to get a full breath.

She'd never told a soul about the heart-crushing, awful guilt that had plagued her for every single day of the past year and a half. It was something she had to face alone. She deserved it.

Rachel had no illusions that, even as a medical resident—heck, even if she'd been a full-blown doctor—she could have physically saved her sister from the asthma attack that had killed her. Not without being there at the onset. But their argument beforehand, the one that had sent Noelle running out of the house so fast she'd left her purse and her inhaler behind…

She slammed a mental door down on that thought, imagining the sound of a metal jail cell clanging shut to accompany it. Nausea boiled up in her gut, and she felt light-headed even though she was lying flat and unmoving. Fighting to regulate her breathing, she dangled her arm over the side of the dock and dipped her fingers into the cool water. But instead of being an escape for her as it was when she was in her boat, the water now felt threatening, unsafe. When she was in her kayak, she felt as if she was part of the bay, connected to it, but here, six inches up, she felt separate. Unwelcome. As if the water was living and breathing…and blaming.

She pushed herself up abruptly, distancing herself from the inky vastness of the bay. She hugged her knees to her chest, the panicked feeling that the guilt always brought subsiding slowly.

Unbidden, Cale's face appeared in her mind's eye. His horrified look as she'd stood before him. The silence.

Embarrassment seared her, made her cheeks burn even as the cool breeze blew over them. She'd practically climbed on him, acted like a desperate loser who couldn't wait to get it on. And she'd been so humiliatingly into it, loving the sweet taste of him, drinking in the way he kissed, treasuring the feel of his hands on her skin. The thrill that had jolted through her when she'd realized he was turned on, as well, when she'd felt his hardness against her... She'd been shameless in that instant. And now she was overpowered by shame.

Her sister's fiancé. The man her sister would have been married to at this very second. The man her sister had died loving.

She couldn't even fathom how she'd made Cale feel by throwing herself at him.

Never again.

Cale was going to be in her life because of the ties between them—the committee she'd committed to, the hospital and, yes, his position as the man who'd planned to spend his life with her sister. Avoiding him would be cowardly, but she wasn't going to seek him out. Wouldn't be calling him and asking him for ice cream again. And she sure as hell wouldn't be touching him and kissing him as if she had a right to.

WHAT CALE REALLY NEEDED was a nice three-alarm fire to occupy his mind. An explosion rocking a deserted factory, maybe, or a mainland warehouse burning to the ground. Something huge that required all his concentration.

As he sat on one of the loungers on the fire station's beachside patio and stared out at an oil tanker light on the dark, indistinguishable horizon, the silence of the fire department's alarm system seemed to mock him.

He'd spent the past twenty-four hours beating himself up for the freak thing that had happened last night with Rachel, and he had yet to work through anything so that it was okay in his mind. There was no way to make any of it—kissing Rachel and liking every last second of it, letting her walk away embarrassed—okay.

He glanced through the wall of windows to the station's common area and realized the baseball game the rest of the crew had been watching must have ended. The TV had been turned off and the room was deserted except for Clay Marlow, who sat on one of the ugly plaid sofas studying for his hazmat certification test. It was after midnight. Most likely, the rest of the guys had retired to their rooms to try to get some shut-eye since it'd been a slow night so far. It was Cale's chance to slip inside without having to talk to anyone.

He went in and headed across the station toward the sleeping quarters without looking in Clay's direction. As he passed the kitchen, though, Dylan's voice reached him from within.

"Rangers won, dude."

Cale grunted an unintelligible response and continued on his way. His colleagues had likely gotten used to his antisocial ways after Noelle's death, but in the past few months, he'd made an effort to come out of it, to be more social. He'd started going out for burgers or beer when he was invited and had been told by his painfully honest sister that he was more pleasant to be around in general. Tonight they probably all thought he was having a relapse of grief and grumpiness…and maybe that was exactly what it was.

He went into his tiny private room in the officers' section and closed the door without turning on the light. He pulled his shirt over his head and hung it on the doorknob so he could find it easily should an alarm come in. Lined his shoes up right by the door and draped his pants at the foot of the bed. Though he was doubtful he'd sleep, he lay on the single bed on his back, not bothering to pull the blankets back over him.

He should never have let Rachel kiss him. A part of him had known that at the time, but that part had been easily crushed by the desire the very first touch of her had awakened in him. By allowing the kiss to go on, by touching her the way he had, by being so undeniably into the moment, he'd led Rachel on. Big-time. He couldn't blame her for being shocked and puzzled when he'd pulled away from her, and then what had he done? Had he tried to explain himself or even assuage her feelings? Oh, hell no. He'd acted like a prick and let her walk away thinking he'd hated every second of it.

He hadn't hated it. At all. Until that moment when he'd realized what he was doing—kissing Noelle's twin sister.

What a weak bastard he was. He hadn't so much as thought about kissing a woman since he'd lost Noelle, not even on the two dates he'd been on, and here he was letting Rachel climb all over him. She may have initiated it, but he'd done plenty to keep it going. Had wanted to keep it going until the inevitable comparisons had filled his mind.

It was wrong and, to use Rachel's word, *twisted.* Kissing sisters was bad enough. Not his style at all. Twins? Yeah, that was tacky as hell. Moving on to the second one because the first one had died? People would have a goddamn field day with that. With good reason.

Had he just been into it because she looked so much like Noelle? The sisters were so opposite, personality-wise, and they had their differences physically, as well, though they were subtle and probably unnoticeable to the casual observer. Cale had always been able to tell them apart easily, but was it their similarities that had drawn him in last night? Was he sick enough in the head that he was searching for Noelle in Rachel?

As bad as that would be, the truth was even less acceptable. He'd known damn well whom he was locking lips with.

He liked Rachel. He had ever since the night he'd met her. The social insecurities that she'd been so open about with him since their very first conversation gave her an honest vulnerability that was impossible not to like. He admired her dedication to her career, respected the way she was so purpose-driven in everything.

And then there was the side of her that was drowning from the death of her twin sister.

Cale was beginning to suspect she hadn't yet gotten through the grieving process that counselors were so damn gung-ho about. Since she'd been back on the island, the two of them had had multiple discussions about Noelle, tough ones filled with memories that hurt like a bitch for both of them, and yet…he'd never seen her shed a tear. She had a knack for changing the subject before talk or memories could go too deep. He wasn't an expert on grief, but he'd done enough reading to know there were steps, lots of them, all of them a gigantic barrel of suck, and he'd been through them. Denial. Anger. Sadness so deep there'd been days he'd struggled to get out of bed to pee. Other steps he couldn't recall but he'd bet money that Rachel hadn't been through them. Hadn't let herself really feel any of the emotions that were supposedly so damn normal and were said to be the key to healing. She didn't stop working long enough to. And while his eyes tended to cross at the mention of psychobabble crap, he didn't doubt there was something to working through the stages of grief in order to move on with one's life.

Rachel was definitely still struggling hard with her

sister's death—there was no question about it. She was a bundle of contradictions. She didn't want to talk about her twin in any detail, and yet she'd dared to take a couple of baby steps on her own—like opening up the bedroom door and looking inside. Volunteering for the fundraising group. Most people probably thought very little about it, but Cale knew how damn hard every single thing was—because he'd lived it. He'd had to do it, too.

She didn't have many friends, and it was obvious to him she could use one. The kiss on the beach—that was just a moment that had spiraled out of control. A little bit of bad judgment. They'd both been wrapped up in the discussion about Noelle and their emotions had taken a wrong turn, convinced them temporarily that there was something there when there really wasn't. It was a mistake that had caught him off guard. It wouldn't happen again. He wouldn't be surprised by a false sense of attraction, and he wouldn't give in if Rachel was. It was all totally controllable.

With that realization, he relaxed a bit, turned on his side and stopped staring toward the ceiling he couldn't actually see in the darkness.

Cale needed to make sure Rachel knew he'd been upset with himself last night, not her. That he liked her and respected her, that they should still go on platonic ice cream dates. There was no reason to let one crazy mistake screw things up between them. It would have meant a lot to Noelle to know that he and Rachel could get to know each other better. From what he could tell, Rachel needed someone, and he was the best person to step in and be there for her.

CHAPTER ELEVEN

RACHEL SHOULD HAVE followed her gut and not ridden with her mom to the benefit-planning meeting. She didn't want to go at all, and had, in fact, manipulated her work schedule so that she'd had a shift on meeting night. It was just her bad luck that this week's meeting had been switched to Thursday. But she knew full well that if she skipped it, Cale would guess it was because she was embarrassed as hell about what had happened last night. God knew she was, absolutely, but she didn't want to advertise it.

Her mom, of course, was adamant about getting there early, which totally cramped Rachel's style of showing up when there were no seats left around the table. It was so much easier to hide—and leave early—when she could sit along the outside of the room near the door. It also made interacting with the other volunteers harder to do, which was the way she preferred it.

"I'll be in in a few minutes," Rachel told her mom as they approached the restroom. "Gonna stop here."

"That's fine," her mom said, distracted by her own thoughts of the upcoming meeting. Rachel breathed out in relief as she entered the deserted ladies' room and her mom's shoes clicked on down the tiled hall of the library's wing of meeting rooms and offices. Now, if only Rachel could find a legitimate excuse to pass the next sixty minutes in here....

A short, hefty woman wearing chained glasses came

in, so Rachel plunked her purse down on the counter and rummaged through it as if she were searching for makeup. The search was futile, as she didn't have anything besides cherry ChapStick in there. She pulled it out and applied it as the woman went in the stall, then fumbled around some more. A brush. Something to do. She ran it through her already untangled hair, making no impact on her appearance.

When the toilet flushed, Rachel scurried into the other stall even though she didn't need it. Waiting it out as the woman washed and dried her hands, which was of course taking aeons, she closed her eyes and wondered what the hell she was doing. Hiding out in a library bathroom stall? For real? She was a highly competent physician. Not a chicken.

Much.

The woman left and Rachel checked her watch. Two minutes till the meeting started. It was better than being ten minutes early.... If she stalled too much longer, her mom just might send a rescue crew to find her.

She walked out, took her time washing her hands and walked at a leisurely pace toward the meeting room.

As soon as she went into the room, she realized her plan to pretend Cale wasn't there was unrealistic and immature. Doubly so when he was looking straight at her and had a hand on the empty chair next to him, obviously indicating she could sit there.

Not. A. Chicken.

She wasn't able to paste a grin on her face, but she did force her legs in his direction and sat down next to him just as her mom started the meeting.

On the bright side, Rachel had avoided small talk with him. What, exactly, could one possibly chat about with

the guy she'd thrown herself at not even forty-eight hours before?

Mariah and Eddie sat on the opposite side of the table toward the other end, but Mariah made a point of smiling at Rachel, and Rachel offered an awkward wave in return. Familiar faces helped somewhat. Even though Noelle's name had already been spoken once, the meeting itself wasn't as bad as it had been last week—so far.

Rachel sat back in her chair, determined to make it all the way through the meeting without wimping out again. She tuned in to hear Trina, one of Noelle's best friends, give her update on volunteers for the event itself. Trina went into detail about how many volunteers she was going to need for every single aspect of the concert. Rachel's attention wandered as she began to relax.

Facing the table straight-on since her mom, at the head of the table, had opened up discussion to the rest of the group, Rachel couldn't help but notice Cale's hand resting on his notepad to her left. His fingers were long, the backs of his hands tanned. The body hair on his arms was a shade lighter than the hair on his head, almost light enough to consider blond, most likely from the sun. She couldn't help thinking about the strength in his fingers, in him, to do his job. Even though he was primarily a firefighter, she knew a lot more about what he did on medical calls, and picturing him in action as she stared at his hands made her shiver. She'd bet in addition to saving lives and putting out fires they could do magic on a woman's body….

God, Rachel!

Her cheeks burned as she reined in her thoughts. Then she made the giant mistake of glancing at his face to see if he'd noticed her fixation. It was too much to ask for him to be sidetracked by something, anything, else—he

was looking straight at her and flashed a heart-gripping smile as if to put her at ease.

Such a beautiful, kind man.

Her sister's man.

Rachel looked away quickly as guilt washed through her and threatened to overwhelm her—and maybe make her puke, to boot.

Focus on the meeting. The benefit. Anything but him...

As the head of the finance committee, a woman she didn't know, started reciting the latest numbers, Rachel straightened in her chair, took the cap off her pen and began taking notes in earnest. The numbers, without context, meant nothing to her, but she was damn well going to get every last one on paper.

When the finance queen took a break for a swallow of bottled water, Rachel checked her watch. Only forty-four minutes and twenty-five seconds to go, if her mom stuck to her plan for an hour-long meeting.

When it finally ended—seven minutes late, not that Rachel was counting each torturous second—she hopped up, wishing she could make a run for it, or do anything other than the thing she'd made up her mind she needed to do. She turned toward Cale and took a covert deep breath. Making contact with his emerald eyes nearly took that breath right back out of her.

"Hi," she said stupidly.

"Hey. Imagine meeting you here. Glad you made it."

"It wasn't as bad as the first one I went to." Unless you counted the horrendous episode of guilt she'd brought on herself. "Can we...?" She gestured to the hallway with her head. "I need to talk to you."

"Sure." He put his hand out for her to precede him.

"I'll be outside," Rachel said to her mom as they walked by her.

"Oh. Is Cale giving you a ride home?" Jackie eyed them with curiosity.

"No," Rachel answered.

"Yes," Cale said at the exact same time. "I can give you a ride if you need one."

She would walk home as soon as she said what she needed to say to him. She went out of the room ahead of him without another word to her mom.

Without thought, Rachel proceeded to the shore, her eyes on a pair of kayaks gliding on the bay as the sun dropped behind the horizon of the mainland. Cale came up beside her and surveyed the awesome scene before them.

"I guess I missed this while I was in the Midwest," Rachel said.

"You guess?"

"I never gave it much thought while I was in school doing my residency. I was always busy," she admitted. "But there's nothing like this in Iowa."

He chuckled. "I don't imagine there is."

She took in the muted colors as dusk descended on them—the lavender and blue-gray of the sky, the same reflected in the water, the dark silhouettes of the towering palms on the opposite shore.

"What did you want to talk to me about?" Cale asked, rattling the calmness she was trying to absorb from the scenery into every cell.

"I'm sorry," she blurted out before her nerves could make her overemotional.

There was a pause before he said anything, but Rachel refused to look at him.

"For?"

As if he didn't know. As if it weren't blatantly hanging there between them like a cringe-worthy neon sign.

He was going to make her say it.

"Let's see," she began, trying to make her tone flippant. "For kissing you. Multiple times. For crawling all over you. For making a fool of myself. Embarrassing both of us. Screwing over my sister." Her pulse throbbed in her temples. "I think that about covers it."

"Is that all?"

"For now. I…I don't know what came over me."

He touched her elbow, nearly sending her into the stratosphere because she wasn't expecting it. He pulled his hand back as if realizing she was tightly wound and that any kind of physical contact between the two of them was, yeah, a sensitive issue.

"Rachel," he said softly, maintaining a good eight inches between their shoulders as they stood side by side. "You are not going to take the blame for any of that—"

"Too late."

"Nope. No one needs to take any blame. It was just… a crazy few minutes."

Crazy *awesome* few minutes, but she couldn't let herself dwell on that. That would just make her sick to her stomach again. Instead, she latched onto what Cale was trying to say. Attempted to excuse what she knew was inexcusable.

"We got caught up in talking about sad things…."

Cale nodded. "We crossed a line we shouldn't have. It was a mistake."

"Huge."

"It won't happen again."

She breathed out and nodded slowly. Absolutely right it wouldn't happen again. Between the look of remorse on his face when he'd pulled away last night and the toxic guilt that had been so overpowering that at times she felt as if she might keel over from it ever since… No. Not going to happen again.

"I wouldn't mind hanging out sometimes, though," Cale continued, and Rachel turned her head sharply toward him. He shrugged. "It's taken me a while to be social again." He gave a short, self-deprecating laugh. "A long while. Over a year. But it's still tough to go out and act happy some nights, you know?"

"So you want to hang with me and be unhappy?"

He laughed again, this time more genuinely. "I don't feel like I have to act around you."

Something about the intimacy of that statement made her heart constrict. She wasn't well seasoned in the art of friendship, with males *or* females, so it was easy to convince herself that was what the flutter was about. "You don't."

"It's comfortable," he said, sounding a little unsure of himself, and that made Rachel want to reach out to him.

She didn't, though.

"I get it," she said as the coil inside her that'd been tightened until it was about to snap slowly unwound. She hadn't realized it until now, but in addition to everything else she'd been feeling all day, she'd been terrified she'd scared him off by bumbling right over that line he'd mentioned. She couldn't have what she wanted with him—for too many reasons to count—but she hated the thought of not having him in her life in some capacity, even if it was just as someone she could sit next to at planning meetings for a few weeks. Anything more would be a gift.

They stood there watching the bay darken for a few minutes, the silence between them almost, like he'd said, comfortable. The small bit that was tense was all her doing—she had no doubt. And she could deal with that.

"I promised your mom I'd get you home," Cale said

once the light had completely disappeared from the surface of the water, turning the bay into a dark abyss. "Ready?"

"I honestly planned to walk."

"Not happening."

"Have you forgotten the Culver stubbornness?"

"Are you chicken to be alone with me now?" Cale's tone was light, and it was obvious he was joking with her, but the word *chicken* hit a raw spot.

"I'm just going to pretend that doesn't sound in the least bit egotistical," Rachel said, throwing it back at him. "Bring it on. Give me a ride, Sir Gallant." She turned and walked toward the parking lot.

"Careful. That kind of sounds dirty." Cale fell into step next to her, and Rachel lightly smacked his arm.

They rode with the windows of the Sport Trac down all the way, the temperate night air blowing through the cab and making it tough to talk. But that was okay. Rachel didn't feel the need for mindless chatter, anyway.

Cale pulled up behind Rachel's mom's Lexus, which sat in the open garage.

"What's your work schedule this weekend?" he asked.

Rachel's heart stumbled. Had she misunderstood everything he'd just said? No way was he going to ask her out…

"Um…"

"I have a favor to ask," he said in a rush, as if realizing what she was thinking.

"I work Saturday night. I have tomorrow and Sunday off. What's the favor?"

In the darkness, she saw him close his eyes briefly and then gaze out the driver's-side window, away from her.

"I need to go to my condo," he said. "To take inventory on all the work that needs to be done. It's time for me to start moving toward living there again. Past time."

He didn't have to remind her that he'd been there only once since Noelle had died or how he'd reacted to it.

"You want me to go with you?" she asked.

Cale finally turned to look at her. "Would you? Maybe Saturday morning before your shift."

"Sure. I can do that."

From what he'd said before, there would be no physical sign of her sister in the condo, only in Cale's memory. Worrying about someone else's battles instead of her own for a while would be a welcome change. If going with him made it a tiny bit easier for him to handle, then she was totally up for that.

As she said good-night and got out of the vehicle, she quashed the obstinate, clueless voice in her head that quietly insisted she would have preferred that he had asked her on a date.

CHAPTER TWELVE

CALE HAD WOKEN up just over an hour ago with a gut ache and a bad feeling about this.

He'd known going to his condo was going to suck the big one, but he hadn't realized just how much, after all this time, it would still knock him on his ass. Why he'd thought even for a second it was a good idea to have Rachel tag along to witness his own personal freak show was beyond him. He would've been much better off facing it alone.

All of this flashed through his mind in forty-five seconds as he stood outside the door with Rachel behind him and made himself stall. He fumbled with the keys on the black-and-gold keychain Noelle had given him, dropped the whole thing, acted as if he wasn't sure which was the right key. He knew damn well which one it was because the thing taunted him every time he happened to notice it. He'd given thought to taking it off his keychain, but that would be a concrete sign he was a wuss. Learning to ignore it had had to suffice.

"Want me to do it?" Rachel asked from behind him in a concerned, well-meaning voice that irritated rather than soothed him.

His response was to shove the key in the hole and open the lock. He pushed open the door as if it had personally offended him.

"Welcome to our humble home," he muttered as he

walked inside, cringing at the sight that met his eyes—solid proof of just how much his last and only venture in had leveled him.

Shame burned in him as he took in the half-demolished wall between the kitchen and dining room. It'd been way too soon for him to come back to this place, and the gamut of emotional crap that had engulfed him had obviously been too much for him to handle. The wall, or what was left of it, was a testament to the rage that had eventually won out over everything else—rage that Noelle had been taken from him too soon, rage that she hadn't had a chance to live out a full life. Rage at so many things.

He'd always intended to take out the wall between the kitchen and dining area in order to open up the space and make it more suitable for entertaining. But he hadn't planned to do it that day over a year ago, and he hadn't had the proper tools or state of mind to do it. Jagged edges and exposed wires jutted everywhere, lacking any sign of professionalism or even remote competence.

The air in the place had gone a little staler and there was dust everywhere. His tools were still scattered over the dining-room table, just waiting for him to pick up where he'd left off. The blinds on the window still hung six inches below the bottom sill on one side and eight or nine inches below it on the other, begging to be replaced.

Rachel stared at the partially destroyed wall in silence, her brows arched in concern. Cale didn't even want to imagine what she must think of him.

Looking to his right toward the living room, he could see the open, year-and-a-half-old *Sports Illustrated* still draped, cover-side up, over the arm of the sofa, half-read. The forty-two-inch flat-screen TV had been less than a month old when Noelle had died, and there it sat now, just like new.

Unable to help himself, Cale walked slowly, apprehensively, to the living room to once again survey the other bits of his life he'd left hanging there. He was testing himself, wondering if he'd handle things any better this time.

The sumptuous brown leather sofa that once had begged him to sink into it now mocked him as he played a searing memory back in his head. The day the furniture had been delivered, he and Noelle had been in a celebratory mood as it and the television were the first pieces they'd bought for their new home. They'd been messing around on the sofa and she'd stopped him, laughing the whole time, and insisted he take her to the bedroom instead of "messing up their new couch."

Cale had never gotten the chance to break in the sofa with his wife-to-be.

The emotional blast was there again but not as violent this time. He ground his jaw from side to side and the muscles were so tight it popped loudly. He cracked his knuckles to keep from taking everything out on the condo again.

He vaguely noticed Rachel as she walked past him, giving him a wide berth, toward the door that opened directly onto the beach.

"I can see why she was so excited," she said, her back to him. From this angle, she could have been Noelle with a haircut. "This place was perfect for her. Her dream."

Without a glance back at him, seemingly—and thankfully—oblivious to Cale's internal struggle, Rachel opened the vertical blinds covering the door and let herself out the door onto the patio.

As if no time had passed and he hadn't spent months grieving and getting closer to acceptance, it all came back to him at once. Sadness. Anger. Loss. So many other ugly feelings. He wanted to curl up in a ball in the corner and hide from it all, and that just ticked him off more.

He kicked the side of the sofa, which of course did nothing but hurt his damn foot. He grabbed the magazine, ripped it in two then threw the pages in the air. Leaves of glossy, four-color paper fluttered to the couch and the floor much too peacefully.

He strode back through the dining area and into the kitchen on the end of the condo opposite from the beach. There on the floor at the base of part of the wall that still stood intact was the hammer he'd taken to the drywall. A hammer, for God's sake. He hadn't had a more appropriate tool for demolition and he hadn't cared. It was the reason for the hack job—well, that and the red fury that had driven him.

He picked up the hammer, fighting to avoid a similar meltdown even as the emotional storm inside of him intensified. Just as he'd feared.

This remodeling project was supposed to be one of joy, one to celebrate a promising future full of love and family and everything he and Noelle had dreamed of. The plan had been to open up the kitchen to the dining room, reconfiguring the cabinets on the other three walls. His fun-loving, social-butterfly fiancée had been looking forward to having parties here—a housewarming, birthdays, holidays, you name it. She'd gone on and on, bubbling over with her characteristic enthusiasm for the possibilities once the kitchen project was finished.

He had no intention of a repeat performance, but he couldn't stifle the urge for one good swing. He twisted, wound up like a pitcher, then gave the center of the intact drywall everything he had. "Son of a bitch!"

"Cale!"

Shit.

He heard the sliding glass door slam shut in the distance and Rachel's footsteps behind him on the tile floor, but he didn't turn to face her. He used all his energy to try to calm himself. He set the hammer on the table—hard—before he could take another shot.

"Cale, what are you doing?" Rachel rushed up to him and touched his arm. He shrugged her off. "No. You can't do this. Not again."

Something in her tone hit him like an incendiary and it was a damn good thing he'd already set the hammer aside, otherwise he might have swung at the wall again as an exclamation point.

"I set the hammer down," he said through gritted teeth.

"Good. You know that doesn't help."

"Maybe you could tell me what the hell *is* going to help." Caught up only in himself, he continued when he should have shut up. "What am I saying? Not exactly your area of expertise."

"What's that supposed to mean?"

He stepped farther away from her and flung open the top of the battered, metal toolbox he'd picked up secondhand. He began tossing in the tools on the table.

"Cale, what's that supposed to mean?" Rachel came around the table to his side.

He wanted to be alone with his pain, needed her to get out of his space. "You're no expert on dealing with your grief."

She stared at him for several seconds—he could feel her gaze burning into the side of his face. The silence grew, and he didn't back down because it was true and he wasn't in the right state of mind to take it back.

"You act all high-and-mighty because you've got such tight control on everything," he continued, well aware this wasn't the time, but not giving half a shit. "But when you get down to it, one of these days, you're going to lose it completely. One of these days, you won't be able to hold it off anymore."

Cale waited for her to react. To yell at him. Cry. Something. She was frozen for so long he was finally forced to look at her. Sure enough, she held on to her composure with every fiber of her being. The muscle in one of her cheeks twitched, and she blinked rapidly several times as if fighting tears. But she kept her control.

He wanted her to blow. To give him a fight. A reason to blow off some more steam. "I don't know why you think you're above breaking down."

She continued to stare at him, mostly statue-still except for the involuntary twitches, but there was so much emotion in her eyes. So much hurt. He wouldn't forget that expression anytime soon. He knew he was being a monster, and yet he couldn't rein himself in.

"Are you done?" she finally asked so quietly he could barely hear her. "Because I am. I'm done. I'm out of here."

He tried to make himself say something. To apologize. Stop her somehow so he could eat the awful things he'd just said to her. His mouth opened but he couldn't form the words.

When the door shut behind her, quietly—she was fully under control and so opposite of the way he was acting—he swore to himself. Remorse washed over him. Damn near suffocated him.

He was such an asshole.

As the maelstrom drained out of him along with every ounce of energy, he gazed at the ceiling and let his heart rate gradually return to normal.

He stood there staring at the physical damage he'd done before today, shame filtering in again at his loss of control. Embarrassing. Both his destruction and the way he'd treated Rachel. It was as though he'd had to prove to himself that asking her here had been a dumb idea.

She hadn't deserved any of that. She was the last person on earth who deserved to be the target of his grief or anger or whatever this ugliness was that seemed to grip him whenever he faced this place.

He had to go after her.

The condo, though a mess, was fixable, but he was afraid the harm he'd done to Noelle's sister, to their tentative friendship or whatever it was they'd managed to forge since she'd been back… Yeah. That was going to take some serious damage control on his part.

CHAPTER THIRTEEN

FOR THE FIRST time ever, the water of the bay was failing her.

Rachel was closer to the mainland shore than the island when she realized how hard she was struggling to clear her mind. That she'd covered so much area in such a short time—and the fatigue she felt in her shoulders already—said it all. She was paddling like a possessed woman, and her brain was attacking what had happened at Cale's condo the same way her paddle was attacking the water. The whole reason she loved to go kayaking was because she didn't have to struggle, mentally or otherwise. It was supposed to relax her. That her main retreat was threatened by...*who knew what* disconcerted her.

Oh, hell. She knew what. The stuff Cale had said to her had been cruel and totally unsettling.

It took a lot of nerve to go spouting accusations at her when he was so clearly messed up. Beating on the wall with a hammer? Slamming tools around? Really? Those were not signs of healthy grieving in her admittedly limited experience.

Yes, she did keep a tight rein on her feelings. About everything. It wasn't just Noelle. Wasn't just sadness. That was the kind of person she was. Just because she didn't show something on the outside didn't mean she wasn't feeling things on the inside. Why didn't people get that? Of course she was dealing with her sadness over her twin sister's death. It was devastating. The absolute worst thing she'd ever gone through in her life. As hard as it had been when her dad had died after suffering an aneurysm when she and Noelle were eight, this was even worse. Noelle had been her other half. But she wasn't about to go around acting pathetic and begging for sympathy. She had her ways of handling her emotions, and it just so happened that none of them involved a hammer.

What hurt more than the words Cale had spewed at her, though, was that when she'd seen the pain on his face, she'd wanted to be a comfort to him, wanted to help him cope somehow. When she'd come rushing in to try, he'd aimed the ugliness of his feelings at her.

He'd invited her to come with him—for support, she'd assumed—and when she'd tried to offer it, he'd done his best to make her feel like an idiot for ever thinking she could help.

She slowed her pace and glided close enough to the mainland that she could see the city park on the shore. The park was deserted, save a group of three. One grade-school-age girl wearing an outgrown T-shirt sat on a bench next to a plump, grandfatherly man. The girl held a hardcover book and the man a folded-in-half magazine. On the grass close to the shore, several feet in front of them, was another little girl with pigtails coming off the sides of her head. She must have been about three or four years old, and she was enthralled by a flock of ducks on the water near the shore. The grandfather glanced up at her every so often and then returned to his reading.

The pigtail girl stood stock-still, gazing at the birds, seeming transfixed, and then suddenly she ran toward them, her arms out, hollering and carrying on and, of course, causing the ducks to take flight. Stopping just before she reached the edge of the shore, she giggled, looked back at her grandpa, who gave her a stern shake of his head, and watched with glee as the birds congregated farther down the shore. As soon as her chaperone's attention was fixed back on his reading material, she galloped forward again, intent on disrupting the ducks' peace.

The girls reminded Rachel of her and her sister when they'd been kids. She, of course, was the one with her nose buried in a book. Noelle was the peace-wrecker.

A gentle slosh of water a few feet behind her kayak made Rachel whip around. As soon as she recognized a shirtless Cale, her peace, like that of the ducks, was shattered. She gritted her teeth, avoided gawking at his bare, very muscular chest and mostly felt annoyed at the intrusion. The little thrill inside her that pulsed faintly but incessantly was obviously just a bad habit, because she was *not* glad to see him.

"What are you doing here?" she asked, returning her attention to the duck-hunting girl, whose grandpa was squatting down next to her, apparently giving her a quiet, caring lecture on the wrongs of scaring the bejeezus out of wildlife.

"Looking for you," Cale said, working to get his kayak even with hers so they were side by side. He lacked grace and skill with the boat, but he eventually managed it.

"How'd you figure out where to track me down?" She'd hopped on a city bus two blocks from his place, lucking out that it'd been going her way at the right moment. There was no way he could have followed her here.

"The swimsuit you were wearing under your clothes and your previously mentioned love for kayaking," he said. "Wasn't hard."

"Did Buck tell you I was out here?"

"If the old guy wearing the Buck's Boat Rentals T-shirt

and smoking a pipe is Buck, yeah. He rented me the boat, too."

"What a traitor." Rachel dipped her paddle in on the opposite side from him and maneuvered her kayak to the left and forward. Away from him.

Cale steered clumsily, but he followed her.

"*Why* did you track me down?" She didn't bother to keep any unfriendliness out of her voice. She'd hate to be accused of having no emotions again.

"Oh, you know," he said flippantly. "Kayak lesson."

"You need one." Curving around more so she faced the island side of the bay, she paddled a few vigorous strokes, leaving him momentarily behind. If she thought for a second that she could outpaddle him to the shore and run away before he could catch up, she would go for it, but no matter how much practice she had, he aced her on arm strength. She'd felt his arm muscles up close and personal.

"Rachel," Cale said, all signs of irreverence gone from his tone. "Quit running away from me. I want to apologize."

"So apologize," she said over her shoulder.

She let up for just a few seconds, her arms and shoulders aching from the frantic trip across the bay, and he was suddenly right beside her again, his boat skimming the side of hers. When he stuck his paddle out and rested it on her boat a couple of inches in front of her abdomen, she looked down at the bottom-of-the-line equipment that Buck—bless his heart—had stuck Cale with and then at his face.

"I'm sorry, Rachel. I never should have said any of that this morning. I was…struggling. I took it out on you. Wrongly so."

"Struggling. Yes, slightly."

"I shouldn't have asked you to go with me."

"Asking was fine. It's pretty obvious you had a hard time handling going into the condo. I didn't mind going with you."

"You only minded the blowing-up version of me," he said, attempting to lighten the tension with a self-deprecating grin. "I knew visiting the condo would be rough, but I never intended to take it out on you." Cale twisted the paddle that still rested on her boat. "This thing is heavy as hell."

"He gave you the worst one."

Cale narrowed his eyes at her as if trying to discern if she meant it and then glared out toward Buck's boathouse. "Crafty old sucker."

"He's got my back," Rachel said cheerfully. Then she sobered and decided to voice what bugged her about his apology. "You said you shouldn't have said what you said to me, but you didn't say you didn't mean it."

Cale pulled his paddle and his gaze away. Obviously, he'd meant what he'd said, and it hadn't been just a random thing during his emotional outburst.

"You think I'm not dealing with my grief?" she asked, her voice climbing higher in pitch.

"It seems like it from where I'm sitting."

"How can you, of all people, even say that?"

"Have you ever let it all out, Rachel? Had some kind of freak fest like I did in my condo—both before and today—or cried yourself to sleep or…lost control for a second?" He shrugged and raised his brows in question.

"Fits of crazy are not the only way to grieve."

"Nope. There's lots. Blocking it out isn't usually considered one, though. I think that's called avoidance."

"I'm not—"

"It's easier not to feel," he interrupted. "I get that. I

don't know how healthy it is to do it on a long-term basis, is all I'm saying."

Irritation had been building up in her since he'd arrived. She wanted to scream. Pondered, again, whether she could beat him to the shore—either one. She wouldn't be picky at this point.

"You want me to lose it?" she asked, her voice sounding half-hysterical. "Is that what you're looking for, Cale? Should I go a little crazy just like you did? Would you consider me normal then? Healthy?"

"That's not—"

She didn't wait to hear what he was going to say. Before he could react, she took her paddle and pressed down on the side of his boat. Within two seconds, it had capsized and Cale was in the drink. Her boat wobbled, but she quickly regained her balance and avoided following him over.

"Haaaa!" Rachel yelled to the sky. When Cale surfaced, she said, half laughing and maybe half-crazy, "Is *that* what you're looking for?"

Cale shook his head like a wet dog, spraying water all over her. "Not exactly."

"You want crazy, I can give you crazy. I just need the right motivation."

"Evidently," he said, shaking his head in disbelief. "How do I get back in this thing?"

"Very carefully." The release must have done some good because Rachel laughed. Or maybe it was just her latent wicked side finally coming out.

She watched his attempts to master the kayak for a couple of minutes, trying not to crack up. He was going at it from the side, and, of course, every time he hoisted his weight on the boat and tried to get his leg in, he went over again. After three failed attempts, he splashed her intentionally.

"Okay, kayak master, what is the trick?" he said, standing on the bottom, the water only about four feet deep there. It became officially impossible to not stare at his chest. His pecs were perfect—not overly huge like a bodybuilder but definitely eye-catching and beautiful. They went well with his considerable biceps, and she couldn't prevent the fantasy of having all those muscles close around her.

She forced her eyes to his face with difficulty. She wasn't supposed to be admiring anything about him. Now or ever.

"Oh, I don't know," she said. "You seem to think I do everything wrong. I probably wouldn't be able to help you."

"If you don't help me, I'll be forced to retaliate." Cale put a hand on her kayak and made it wobble.

While Rachel had had years of practice and was pretty good at staying upright, she didn't stand a chance if he decided to deliberately tip her.

"Okay, okay. Give me your paddle."

"Right. So you can strand me out here or force me to use this thing as a kickboard to get back to good ol' Buck's? I don't think so."

"You don't trust me?" she said, acting overly innocent.

"I *used* to trust you."

"I'll hold your paddle while you get in and then I'll give it right back."

He sized her up, his eyes roving from her face, down over the top of her tankini swimsuit and back up to her eyes again. At last, he handed over the paddle. "I suppose I can swim to shore if I have to."

"Don't they teach you to get in a kayak in the fire department?" She lined up his paddle with hers and held them crosswise to the kayak in an attempt to give herself better balance should he rock it again.

He laughed. "Of course. You're familiar with water rescue from a kayak?"

"Grab it right here," she instructed, pointing at the very back of the kayak. "Go up on your chest there and let it steady."

He did what she said and ended up back in the water.

"Easy," she warned. "Not so overzealous. Try it again."

"You're enjoying this way too much," Cale said, guiding his kayak a few feet away from her, as if it were her fault he'd failed yet again.

"It's a little entertaining. Think of it as a mood lightener."

"For you."

"I'll hold the front if you want me to."

"I don't." He heaved himself up again, this time with a little less power, and managed to balance himself over the back end.

Rachel walked him through sitting up on the back and then sliding his way forward inch by inch. When he was finally situated back in the kayak, he breathed out. "That wasn't the kayaking lesson I had in mind originally."

"Always good to learn new things."

"Your generosity is unrivaled." He held his hand out and she returned his paddle. They sat for a few minutes in silence and her attention switched from him to the girls in the park onshore, more distant now. They were both sitting on the bench, one on either side of their grandpa.

"I hate to get back to being serious," Cale said after a while, "but I'm sorry I ruined your morning, Rachel. And your kayak outing. God knows I'm not an expert on how to handle things, but...I worry about you."

"Said the man who single-handedly destroyed a wall with a hammer."

"That was months ago. I was much calmer today. Sometimes you have to block out the bad stuff, but if you never let it in, you're never going to get through it. Don't you want to feel a little better, have it get somewhat easier to handle thinking about Noelle?"

Like he wouldn't believe, she did. But…letting in that pain without filtering it at all? No. She wasn't sure she could ever handle that and live to tell about it. With enough time, her way of dealing with her grief would be just as effective. She hoped.

"I do what I need to do to get through," Rachel said, a lump developing in her throat. All this time, she'd fought not to lose control, afraid that if she ever did, she wouldn't be able to surface for days. It was self-preservation, the only way she knew to handle her loss. But now Cale planted doubts in her mind.

Their boats were side by side, touching. Cale was staring at her, his expression sympathetic. She almost preferred having him rant at her because sympathy made her want to lose it. As she'd already pointed out, she wasn't up for that. He reached out and put his hand around hers where she held on to her paddle.

"I rented this godforsaken boat to tell you I'm sorry for the things I said at my condo. I never meant to upset you more, but that seems to be about all I can do, huh?"

"You do have a knack for it," Rachel said, endeavoring to lighten the mood. So maybe she was an escapist, she acknowledged.

"You're the doctor…. Doesn't it have something to do with the Y chromosome?"

"Cop-out," she said, stifling a grin. "It has nothing

to do with genetic makeup and everything to do with personality."

"Oooh, that's where you're gonna go? And here I was about to offer reparations."

"Such as?"

"I was going to give you a head start on our race back to Buck the shyster's. But not now. And you know why?"

Trying not to laugh, she waited for him to answer his own question.

"Because I have a Y chromosome and Y chromosomes make men want to win."

Rachel rolled her eyes. "Personality again. But I'll take the challenge. To the dock."

"So I'm forgiven?" he asked. "Everything's good with us?"

"Until the next time you accuse me of grieving wrong, everything's good."

As they lined up side by side, with Cale making sure the noses of their kayaks were precisely even, Rachel kept a smile on her face. Everything between them did appear to be fine, and for that she was thankful. But what he'd said about working through things, about it never getting any easier for her, had her questioning herself. And that was not a familiar place to be for Dr. Rachel Culver.

CHAPTER FOURTEEN

"NOW YOU'VE got new miniblinds for me, huh?" Cale's mother said as she sauntered into the guest bedroom of her condo. "Was there something wrong with the old ones?"

"Only if you wanted them to actually cover the window completely. There were three slats toward the bottom that were damaged." Cale reached above his head and tightened one of the screws on the bracket.

Ronnie sat heavily, as was her way now, in the flowered armchair in the corner. "I hadn't noticed, but thank you for taking care of that. Thank you for everything you've done, Cale."

"Happy to do it." He finished with the bracket on one side, lowered his arms and studied his mom. She looked worn-out. He'd been here at their new condo every day he hadn't been on duty at the fire station, trying to help them put the place together. Trying to alleviate the burden for his mom, knowing full well his dad was of little or no help with the physical stuff.

"You've spent too much time here," she said. "Too much time on us these past few months."

"I don't mind, Mom."

Getting his parents relocated after his dad's accident had been a priority, one he'd worked toward for close to six months. The ranch was too far from medical services. Hell, his mom had had to drive forty-five minutes on a good day just to get groceries, and she'd ended up doing it alone since getting his dad in and out of the van was too much for her. The past few months had put about ten years on Ronnie, even though Cale had made the nine-hour drive regularly, whenever he had three days off at a time from work, in order to do what he could for them.

"You're young, son of mine. You should be out painting the town, not taking care of your decrepit folks."

Cale chuckled. "Painting the town, huh? I don't think people do that anymore."

"You've always been the guy who takes care of everybody else," she continued, ignoring his smart-aleck response, "and I appreciate everything you've done for us. Your father does, too. But we're here in San Amaro now. We're fine. Your social life must be nonexistent, Cale."

"I go out sometimes."

She always pointed out how he was a caretaker, the one to go out of his way whenever someone needed help. He didn't think much about it—it was just the way he was. But...maybe that explained why he was drawn to Rachel so much. There was no doubt in his mind she was going through a rough time now that she was back in town and was faced more directly with Noelle's death.

"When?" his mom asked. "For the three weeks we've lived here, you haven't had a moment that you weren't fixing up our home or working at the fire station, have you?"

"I went kayaking just the other day," he blurted out.

"Kayaking? Who did you do that with?"

"Noelle's sister. She's a doctor now. Only been back in town for about a month and doesn't have many friends."

"I remember Noelle talking about her when you two came out to the ranch for the weekend. They were twins, right?"

"Identical," he said reluctantly. He didn't want his mom's mind going...*there*. "She's having a hard time, I think." He rushed on, maybe to distract her from jumping to conclusions. "It's like Noelle's death is just starting to sink in now that she's back on the island and living in her family home."

His mom frowned and shook her head sympathetically. "Poor thing. It's good of you to befriend her." Her frown turned into a bittersweet half grin. "See what I mean? You're doing it again."

"It's not because I feel sorry for her." He wasn't sure why he protested, especially when he risked having his mom suspect he was interested in Rachel as more than a friend. In spite of the kisses on the beach, that wasn't what he wanted.

Was it?

He shook his head. Hell no. It couldn't be. That would be ten shades of twisted.

"You're not focusing on her to avoid things yourself, are you?"

The suggestion grated on him and he had to temper his reaction.

"I went through hell, Mom." He shook his head, choosing his words carefully because he knew, on some level, she was looking out for him. But... "It's been a year and a half—more than that—and I've worked through a dozen or two stages of grief. Faced it head-on because I can't see how else to get through it and start feeling like maybe I can get up in the morning and get through a whole day without being flattened by a thought of Noelle..." His throat threatened to swell up and cut off his oxygen supply.

"I know you have, Cale. I wasn't suggesting that you weren't."

He turned his attention back to attaching the blinds to the brackets so his mom wouldn't see what the topic was doing to him.

"You've come a long way. I know it's been hard," she continued. "But you don't really have your life back yet. You used to love to play beach volleyball, didn't you? Weren't you in a league of some kind?"

"I played on the department's intramural league." He'd liked playing, but when Noelle had died, the thought of going out and horsing around, carrying on…caring about something as petty as a game… It had turned his stomach, to put it mildly. "I'll go back to it someday. Soon," he added in an attempt to appease her. He hadn't given much thought to looking up the team's schedule or seeing if they needed another body. He probably should.

Her compassionate look morphed into the stern-mom look. "Do. It'll be good for you. You need some fun in your life."

Cale got the blinds attached and lowered them. He tested them out, opening and closing the slats a couple of times.

Fun was a tall order.

"And another thing…"

Cale closed his eyes. Sometimes—no, most times—it was better not to get his mom started. It appeared it was too late for that today, though.

"Your condo."

"What about my condo?" As if he didn't know.

"It's time, Cale. Your father and I are fine. The few boxes we have left to unpack will be there. I can tackle them when I feel like it. You've done all the updates to this place that we wanted and more."

He could feel her staring at him, stern look still in place. Sometimes he hated that look.

"Did Mariah say something to you?" he asked guiltily.

"She didn't have to."

"I know. I need to get out of her apartment." The thought of living in his condo, of sleeping in that bed, turned his stomach, but maybe once he spent time in it just working on the remodel, it would get easier.

"Maybe it's time to consider selling."

The suggestion panicked him. "No way. It's a great place. Tons of potential. I started working on it last weekend." Never mind that "working on it" was an exaggeration.

"Why don't you let us pay to have someone help you with the work?" his mom asked.

He shook his head. "I've got it, Mom. I want to do it." Cale sat on the bed, suddenly exhausted—from the conversation, not the task. "I get it, okay?" he said gently. "I've been letting a lot of things slide. I've known I needed to jump back into them, but sometimes it's easier just to stick with the status quo."

"We just want you to find happiness, Cale. You've been through so much…."

"I get what you're saying, Mom," he said, appreciating her intention but wanting to avoid the mushiness. And any mention of finding a girl, which he suspected would be next. "I hear you. I'll see if I can get my act together."

If he reassured her enough, maybe he'd believe it, too.

"See that you do. And if we can help you somehow, you let us know."

Needing help wasn't his way. His mom was right—though he'd taken steps to come out of his reclusive sadness, he had a long way to go to get his life back. He'd been patting himself on the back for the occasional night out with the guys, even if they were few and far between. But he had to admit that he'd plateaued in his recovery.

He'd just been waiting for something to push him. Something like a kick in the butt from his no-nonsense mom.

It didn't slip his notice that if he was going to preach to Rachel to stop avoiding, then he better walk the walk himself. Maybe if he faked it for long enough, he could get through the rest of his reentry relatively unscathed.

CHAPTER FIFTEEN

"TELL ME AGAIN—what part of this is relaxing?" Rachel asked her mom.

"You need to use a fork to cream that together," her mom said, pointing at the bowl of sugar and butter on the counter in front of Rachel. Jackie surreptitiously licked a dab of brown-sugar-nut topping off her finger as she directed their Saturday-morning undertaking.

"I saw that," Rachel said. "Even a kitchen-phobe like me knows you aren't supposed to lick your fingers till you're done."

"This stuff is to-die-for. The girls are going to demolish these cupcakes at the dinner tomorrow. That looks good."

"You know there's a cupcake shop on the mainland about a mile from the hospital, don't you?"

"Take a deep breath, honey. Enjoy the time away from work. Cupcakes are about the journey."

"You've lost your mind. I need to be catching up on my reading," Rachel said.

"Now, the bananas you mashed? Add those and the vanilla. Mush it all together and mix it with the hand mixer."

Rachel used a spatula to dump the fruit into the bowl and then measured out the vanilla. "This looks like baby puke."

She put the two beaters on the mixer, stuck them in the goop and switched the appliance on to Medium. The doorbell sounded over the noise of the mixer, and her mom sent her a questioning look and then, after licking her fingers clean, headed toward the living room to see who it was.

When the glop was thoroughly combined, Rachel turned off the mixer, not even remotely tempted to lick her own fingers. Then the visitor's voice coming from the living room caused her heart to speed up without her permission.

Crap. What was Cale doing here? And why couldn't she handle even the sound of his voice without getting all messed up inside?

Ignore, ignore, ignore. He'll be gone momentarily.

Unless, of course, it was her he wanted to talk to, she amended, as their footsteps and chatter moved toward the kitchen.

"Rachel, look who's here," her mom said, cheery as can be.

"Hi, Cale," she managed to say without taking her eyes from the eggs she cracked into the mixture.

"Hey, Rachel." He leaned against the counter several feet from her. "How's it going?"

"My mom's putting me through a round of torture."

Jackie resumed her spot on the other side of the sink and started spooning the sugar-nut topping into each section of the cupcake pan. "You'd enjoy it if you'd let yourself."

"What are you making?" Cale asked, eyeing the baby-puke-with-eggs-on-top mixture.

"Banana-walnut cupcakes," Rachel's mom said. "With brown-sugar-walnut topping and a banana-cream filling. We'll save one for you when they're done."

"Which, at this rate, should be early fall," Rachel said.

"She's always been such a go-getter, but slap an ounce

of domesticity in front of her and she goes all tachycardic," her mom said.

The baking had nothing to do with Rachel's rapid heartbeat. More accurately, having her twin sister's fiancé, whom she had frequent naughty dreams about, show up made Rachel go all tachycardic.

Cale laughed and Rachel threw the eggshells in the sink.

"I came by to see if you would go to a small get-together with me," Cale said to Rachel. "Evan Drake is one of the guys I work with and he and his wife are taking their trawler yacht out in about half an hour. Sorry the invitation is so last-minute, but I hadn't planned to go until my mom recently made a very emphatic point that I needed to go out and have fun more often."

The two sides within her warred—the one that longed to spend the day with him and the one that acknowledged it was much smarter to stay home and read her medical journals. Or even bake.

"I'm kind of up to my elbows in torture right now," she said. "And then I have a good twenty hours of reading to catch up on."

"Oh, no," her mom said authoritatively. "No, you don't. I've got the cupcakes covered, and you can read later. You need to get out just as much as Cale does. Probably more."

Rachel opened her mouth to argue but closed it without a word, not wanting to debate with her in front of Cale. After a glare at her mom, she set the mixer down and faced him. "I'm not much of a partygoer."

"It's not really a party. Think of it as a boat ride on the gulf."

Rachel's mom walked over to her and took the mixer from in front of her. "Out."

"Now?" Rachel asked in disbelief. "You practically forced me in here an hour ago."

"And now I'm forcing you out. Go with Cale. Get some fresh air. The journals will be there when you get back, I promise."

Rachel stared at her mom for a handful of seconds. To refuse to go at this point would be beyond rude. She didn't have that in her, and her mom knew that. Slowly, she pivoted around to Cale. "I guess I'm going on a boat ride." She forced a smile.

"Good. Just put on a swimsuit and something over it. I've got everything else we'll need."

A swimsuit. Didn't that just make everything a touch more fabulous? Her smile was still pasted in place as she nodded. "You got it."

She'd kill her mother later.

CALE SUSPECTED INVITING Rachel to go with him to Evan and Selena Drake's party was a mistake right after they got to the marina and walked up to the Drakes' trawler yacht.

He hadn't had a chance to warn Evan he was bringing someone. Although his friend had made it clear Cale was welcome to bring a guest, he realized a little heads-up would have proven wise in this particular circumstance when he caught Derek Severson and Evan, who'd both known Noelle, exchanging a wide-eyed look up on the flybridge as Cale and Rachel climbed aboard into the midst of eight or nine people on the roomy aft deck.

"Cale, you made it," Selena said and took his hand. Macey Severson, Derek's wife, looked subtly shell-shocked until he was able to introduce Rachel.

"Everyone, this is Dr. Rachel Culver—"

"Noelle's sister," Clay Marlow announced, as understanding obviously dawned on him.

Cale couldn't imagine how Rachel felt to repeatedly have people direct that momentarily stunned expression at her.

She smiled just enough that no one else was likely able to tell she wanted to throw up from nerves, but Cale could see it. He put his arm around her waist, hoping to reassure her.

"Since this is a no-name-tags affair, pay close attention," he told her in a mock-serious voice. "Up top is the captain, Evan Drake, the fire station's former playboy until he got snapped up by Selena." He gestured at Selena, who smiled warmly to welcome Rachel. "Derek Severson is up there with Evan."

"Nice to meet you," Derek called down, lifting his aviator shades so she could see his face.

"Derek, like the rest of these guys, is a firefighter, and he and his wife, Macey, own the Shell Shack bar. Do you know it?"

"I've heard of it," Rachel said. "I'm embarrassed to say I've never been there."

A round of exaggerated disbelief and phony outrage went up around them. "Island mainstay!" Evan called.

"Fire-department mainstay," Clay added and everyone laughed. "Make sure Cale takes you there. Best bar on the island, by far."

"It's our food that makes us famous, right?" Macey, who was a lot of months pregnant, said.

"That and your Sandblaster," Cale said. "It's a triple-size drink with about a dozen types of alcohol in it. It's feared and revered far beyond the island," he explained to Rachel. "This is Clay Marlow and his wife, Andie. They have a daughter who's…how old?"

"Seven going on sixteen," Clay said. "She's staying with my sister today."

"She'd much rather be on a boat ride having all her daddy's firefighter colleagues spoil her," Andie, who had multiple intricate tattoos curling out from under her short sleeves, said.

"Nice to meet you all," Rachel said stiffly. "I really like Cale's idea of name tags. I'm used to having people's names readily available on their medical charts."

Everyone laughed and Cale squeezed her waist briefly, again to try to put her at ease.

"What kind of a doctor are you, Rachel?" Macey asked.

"Emergency medicine. I'm sure I'll see some of you guys bringing in patients to the E.R." Rachel nodded to the men.

"Not an ob-gyn," Derek hollered to Macey, "so keep your legs crossed while we're out on the gulf."

"Baby's not coming for two months, Mr. Impatient," Macey said. "Two months, you hear that?"

"Unless baby has other plans and decides to come before that," Selena said. "But we'll cross our fingers she'll stay put for a while."

"I could get you through childbirth if I had to," Rachel said confidently. "No worries."

"Faith and Joe could have come after all, then," Evan said.

"Joe is one of the captains at the department. His wife, Faith, is due in a couple of weeks," Selena explained.

"I saw them the other day," Clay said. "She's ready to pop."

"Poor Joe," Evan said with a look of dread.

Rachel sidled closer to Cale as the jokes continued,

and Cale assured himself the reason that made him happy was because it meant she trusted him. That was all.

As soon as Scott Pataki and his girlfriend, Mercedes Stone, arrived with Mercedes's sister Charlie in tow, they set loose the moorings and headed out toward the Gulf of Mexico.

The women went down to the galley to set the food out, and they took Rachel with them. She went with a single unsure look at Cale before descending the flight of steps. Scott went with them to check out the cabin since he hadn't been on the *Fire and Ice Cream* before.

Cale took a seat on one of the loungers on the deck, beer in hand, and told himself Rachel was an extremely competent woman and would hold her own just fine with the others.

Derek came down from the flybridge, leaving Evan to drive, and sat across from Cale, next to Clay.

"So," Derek said, leaning forward and holding a beer between his knees. "You're dating Rachel now?" The look on Derek's face said so much more than his tone, which he kept casual and only marginally curious. The subtle wrinkle between his brows said he was trying to wrap his brain around the concept.

"No," Cale said quickly. "She just moved back to the island and doesn't know many people. We're just friends."

"She seems shy," Clay said.

"A lot of people would, coming in to this crowd," Evan said from above them.

"For all her confidence professionally," Cale told them, "she's not really comfortable socially. I don't know why."

"The opposite of Noelle, huh?" Derek said sympathetically.

"Like you wouldn't believe." Cale grinned and shook his head. "Hard to imagine they shared a womb."

"Must be...awkward to hang out with her. She looks so much like Noelle."

"I don't know if *awkward* is the word. They're different to me somehow, even though most people couldn't tell the difference between them. But there are times when I see Rachel from a distance and..." He shook his head, remembering the effect the first time he'd seen her in the E.R. "Sometimes it's a little haunting."

Cale exhaled quietly in relief when the subject changed. Their fascination with the whole twin bit just made it more solid in his mind that he and Rachel could never be anything but friends. Not that he was looking to go beyond that, with her or anyone.

NOELLE WOULD HAVE loved this, Rachel thought two hours later, after they'd all stuffed themselves with barbecue pork sandwiches, potato salad, corn on the cob, fresh fruit, coleslaw and brownies. Her twin would have fit in perfectly with this group—and apparently had, based on some of the things the others had told her about her sister.

Strangely, though Rachel was far from the life of the party, she was beginning to really enjoy herself. She'd be loath to admit it to her mom, but all of Cale's firefighter and paramedic buddies seemed like genuinely good guys, and their wives and girlfriends had mastered the art of making her feel welcome without fussing over her.

Rachel and the other women emerged from the cabin after putting away scarce leftovers and ascended to the largest deck, where there were a few lounge chairs, built-in benches, a cooler of drinks and a couple of small tables tucked in the corners holding beverage coasters and bowls of nuts and M&M's. Two of the guys were on the top navigational deck, which she'd been told was called the flybridge, and the others, including Cale, were relaxing on the deck.

Rachel's debut today had been rocky, most likely due to her own self-doubt. When she and Cale had arrived, she'd seen the looks from just about all of his friends, brief and disguised though they'd been. Cale hadn't had to tell her that everyone here had been acquainted with her twin sister. However, they'd gotten over their initial shock at her similar appearance quickly.

Then there was the subsequent surprise for Cale's friends when, after just a few minutes with Rachel, they figured out that, unlike Noelle, she didn't like being the center of attention and had no crowd-entertainment skills to speak of. Again, everyone had adjusted their thinking and seemed to be okay with her sticking to the fringes of group conversations.

One-on-one, Rachel did better. Earlier, she and Andie had talked about Andie's marine biology classes and her volunteer work at the sea-turtle rescue center on the island. And during lunch, she'd gotten involved in a discussion with Scott, a former paramedic, about some of the things he'd run into on emergency medical calls. Rachel had done ride-alongs with paramedics a few years back, but the stories Scott told were like nothing she'd experienced. It fascinated her to hear what sometimes went on before the EMS people even got the patient to her and the team at the hospital.

"Where's my baby mama?" Derek asked the group when he noticed Macey wasn't with the women.

"She's resting," Andie said. "Her ankles are a little swollen and she was roasting out here in the sun earlier."

"I'll go check on her," Derek said, trying to hide his adorable overconcern as he headed down to the cabin.

"He's even worse than Evan was," Selena said, shooting a loving look up to her husband. "You might need to sit him down and have a talk, hon."

Evan chuckled. "Already did, darlin'. The guy is hopeless. Can't wait to see how he handles labor."

"Not gonna be pretty," Clay said.

As Selena, Andie, Mercedes and Rachel claimed the four lounge chairs, Mercedes's sister Charlie climbed up to the flybridge and asked Evan to teach her to drive the boat. Rachel sat sideways on her chair and took the opportunity to soak in the view while the other women chatted.

Cale came over to her, looking concerned, as he had several times throughout lunch. "Would you like a refill on your wine yet?" he asked.

She glanced at her nearly empty glass and shook her head. "I'm okay. Actually, I'll get myself a bottled water."

"I've got it," he said, heading to the cooler in the corner before she could get up. He came back over and handed it to her before settling on a bench seat off to the side.

The poor guy… He obviously hadn't thought about what he was getting himself into when he'd invited Rachel to join him today. Instead of being able to enjoy himself and let loose, he seemed to feel obligated to make sure she was okay—and wasn't understanding that she was, in fact, doing fine.

He'd been amazingly kind, making a point of sticking close to Rachel, engaging her in conversations with the others when he noticed she was uninvolved. He was again—or rather, still—the superconsiderate guy she'd started crushing on that very first night they'd met.

In other words, he was an awesome "date" and a perfect gentleman, just like Rachel knew he would be. It was easy to get carried away with thoughts of him instead of paying attention to the conversations around her. Then she had to reel herself in and remind herself of the fundamental reason her thoughts were pointless.

He'd loved Noelle.

Even if Rachel could somehow ever lay aside the guilt over her sister's death and the cause of their argument that had led to it that night, it was like some kind of algebraic law working against her. If A was attracted to B, and B was the opposite of C, then A would never be attracted to C.

"Are you doing okay, Rachel?" Selena asked, leaning forward in her chair. "Do you need sunscreen?"

Rachel realized she was still sitting on the edge of her lounge chair, staring at the scenery, while everyone else had shed their cute, trendy sundresses to don their swimsuits.

"I'm fine," she said with what she hoped looked like an easy smile as she tried not to cringe yet again over her out-of-place tank-and-shorts combo. "Just taking it all in. It's beautiful out here. In all the years growing up on the island, I've never seen it from this perspective. I've only kayaked in the bay."

They were cruising along the gulf, parallel to the shore of the island but a few hundred yards out. The large hotels were visible, but the people on the beach were barely discernible dots of color. A pair of kite surfers bounced along the water's surface on the north end of the island, their huge, arched kites patches of vivid color against the light blue sky.

"It's easy to fall in love with," Selena said. "It was kind of part of the package deal when I married Evan, but I've grown to love it out here. Our son, Christian, does, as well. Evan lets him sit on his lap and drive."

The others joined in the conversation, recalling their

first time out on the gulf or their favorite spots on the water, and Rachel settled back into her lounger, content to listen in.

Hoping to escape notice, she lifted her tank top over her head and worked her shorts off as surreptitiously as possible. When she glanced up, she caught Cale watching her. While Noelle would have loved the attention, it made Rachel wish for a big stadium blanket to cover herself.

Yet again, it seemed the only thing she and her sister had had in common beyond their looks was their feelings for this man.

CALE WAS SURE NOW—he shouldn't have brought Rachel.

Not when his body reacted to seeing her in her non-skimpy, very plain, navy blue swimsuit the way it did.

Plus there was the fact that he was sure she wasn't having much fun.

She'd eaten only a small amount at lunch and was still nursing her first glass of chardonnay as if her life depended on staying sober. Not that Cale was trying to get her drunk, but if she would just go a little easier on herself, she would fit in better and have a good time.

Cale tried to tune in to the conversation Scott and Derek were having next to him about commercial development on the north end of the island. Scott was the manager of a newly opened horse stable in that area, and Derek was curious about a new bar that had gone in nearby, and whether it would pose any competition for the Shell Shack.

As Cale didn't have any immediate concerns or knowledge about the subject, his attention drifted. He caught his gaze veering back to Rachel and the smooth, untanned skin of her chest above the modest neckline of her suit. A delicate silver chain with a simple R-shaped charm hung around her neck, catching the sun and sparkling.

She stretched her short, toned legs out in front of her and leaned her head back. He noticed her toenails, unlike the other women's, were unpainted. Maybe that was to compensate for Noelle's tendency to go overboard and indulge in serious artistry on her nails—she'd spent loads of money on weekly pedicures and had always come back with multicolored designs. There was something to be said for the natural look, he thought, though Noelle's desire for foot art had never bothered him.

Shaking his head, he silently swore at himself for his constant comparisons of the sisters. He'd not spent much effort comparing them when Noelle was still alive. Why start now? That line of thought wasn't relevant to anything. Was it a yet-to-be-identified stage of grieving a twin? He scoffed.

No. It was just stupid and pointless.

He leaned back against the wall, stretching his legs out in front of him and noticing Scott and Derek had meandered away from talk about business and development. Again, he tried to get involved in the conversation but found his attention back on Rachel in no time.

She wasn't talking to anyone, didn't even seem to be paying attention to the women next to her. As he stared at her, she checked her watch, no doubt more than ready to escape this gathering of his friends.

Cale took a final drink of his beer and got up to help himself to a bottled water. Might as well be sober and ready to drive as soon as they got back to the marina. Then he could end her suffering and take her home. He just hoped she didn't hate him too much by then.

CHAPTER SIXTEEN

"THAT WASN'T MUCH FUN for you, was it?" Rachel said as soon as they got into Cale's Sport Trac.

Confused, he furrowed his brows and looked at her. "What?"

"You were too worried about making sure I was okay to enjoy it yourself."

"No..." Cale began automatically. Although...maybe? Yeah. She'd pretty much hit it. He shoved the keys in the ignition and started the engine, then exhaled loudly. "I shouldn't have forced you to go with me, Rachel. I'm sorry."

"*Forced* is a little strong, don't you think?" she asked with a half grin. "If anyone pushed me, it was my mom. And I'm glad she did."

"I know that was way out of your comfort zone and... What?" He'd just backed out of the parking space but now he braked and whipped his head toward her. "What did you just say?"

"I said I'm glad she did." Rachel repeated it emphatically. "It was fun."

"It was...fun." He'd stopped drinking two long hours ago and had had only two beers before that. And yet he was having trouble making sense of anything Rachel said. "You had fun? Seriously?"

"I'll admit, I was so nervous when we got there I considered jumping in the bay and disappearing for a couple of minutes. But yeah. It turned out okay. I like your friends, really."

"If I looked worried, it was because I figured you were miserable."

"Let me get this straight," Rachel said, tilting her head. "You didn't have fun because you were sure that I wasn't having fun. And yet, I *did* have fun, so you had no fun for no reason."

Cale glanced at her as he drove, trying to make sense of both her words and her mood. "If you say so. Look, you can level with me. I can take the truth. I knew going into that that you don't like big social events, especially when you don't know anyone. I was thinking it would be good for you to meet some people who weren't depending on you to save their lives immediately."

"All true. But like I said, your people were friendly and, once they realized I'm not the same as Noelle and didn't expect me to be the life of the party, I was able to relax a little."

He shook his head slowly, not convinced. "You didn't look like you were having fun."

"And what would that look like, exactly?"

"You know…laughing. Taking part in the conversations. Loosening up a bit and having a couple of drinks. Not checking your watch every few minutes."

Rachel leaned back against the headrest, closed her eyes and made a sound that sounded sort of like a hollow laugh. But somehow he didn't think she was happy with him at the moment. She didn't explain herself, though.

"What?" he asked yet again.

She looked out her window at who knew what when he stopped at a red light. It took close to a minute for the light to turn green, and yet she still ignored him. He started up again, beginning to think this short, three-mile drive was the longest of his life.

"Whatever you're thinking, just say it, Rachel."

She turned her gaze from outside to her lap. Stared at it pensively, as if debating whether to do as he'd suggested.

"That would be Noelle," she said at long last in a voice he could barely hear over the sound of the engine.

He opened his mouth to question her but paused. Tried to figure out what he wasn't understanding.

She turned her head in his direction and spoke a little louder, still not looking directly at him. "You described Noelle, Cale. Laughing, being in the middle of the fray, drinking freely…that's how my sister had a good time."

A bittersweet smile tugged at his mouth. "Yeah. True."

"Not me." Her voice was louder now. More emphatic. "That's not me. You're trying to make me into her."

"I'm not… No way, Rachel. I'm not trying to make you into anything." His voice rose a touch in volume. "If anyone knows how different you two were, it's me."

As he said it, they reached the Culver home. He pulled up alongside the curb and put his SUV into Park.

"You say that, but…" She shook her head sadly. "If you really knew, you'd realize that being in the middle of a group conversation makes me nervous. Listening to it, maybe throwing in a comment or two when I'm so moved, that's where I'm comfortable."

"Okay—"

"One-on-one conversations, totally different thing," she continued. "I had a wonderful talk with Andie. Just the two of us."

"Great," he managed to say, sensing that he wasn't going to win this, nor was he going to slow down her tirade. "I'm glad to hear it."

"And Scott—"

"Yeah," Cale said. "The lunch discussion? I caught parts of it. I'm sorry he was being so graphic. Sometimes in the fire department we tend to forget what normal people consider appropriate lunch conversation material."

"Normal? Hello, I'm an emergency-medicine doctor. Pretty sure I can take a lot more of the gruesome and bizarre than a 'normal person.' I loved talking to Scott, actually. One of the highlights of the afternoon."

"Okay, then..."

"And having a couple of drinks?" she continued. "That doesn't happen to be fun to me anymore. These days, I can't afford to lose any brain cells. Don't enjoy the feeling of losing control. I learned my limits long ago—the hard way."

"That's...smart." Just like her. Her brains had always awed him and intimidated him a little. Maybe more than a little.

"My single glass of wine had nothing to do with being too bored or miserable or whatever you were thinking. What else?"

"What else?"

"Ah, the watch. I was keeping track of how long until I needed to put sunscreen on. More than sixty minutes and I would burn to a crisp, but I wanted to get some color as well as some vitamin D."

"Makes perfect sense," he mumbled, feeling like a chastised kindergartner. He suspected he deserved it.

"I think..." She cut herself off as she narrowed her eyes at him. She clenched her jaw and looked away. Leaned forward as she collected her bag. "We've tried this, Cale. This friendship thing. It's not working. You're a good person, but I think you're looking too hard to find my sister in me. I don't think we should 'hang out,' as you put it, anymore."

She opened the door and lowered her right foot to the running board.

"Thanks for dragging me along today," she said. With that, she slid down from the high seat, shut the door and walked off without looking back at him.

Cale's mouth hung open as he watched her go up the stairs at the back of the garage and disappear into the main level of the house.

She didn't want to see him again?

And the thing that unnerved him the most was the way the bottom seemed to drop out of his gut. It was as if… almost as if she'd broken up with him. But they hadn't been together. Would never be together.

His disappointment was way out of proportion, verging on ridiculous. As he'd made so readily apparent, he didn't even know her that well. Not the real Rachel Culver.

Feeling as if his head was spinning, he glanced up at the living-room windows and realized her face was there, peering out at him for a moment before disappearing.

He quickly shoved the Sport Trac into gear and drove away, not wanting her to know she'd left him reeling, sitting there like a dejected hound with his mouth hanging open.

He pointed the truck toward home—his sister's home, technically—and wondered when he'd become such a pretender. Inexplicably, he recalled the time when he was eight years old and had been called out for having an imaginary friend he'd insisted to his mom was real.

What the hell?

He'd thought he'd been doing so well with his grief, working through it, feeling a little better with every passing month. But he was still camped out at his sister's house and now… Was Rachel right? Had he been trying to see Noelle in her, as she'd accused?

Cale shook his head. "Hell no." He said the words out loud and then repeated them, louder still.

He damn well knew the difference between the woman who had been his fun-loving, easygoing fiancée and her serious, uptight sister. He'd been going out of his way to be nice to Rachel, in fact. And this was what he got in return?

He'd known the two women were opposites from the night he'd first met them at a party. Rachel had been cowering outside in the shadows while Noelle was in the middle of a group in the kitchen, egging on one of his buddies in drinking tequila shots. Noisy, laughing, happy. Bubbling over with her joie de vivre. She made the people around her feel good just by being herself.

And today, as Rachel had pointed out, he'd not particularly enjoyed himself, all because he was worried about her having a good time.

Opposites.

Rachel was introverted and scary-smart. So smart, as her overly technical—not to mention gruesome—conversation with Scott Pataki at lunch had emphasized, that sometimes she made people feel as though she could think circles around them.

She wasn't exactly spontaneous, as her severe hesitation this morning when he'd invited her out had proven, and she wasn't a wizard in the kitchen. Far from it, judging by her reaction to her mom's insistence on baking. She was far more concerned about her career. Single-minded in her ambition, as a matter of fact, to the extent that her supervisor had to cut her off from taking too many extra shifts. What room did that leave for relationships?

He whipped into his parking space at the apartment building, turned off the engine and swore crudely.

Where had that last thought come from? Relationships? What did he care what the repercussions of Rachel's drive and personality were on a relationship?

The last thing he wanted out of life right now—and for the foreseeable future—was a relationship. Of any type, really. A relationship meant you were hooked. Attached. Vulnerable.

Just setting yourself up for the possibility of losing someone.

Yeah, he was so not up for that. With Rachel or anyone else. On a romantic level or otherwise. He had his friends—mainly the guys at the station. Had his mom, dad and sister. Those were the only people he needed to be close to in his life.

If Rachel wanted him to back off, he would do exactly that. No problem whatsoever.

Having come to that conclusion, he got out of the truck and headed inside, pushing away the question of why, exactly, he'd worried so much about trying to make her happy.

HARLEQUIN® READER SERVICE—Here's how it works:

Accepting your 2 free books and 2 free gifts (gifts valued at approximately $10.00) places you under no obligation to buy anything. You may keep the books and gifts and return the shipping statement marked "cancel". If you do not cancel, about a month later we'll send you 6 additional books and bill you just $4.94 each for the regular-print edition or $5.69 each for the larger-print edition in the U.S. or $5.24 each for the regular-print edition or $5.99 each for the larger-print edition in Canada. That is a savings of at least 14% off the cover price. It's quite a bargain! Shipping and handling is just 50¢ per book in the U.S. and 75¢ per book in Canada.* You may cancel at any time, but if you choose to continue, every month we'll send you 6 more books, which you may either purchase at the discount price or return to us and cancel your subscription.

*Terms and prices subject to change without notice. Prices do not include applicable taxes. Sales tax applicable in N.Y. Canadian residents will be charged applicable taxes. Offer not valid in Quebec. Credit or debit balances in a customer's account(s) may be offset by any other outstanding balance owed by or to the customer. Please allow 4 to 6 weeks for delivery. Offer available while quantities last. All orders subject to credit approval. Books received may not be as shown.

▼ If offer card is missing write to: Harlequin Reader Service, P.O. Box 1867, Buffalo, NY 14240-1867 or visit www.ReaderService.com ▼

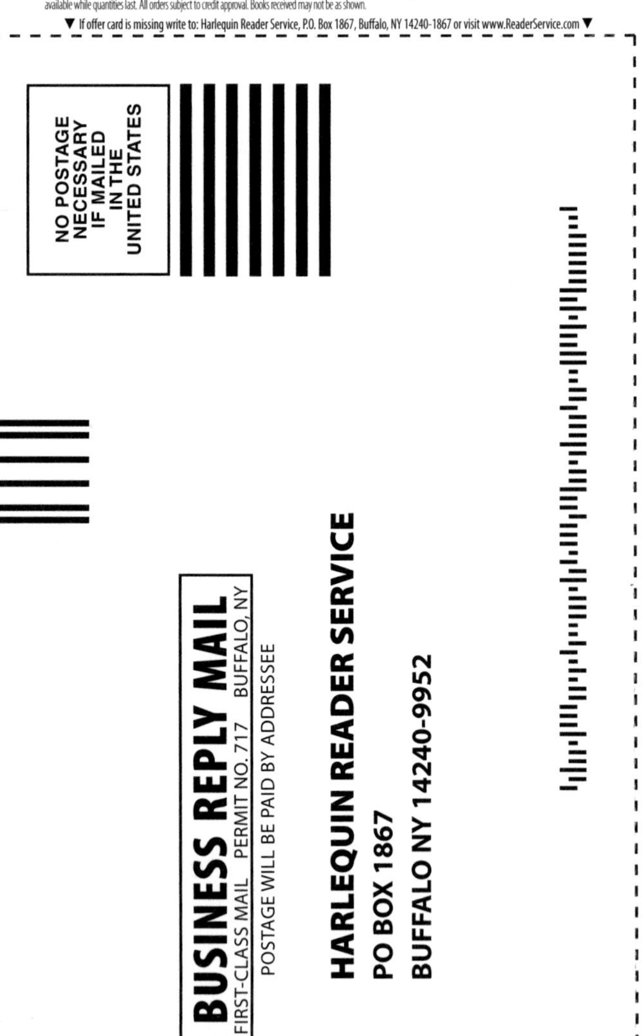

CHAPTER SEVENTEEN

A LOT OF THE GUYS on the fire side of the department dreaded the required EMS shifts, but Cale didn't mind them once a month. They were different, with a different kind of thrill from the usual fire calls. Both guaranteed a dosage of the unexpected, but, maybe because he only did medical once a month, Cale felt as though he had to be on top of his game every second he worked as an EMT. Didn't matter that it was standard for the two sides to accompany each other on every call. When he was the medical guy, it was suddenly on him—and his partner. Today, like most times, Cale was with Rafe Sandoval, a captain, department veteran and one of the very best paramedics.

Since Cale didn't do medical calls every day, he still found himself going over possible scenarios, reviewing relevant procedures in his head on the way to every alarm. Now was no exception. His adrenaline had kicked in the second the alarm had sounded throughout the station.

The night was extra dark because of cloud cover. The streets were damp from a recent rain. Moisture could be seen rising from the pavement in the beam of the ambulance headlights in certain spots as Cale and Rafe emerged from the station garage and took off. They raced, sirens screaming, toward the address on the print-out for an older, one-star motel that was as landlocked as something could be on the island.

"Twenty-three-year-old female," Rafe recited as Cale drove. "Acute asthma attack. Lost consciousness. They said they've got her outside in the parking lot. Shouldn't be hard to spot."

A shock of coldness shot through Cale's veins at the mention of asthma. He'd only been on one asthma call since Noelle's death. That one had been a thirteen-year-old boy and had had a happy ending. He said a silent plea that this one would, as well. It was up to him and Rafe, and the first thing that had to happen was that they had to get there, in spite of the heavy summer-night tourist traffic and the weather.

Getting off the main road to the side street the motel was on took about forty-five seconds longer than Cale would have liked, but short of careening down the sidewalk, there was nothing he could do about it but lay on the horn and cuss futilely into the cab.

"There," Rafe said, pointing at a group of people gathered in a circle to the side of the lot. An older man approached, gesturing frantically at them from the outskirts of the group.

Cale pulled up and he and Rafe hopped out. Rafe took the airway kit and the heart monitor and ran to the crowd while Cale grabbed the medical bag. He heard a woman's plaintive, desperate cry for them to hurry and then the fire engine drove into the lot behind them with its noisy diesel engine. The guys in the engine would bring the spine board and other necessary equipment to the patient.

When Cale joined his partner, Rafe had already done an initial assessment. "Nonbreather," he said. "Set up the O2 and get an IV line started."

"Back up, everyone," Cale said sternly.

Cale immediately started to follow Rafe's directions while Rafe prepped the bag valve mask. Cale's heart was pounding jackrabbit-fast, even more so than during the usual life-threatening call. He didn't take the time to acknowledge why. Couldn't. This woman's life depended on him doing everything he could to keep her alive.

It didn't take long for sweat to coat Cale's body beneath his uniform as he and Rafe continued to work on the woman, with less and less optimism.

"We need to get her to the hospital ASAP," Rafe said, his voice grave when none of their procedures were making a difference in the woman's condition. "Joe!"

Rafe tersely updated the fire captain, who'd been standing right behind him, on the situation, and Joe assigned Nate, one of his fire crew on scene, to drive the ambulance since Rafe and Cale would have their hands full in the back.

Rafe continued to work on the patient and they got her on the spine board. As soon as the three of them were in the back of the ambulance, they started backing up.

His own pulse hammering, Cale yelled up to Nate to avoid Gulf Boulevard at all costs. If they got caught up in that traffic again, this woman didn't stand a chance.

They reached the hospital on the mainland without Cale even noticing they'd crossed the bridge over the bay. The hospital personnel had been radioed on the way in and would be waiting for the patient at the door. He focused on none of that, though, only on getting a response, a change, anything positive from the patient. Rafe continued to work on her as they slid the gurney out and rolled her to the entrance. Cale updated the nurses who hurried alongside them, filling them in on what they'd attempted as well as the results—or lack thereof—in the minutes since the radio report.

As soon as the patient was in an exam room, things got even more chaotic—if that were possible. Rafe was the lead on this call, and Cale was only in the way at this point, so he stepped aside, swallowing hard. The mood in the tiny room was panicked and somber at once, and even someone who wasn't trained in what was happening and hadn't been involved on the call would grasp that it was going to take a miracle for a happy ending.

As he backed into the wall, making the mental transition between being wholly responsible for this woman's life and letting others take over, he swore under his breath the most vulgar stream of words he could concoct when he finally had the chance to observe and realized…

The doctor on duty was Rachel.

Unless there was a major turnaround, this situation had the potential to seriously mess with her head like other patient deaths hadn't.

Though Cale was out in the E.R. hallway, sagging against the wall a short distance down from the room with the asthma patient, he knew the minute Rachel called the death. The frenzied din of medical personnel had petered out, and the energy in the air had disappeared.

He knocked his head back against the wall in defeat.

The woman's family members were crowded into a private room, and as Cale looked in that direction, he fought to get air past the choking lump in his throat to his lungs, all too aware of the devastation they were about to have thrust upon them.

Rachel emerged from the exam room, her face as white as the drab, institutional walls around her. Generally speaking, her professional demeanor remained intact. However, there was a second when Cale saw it falter, saw her swallow, close her eyes for a moment longer than a blink and exhale slowly, as if to expel any personal pain so she could carry on with the task at hand.

She looked up then, met his eyes for the briefest instant, and there was no mistaking the toll the past half hour had taken on her.

Without so much as a nod of acknowledgment, Rachel walked in the opposite direction from him, toward the room where the family waited, undoubtedly to deliver the most difficult news to the family of the twenty-three-year-old woman who had, like Noelle, inexplicably, unfairly lost her brief battle.

"Paperwork's done," Rafe said, coming from the nurse's station around the corner. "Let's get out of here. We've got an ambulance to restock."

Cale didn't immediately move, feeling hollow and so damn tired.

"Standing here isn't going to do anybody any good," Rafe said gently.

Cale glanced back toward the room Rachel was now in, thinking she shouldn't have to handle this alone. That she needed someone to be there for her. But…no. The likelihood of her breaking down while on duty was next to nothing. The queen of blocking out the hard stuff would soldier on at least until the end of her shift—he was sure of it.

FOR ONCE, RACHEL WAS out the door of the hospital less than ten minutes after her shift ended. She didn't bother to change out of her scrubs, didn't grab anything to eat, didn't hang around to get any extra work done. She didn't say a word to anyone, either.

Her training had come through for her throughout the night after the asthma patient, allowing her to function on automatic for the most part, and in the times of extreme emergency, adrenaline had pulled her through.

It was a rainy morning out, the sun lazing around somewhere beneath the thick cloud cover, but she had her sunglasses in place over her eyes before she left the building anyway. Her jaw was set with determination to get out of there unscathed.

The silence when she got in her car was deafening. Punching the radio on, it struck her that she hadn't bothered to check out the radio stations once during the month she'd been back on the island. Who knew if they were the same as they'd been when she'd been a teenager? Come to think of it, who cared?

She hit the scan button and stopped it at the first pop station then cranked up the volume until the steering wheel vibrated. Taking care to look behind her, she backed out and left the staff lot. At the first stop sign, she finally noticed the blaring music. It was upbeat and happy. Nauseating. She smacked the power back off, preferring the silence to someone's joyful declarations of love.

The entire drive home, she held strictly to the speed limit in spite of a burning need deep down to floor the pedal, whip recklessly around corners and dodge vehicles. Or maybe not dodge them. Maybe hit them.

She was hanging on to control by a microscopic thread. As if she was grasping for dear life, dangling over a bottomless canyon that would engulf her in its darkness and never spit her out. Never let her hit the canyon floor.

She clung to that thread harder yet when she let herself into the empty house.

Rachel stared at the kitchen, feeling disoriented, unsure what to do next. She was too keyed up to sleep, and besides, she was afraid of what might sneak up on her in her dreams. It was easier to stay vigilant when her eyes were open.

Out of habit, she went to the refrigerator and opened it. Searched for a gourmet something her mom might have whipped up and then remembered her mother had left town for a weeklong conference before sunrise this morning. Rachel had been at work for a twelve-hour shift and she hadn't had so much as a snack. She should be hungry, right? She should eat.

But the thought of food hitting her stomach made her want to hurl. She closed the fridge, again at a loss for what to do. Because, God knew, she had to do *something.*

A shower. She needed to be clean. Needed to wash the awful night off. That would help.

With a nod of reassurance to herself, she climbed the stairs, went into her brother's room and opened the dresser drawer for clothes. Comfort clothes. A pair of pink-and-yellow boxers and an ancient, faded, touristy San Amaro Island T-shirt.

Once in the bathroom, she dropped the clothes on the floor, stripped out of her scrubs and waited for the water to heat. When she stepped in, she turned the water temperature up higher yet, needing it to scald her skin, cleanse her. She didn't allow her mind to veer to what she needed to cleanse herself of. Couldn't let herself reflect on…anything.

It was too easy for thoughts to invade in the shower, though. It had always been her thinking place, her one sanctuary to process the other twenty-three and a half hours of her day. To slow down momentarily and catch up mentally.

Today, she decided she wanted none of it.

Without soaping or shampooing, she flipped the water off and hurried out of the glass-doored stall. In spite of the shortness of her time under the hot water, her skin was pink from it as she toweled herself off. Then she swiped her towel over a spot on the mirror to clear the steam and squinted at her reflection, only half-aware that she was looking for her sister.

She knew that wasn't Noelle staring back at her, and yet… She didn't let herself think too much. Just allowed the relief to seep through her, clinging to the reminder that the sadness that'd been hovering just beneath the surface since the young woman's death last night…*that* was not her grief. It was someone else's. Hers was not fresh or new or different. She knew how to handle her sorrow. It wasn't a friend, but it was familiar.

"It wasn't you, Noelle," she said hoarsely to the reflection. "Not last night."

Breathing a little easier, she pulled on the shorts and shirt, ran a comb through her hair and escaped the steamy bathroom.

She could handle this. Whatever *this* was.

Outside of Sawyer's room, she paused. She threw her dirty scrubs on the floor just inside. Inhaling deeply, slowly, she pivoted and faced the door of her and Noelle's room.

It was still open, but Rachel had managed to keep her gaze averted every single time she'd walked by it, out of sheer determination. And, okay, she'd admit it…fear.

Apparently, she'd had enough of cowering for one day.

Without giving herself time to think about it, propelled by the realization she'd had in the bathroom, she plowed into the room.

CHAPTER EIGHTEEN

RACHEL HAD THOUGHT barreling into the room quickly would be easier, like ripping off a bandage all at once instead of drawing out the pain skin cell by skin cell with a gradual removal. She stopped in the center of the bedroom and spun in a slow circle, her eyes not focusing on any one thing.

It felt as if there were a vacuum in the room that sucked every last molecule of oxygen out of her lungs, leaving her unable to breathe or function.

Everything hit her at once. Everything. The smell of the stale, dusty air and a hint of the baby-powder scent that had been Noelle's body lotion. The almost painful silence. The sights—all the things she'd noticed the last time she'd come in here and so much more she hadn't. She was fixated on Noelle's side of the room, unable to look away. Like a gruesome traffic accident.

She could do this. Though what *this* was, exactly, she wasn't sure. Sort through her sister's belongings? Decide what items had no more use and what she or others might cherish?

Putting things into boxes would be measurable action. Progress.

Realizing that if she left the room to find an empty box, she would likely never make it back across the threshold, she went to the closet, which was on Noelle's half of the room, and slid the door open. Rachel's share—

the right side—was, of course, neat and half-empty. On the floor was a stack of shoeboxes. Rachel pulled the stack out and, one by one, opened each box and dumped out the old, seldom-worn dress shoes into a pile on the closet floor. The three boxes wouldn't be enough for Noelle's belongings, but they would get her started with the little stuff.

Energized—relatively speaking—by having a concrete task, she went to the desk on her own side of the room and retrieved the empty wastebasket from beneath it. She carried it back and set it on the floor between Noelle's twin-size bed and her vanity table.

The vanity was the easiest place to start. The makeup that was still lying on top of it was no longer good for anything, so Rachel sat in the dainty chair and busied herself tossing it, piece by piece, into the wastebasket, not allowing any thoughts about whose it was or why it was only half-used to barge in.

As she was systematically picking up each item, one in particular caught her attention and broke through her determination to not really see what she was handling—the bright green, sparkly eye shadow. It was so obnoxious and so uniquely Noelle. Rachel dipped her index finger into the powder and smoothed a streak onto the back of her hand. A bittersweet grin tugged at her lips as she remembered the first time she'd seen her sister wearing it, on a visit home from med school. Though Noelle had looked beautiful, as she always did either because of or in spite of her daring style choices, Rachel had joked about her aspirations of setting alien fashion trends. Noelle, of course, had come back with some insult about Rachel's trademark "natural" look. Neither had thought more about the good-natured exchange. Rachel herself had never expected it to become a poignant memory that would threaten her composure.

Swallowing back the surge of emotion, she clamped her jaw against feeling too much and threw the eye shadow in the trash.

When the top of the vanity was bare, she opened the drawers to find Noelle's extensive jewelry collection. Most of it was inexpensive costume jewelry and simple sterling-silver pieces, but none of it belonged in the trash. She stared at it for a couple minutes, overwhelmed. This was something she and her mom would need to sort through together and decide what to do with it.

As she started to push the drawer closed, one of the necklaces caught her eye. She pulled it out and held up the silver N-shaped charm—a match to the *R* that Rachel wore around her neck. This one was easy. After unfastening her own necklace, she removed the *N* and added it to the chain that held her initial. She set the empty chain back in the drawer and put hers back on, fingering the two letters for several seconds before jumping up.

Rachel eyed the door and reminded herself she could handle this. She *was* handling it. Though her throat felt as if a ball of clay had lodged in it and her pulse pounded in her temples, she was…okay…ish.

She lost track of time as she tackled the two shelves of Noelle's bookcase. The top shelf was full of stuffed animals from her sister's childhood and her high school yearbooks—identical to the ones Rachel had stored in a box somewhere in the garage. These went in a pile on the floor since they were too big for a shoebox.

The bottom shelf was the lump sum of reading material her sister had owned—yet another way they were so different. The stack of magazines, current over a year and a half ago, was such a display of her sister's personality it made Rachel's chest tighten. Celebrity mags, guides to hairstyles, women's fashion magazines, one on exotic travel adventures. Not that Noelle had done a lot of exotic traveling, but she'd dreamed of it. Just one of many things she'd never gotten the chance to do.

Rachel squeezed her eyes closed against the drops of moisture that threatened—not tears, dammit—and lifted her chin, fighting the pain that was so acute it was both physical and emotional. She stood and paced back and forth from the bookshelf to the center of the room several times, trying to get air, wiping at her eyes. She bent at the waist, grasping her middle, her lips pursed.

Just half a shelf. She could get through the rest of it and call it a productive day. Walk out of here with the knowledge that she'd faced a pretty giant demon. She only needed to sort a few more books.

She bit her lip and stared down at the remaining books, maybe two dozen of them. The temptation was there to just shove them in a box without a glance but she needed to make sure there was nothing there to hold on to. She owed her sister that, and so much more.

Crouching in front of the shelf, she went through the books, checking for personal inscriptions that'd been scribbled in the front covers. Both Rachel and her mom were notorious for writing such things whenever they gave books as gifts. There were volumes of real-life paranormal tales, ghost stories, a couple on UFOs. She removed the last of a handful of celebrity biographies and noticed one more small book that'd been hidden behind the hardcovers.

"No," Rachel said sadly. "Damn."

Noelle's diary.

It, more than anything else in that bookshelf, was so personal, so brimming with Noelle. Even though Rachel had never read her sister's diaries—mostly because she feared there were booby traps and she'd get caught—she recognized that Noelle's innermost thoughts were contained in these pages. A private account of everything that had been important to her.

Rachel flipped open the cover, not really intending to read the pages right now but wondering if there was a date or some other frame of reference to how old the journal was.

What she found made her cover her mouth with her palm and then pinch her lips as hard as she could. And still, she barely noticed the physical pain.

Private. Keep Out! That means you, Rachel Ann Culver. Don't think I won't find out if you've snooped!

The words were scrawled in Noelle's distinctive, looping handwriting, complete with outlandish curvy capital letters, in a glittery, blue gel pen so characteristic of her.

It looked as if she could have written it last week. Seeing the style of handwriting that Rachel knew so, so well, had sometimes envied for its free-spirited fanciness, in fact, was like a physical blow to the chest. And once the initial impact was over, it felt as though a boa constrictor had got hold of her, was wrapping itself around her and squeezing, squeezing, suffocating, stealing the air from her.

Stricken, unable to fight anymore, Rachel closed the diary and hugged it to her chest, falling back onto Noelle's disheveled bed. And then she did what she could no longer prevent. What she hadn't done for nineteen months and six days.

She let the tears come.

CHAPTER NINETEEN

CALE HAD HAD all night on duty to debate with himself, and he'd decided to hell with honoring Rachel's wishes. To hell with leaving her alone.

When his shift with the asthma patient had ended, he'd gone home, taken a shower and gotten some breakfast after a busy night that had left no time to grab a bite to eat. He was relieved to see Rachel's Honda in the open garage at her house. Even though it'd been almost two hours since she'd gotten off work, it wasn't unheard of for her to still be at the hospital this much later.

He made his way through the light rain up the wet stairs toward the Culvers' front door. It appeared that Rachel was alone, since hers was the only vehicle on the property. It didn't surprise him, but it did concern him. Today might not be a good day for her to be alone.

When he got to the door, he knocked and waited. He rang the doorbell, beginning to wonder if she'd gone to sleep, as most people would do after working an overnight. Somehow he didn't think she'd be able to sleep after what had happened last night, though.

After ringing the bell twice more, he tried the knob and found the door locked. The misty rain had picked up, and water dripped down his face from his hair. He went back down the stairs, into the garage and up those steps to the door that led to the kitchen. Without bothering to knock, he turned the handle and was relieved when it opened.

"Rachel?"

There was no sign that she'd been in the spotless kitchen.

"Rachel, where are you?" he called again as he walked into the deserted living room. Hearing a faint sound from above, he took the stairs two at a time, keeping his step light and quiet so as not to scare her if she was sleeping.

At the top of the stairs, he stepped into Sawyer's bedroom, knowing she'd claimed it as hers for the time being. It was empty, as well, so he stopped and listened for a second, then turned and crossed the hall.

What he saw when he cleared the doorway stopped him cold for a fraction of a second, and then he rushed forward.

"Rachel, baby, what happened?" His heart raced as his mind sifted at lightning speed through possibilities of injuries or accidents that might be the cause of her condition.

She was doubled over on the bed—Noelle's bed—her back to him, sobbing uncontrollably. Fighting for air. Or maybe…hyperventilating? She gave no indication that she'd heard him come in.

He sat on the bed next to her and touched her shoulder from behind, still not certain she knew he was there but beginning to sense this was no physical pain she was dealing with.

"Are you hurt?" he asked quietly, close to her ear, as he wrapped his arms around her from behind.

To his surprise—and adding to his concern—Rachel, the woman who seemed determined to handle her personal pain on her own, turned around and curled into him, grasping his shirt as if she were afraid she might sink into quicksand if she let go.

Cale cradled her to his chest and pressed his lips to her temple. "Shh, baby. You need to slow down. It's okay. I'm here."

"Can't…stop…" she said between gasps. "Can't… stand it… Help…me…"

He pulled her head away from him and forced eye contact. "You're hyperventilating, Rachel. You need to slow your breathing down. Everything's okay. Hear me?" He stared into her beautiful blue eyes and saw so much pain and sadness in them his chest constricted with the need to take the bad stuff away. "It's okay, baby. Shh. Deep breaths."

She tried to do what he said, nodding her head and inhaling slowly. Her breath hitched a few times. Cale continued to coach her through several slow, counted breaths, and she seemed to calm down a little.

He eased his way farther onto the bed on his side and pulled her with him, keeping his arms around her. She felt so small and vulnerable, her shoulders still jerking periodically as she continued to work to calm her breathing. Holding her tighter, he inhaled deeply, his nose buried in her hair, and felt the softness of her body beneath his fingertips.

He hadn't held a woman this way for so long. He was supposed to be comforting her, but, God, it felt good. *She* felt good. He hadn't realized how much he'd missed being this close to another human being.

And it felt twice as good to be needed. Not that he wished whatever Rachel was going through right now on her or anyone, but focusing on what she needed gave him purpose like he hadn't had in months. It dragged him out of his own problems. Until this moment, he hadn't realized how wrapped up in them he still was, even after all this time.

When Rachel seemed to regain control of her breathing, he squeezed her closer and kissed her forehead. "Tell me what happened," he said in a gentle voice. He could guess a lot of it but didn't want to jump to the wrong conclusions.

Rachel slowly, stutteringly told him how she'd been trying to keep it together ever since the asthma patient and how coming home to an empty house had magnified everything that she was trying to fight off—the girl's death, the similarities to Noelle…

"She even kind of looked like her," Rachel said in a wrung-out voice. "A little bit. Blond hair. Skinny. I bet she had a pretty smile."

Her breath hitched again and she ducked her head deeper into Cale's chest. He rubbed her neck. Ran his fingers through her damp hair.

"You know there was no hope for her last night, right?" he asked.

Rachel nodded, her eyes closed tightly. "Just like Noelle…"

"She was too far gone when we got to her." Cale hated those cases, but over the years, he'd gotten better at accepting them. Generally speaking. Last night's was tougher.

"After I got out of the shower, it hit me that all the stuff I was bottling up inside since last night was not based on reality," Rachel said. "I was mixing up Noelle and that girl in my head."

"Believe me, I had some of the same thoughts."

"You did?"

He nodded, the sadness intensifying again. "Hard not to."

"When I realized they were different..." She broke off and shook her head. "This must all sound crazy. When I remembered that Noelle hadn't just died and I didn't have a fresh loss to try to handle, I had this overwhelming relief. So I thought I could handle...this." She flung a hand blindly toward the rest of the room.

"Your first time in?"

As she nodded, she began silently sobbing again, her shoulders heaving. Seconds later, her sobs weren't silent; they were huge, heartbreaking sounds of grief, as if the levee had busted and there was nothing holding back months' worth of pain.

Cale felt her bone-deep sadness on every level, had lived it and breathed it for so many months. Even though his grief had lessened with time, as he'd worked through it, now it came back, fresh and raw. He let the moisture in the corners of his eyes gather, refusing to take his hands away from Rachel.

He had no idea how much later it was when her sobs became fewer and further between. Quieter. Her breaths evened out again, though this time, she hadn't hyperventilated. Cale rubbed light circles on her back.

"S-s-sorry," she said shakily. "I didn't mean to cry all over you."

"Maybe you needed to. How long has it been since you let go like that?"

Rachel pulled a corner of the sheet from between them and wiped her swollen eyes with it. She shook her head.

"No?" he asked, confused.

As she studied the sheet intently, she shook her head again, and he saw her lower lip tremble before she admitted, "I haven't. Cried. Not since getting the awful news that night..."

Oh, shit. "At all? Or do you mean you just haven't cried so much?"

"Not at all." And the tears started again. "It hurts… too much…."

"I know," he whispered, aching for her. "It's okay, baby, just get it out. Let it come out. I get it. I understand."

All of a sudden, Rachel stiffened and rolled away from him. She sat up on the edge of the bed with her back to him.

"Rach? What happened? Come back here."

He put his hand on her slender waist, but she jumped off the bed, shaking her head and putting distance between them.

"Oh, gaaaawd," she said, as if she had some new unbearable physical pain. "Nooo. You don't understand at all."

He frowned and sat up. "There's a little difference between being her boyfriend and being her twin, I'm sure. But the sense of loss is similar."

She took a throw pillow from the other bed and hugged it to her chest desperately. If it had been alive, she would have squeezed the life out of it.

"Rachel, if you haven't cried until now, you have so much sadness to get out. I know how much I've been through since it happened and—"

"Stop it. Cale, just stop," she said hoarsely. "You can't begin to understand. It's not just the wrenching sadness that makes me want to curl up in a ball and die. It's…" She pulled the pillow up and buried her face in it.

He couldn't imagine what she was trying to say, but though he wanted to go to her and touch her, reason with her, he sensed that wouldn't go over well at this particular moment. "What, Rachel? It's what?"

She lowered the pillow, went to the window and absently turned the stem on the blinds until the slats let in what little bit of clouded-over daylight there was. Shaking her head subtly, slowly, she let the seconds tick by. "Guilt," she finally choked out. "I have this horrible, awful guilt."

Cale stood abruptly, because, of all the things he thought she might say, that was absolutely not one of them.

"Why, Rachel? You have nothing to feel guilty for. You weren't there. You couldn't have saved her."

He could just imagine the things that went through her head, back then and now, as someone who was trained to save lives. It was something he'd had to learn to get over when he'd first started going on medical rotations. Being trained to save a life did not equate to being able to save everyone. And Noelle had died alone in her car. Rachel hadn't ever had the chance. By the time anyone knew Noelle had had an asthma attack, it'd been too late. By hours.

"It was my fault she was by herself," Rachel said, her voice haunted.

Cale stepped up behind her, stopped six inches away from her. He reached out to touch her shoulder, his hand hovering above it, but she glanced down at it and stepped to the side angrily.

"She ran out of the house because of the argument we had, Cale. Because of…what I told her." She let out a long, pained groan.

Cale put his hands on her waist again with the intent of pulling her to him.

"Come here, Rachel. You don't have to feel this way by yourself."

The pillow dropped to the floor but Rachel didn't move. But she didn't fight him, either, so he moved to her and wrapped his arms around her from behind. Her obvious pain was killing him. He knew he couldn't take it away, but he had to do whatever he could to lessen it. Give her some measure of comfort. It wasn't just that he felt he had to. He wanted to. Like he hadn't wanted anything for a very long time.

RACHEL COULDN'T UTTER the rest out loud. She just wanted to wilt and become unconscious so she didn't have to feel anymore.

Cale's arms around her, supporting her, were such a relief. He was so strong compared to her. Physically and emotionally. The fact that he was still standing here after she'd cried all over him and made a blubbering fool of herself spoke volumes about the man he was. Not that she had experience with many different men, but she was pretty sure her scene would have sent the vast majority of them running.

But then, she wasn't at all surprised.

Weakly, she turned around and ducked into his chest, drinking in the security his body and his acceptance afforded her. Her cheek rested on his rigid pectoral muscle as if on a firm pillow. She never wanted to move.

"How are you doing?" he asked a few minutes later in a near whisper. "Any better?"

She didn't figure she would ever be better. Every inch of her body ached, and she wasn't sure she would be able to stand much longer if he hadn't been holding her up. Her head throbbed, and her heart literally hurt. "I'm so tired, Cale."

"I know. Come here."

Before she could react, he bent and picked her up, sliding one arm beneath her knees and the other one around her shoulders.

"Let's get you to bed."

Rachel threw her arms around his neck and rested her head on his shoulder, knowing in some tired part of her mind that she should protest but…bed sounded like a gargantuan relief. She only wanted to sleep. For days.

She closed her eyes, oblivious to everything except how heavy her lids were. Her body shifted slightly with every step Cale took. When he lowered her, she blinked open her eyes and saw he was setting her in Sawyer's bed. The blinds were closed and the room was wonderfully dim. Cool from the air conditioner. So much more comfortable than the other room, with its awful thoughts and agonizing memories, where even the air seemed… tainted. Her lids drifted shut again.

When Cale started to straighten, acute fear jabbed at her, jolting her out of her daze. She tightened her hands around his neck. "Please," she begged, stunned by the force of yet more emotions when she'd thought she was drained. "Don't leave me by myself, Cale."

"You got it, baby. I'm not going anywhere."

He gently pulled the bedding out from under her and crawled up onto the twin-size captain's bed next to her, covering them both with the lightweight blanket. He drew her close to his body and pressed his lips to her forehead.

"Okay?" he whispered.

"'Kay." She closed her eyes again and let sleep mercifully drag her under.

CHAPTER TWENTY

CALE AWOKE TO a low-key, drawn-out rumble of thunder. Before his eyes were even open, he breathed in Rachel and moved his hand to her waist, keeping his touch light, cherishing the feel of her skin beneath his fingers where her T-shirt had crept up. Her head was tucked under his chin, and he burrowed into her silky hair.

His first coherent thought was how good it felt to wake up not alone for once. With Rachel.

The sadness from last night and this morning had faded and was reduced to a fuzziness around the edges, a weight that was no longer directly bearing down on him. Contentment had pushed it aside. Contentment and purpose. Usefulness he hadn't felt for some time.

Rachel had needed him earlier. She likely still would when she woke up and faced the grief she'd only just begun to reckon with. He remembered the raw sensation of that only too well and wished he could alleviate it for her. He couldn't, he knew. No one could. But the two of them could find comfort in each other—they had already.

He wanted that. Wanted it for her and he wanted it for himself. It was hard to explain, even to himself, but witnessing Rachel this morning, being the one person she turned to, the one she trusted enough to open up and reveal her vulnerable side to… It had affected him on a soul-deep level. The connection between them was like nothing he'd experienced before, and though it'd been initiated with a painful loss, there was more to it than that.

Cale watched her sleep in the dim, rainy afternoon light, studied the way her makeup-free lashes rested on the pale skin of her face. Blond strands fell across her cheek, and he brushed them away. Rachel stirred, inhaling deeply and emitting a soft moan as she breathed out. It twisted something deep inside of him. He kissed her forehead, keeping his touch whisper-soft and allowing his lips to rest on her flesh for several seconds.

She curled into him and ran her hand drowsily, possessively, up his chest without opening her eyes. In that moment, heat began pulsing through his veins, and he was forced to acknowledge that there were more than just platonic feelings going on here. He wanted to do more than hold Rachel, more than assuage her sadness. He wanted…her.

She needed to sleep, though, more than anything. And who knew how she really felt about him? Never mind all the other arguments he could come up with if he gave his brain free rein. He raised his mouth from her forehead and ducked his chin so that their faces were so close he could feel her breath—but not quite touching. He shut his eyes and did his best to ignore the urge to pull her closer.

Rachel moved again, made another sleepy, sexy sound. Nuzzled her nose next to his. Her eyes blinked partially open and he held himself stock-still, knowing if he dropped his guard for a second, his lips would be on hers.

Then they were anyway.

And Cale could swear he wasn't the one who'd moved that last half inch.

Rachel's grasp tightened on his shirt, and she pulled him toward her. She moved her other hand to the back of his neck aggressively as they kissed, making it clear she was into this and aware of what was happening, if still drowsy. She wedged her knee between his legs, entwining their bodies intimately.

Within moments, the intensity of the kiss notched up times twenty. Their tongues met. Tangled. Teeth tapped together clumsily as they tried to work themselves closer still, to deepen their connection.

Reason and thought escaped Cale as a primal need like he'd never experienced took over. Yes, it was physical, but it went far beyond. He wanted to climb inside of her and heal her, make everything in her world right and have her do the same for him.

Their bodies aligned, and they rolled so she was beneath him, clinging to him. It was all he could do to support part of his weight with his arms. She seemed so fragile under his body, and yet, in spite of her softness, he knew she had a thread of steel in her that made her stronger than he could ever dream of being.

"Rachel," he whispered reverently and then crushed their lips together again.

RACHEL REVELED IN THE storm of delicious physical sensations Cale aroused, in the weight of him on top of her. The feel of his skin as she inched his shirt up and ran her hands over him, his taut abdomen, muscled chest, strong back, broad shoulders.

She shut down the pesky little voice that questioned what she was doing, reassuring herself that there was nothing wrong with a few moments of glorious escape from the shadows that had weighed her down even in sleep. She needed this closeness like she'd never needed anyone before.

He lifted his head, breaking the contact of their mouths, and she pulled him back to her, afraid of losing the link between them, the security, the affection. Being so close to him made her feel safe, as if the horrible stuff she knew hovered just out of her consciousness at the moment couldn't get to her.

He lifted her T-shirt, baring her so that they were skin-on-skin from the waist up. The heat of his flesh made her crave even more of him, made her long for him to take her higher, to soothe the hollow ache inside of her.

His hands explored her body, caressing, rubbing, palming her breasts, making her feel so feminine and desirable, she knew she would never get enough of him.

As she pulled his shirt over his head, he leaned to the side to help her. Their eyes met, and his held an unspoken question.

Rachel couldn't fathom any question, couldn't imagine letting him walk away now. She wanted all of him, needed him to fill her, make her feel alive, give her hope. There was no thinking of anything else—she couldn't let herself.

Instead of responding to him with words, she lifted her own shirt the rest of the way off, then reached lower and worked her shorts down her legs, baring herself to him completely.

His gaze shifted to her body, and she felt his eyes burning her up, sharpening the ache low in her abdomen. She lifted one knee and urged him back on top of her, nestling him between her legs and soaking up the gratification of his drawn-out, needy moan.

She slid her hands beneath his waistband in back, kneaded his butt with both hands as she drew him as close to her as physically possible. And yet she still yearned for more, needed more.

All it took was for her to unsnap his shorts. He reached down and took over the task. His zipper lowered with the unmistakable sound of metal letting go, freeing him. In a single motion, he arched himself and slid his shorts to his ankles, kicked them to the floor.

His mouth was on hers again even before his body was, his tongue plunging between her lips, demanding and insistent. He tasted earthy, masculine…safe. Like a refuge.

The sensation of his hardness against her, pressing into the juncture of her thighs where she was damp and throbbing for him, elicited an unfamiliar, lustful sound from deep in her throat. Unable to deny her pulsing need, she opened herself to him, her hands on his beautiful, toned butt again, urging him closer.

When he entered her, her eyes filled with tears that contained both relief and need at once. She bit her lip against the momentary sting as her body adjusted to his size. He stilled, as if waiting for her to be comfortable, and when the heat inside of her climbed feverishly, outweighing any discomfort, she moved her hips suggestively and nibbled at his shoulder.

Finding her mouth with his again, he began to move inside of her, gently at first, inch by incredible inch, until she couldn't stay quiet.

"More," she whispered.

"Yesss."

They fell easily into a rhythm, their bodies working together as if they had an age-old intimate knowledge of each other. Her body began to tingle and burn in no time and their pace quickened, became more urgent as he slid in and out of her. She clung to him, her mind stopping, letting the physical sensations take over. Taking, giving, needing…finally tumbling over the edge in a climax that turned her inside out. Her senses were overwhelmed as she held on to him for all she was worth. Moments later, he thrust into her a final time, a sexy groan of ecstasy rumbling from his chest.

Rachel closed her eyes and slowly regained her senses, came down from the ecstasy bit by bit. Her breathing slowed, as did his, and her heart rate gradually returned to normal. The sheen of sweat on her body eventually made her shiver in the chilly room.

He rotated to his side, pulling her with him and drawing the blankets back around them.

He kissed her forehead as if she were the most precious thing in the universe. "Rachel," he said in a growly, gravelly voice.

An alarm went off in her dazed, satiated mind when Cale spoke her name.

Cale.

He was beautiful with his sleep-tousled hair and his stubble-rough chin. Tender and caring in the way he touched her, caressed her face, pressed sporadic kisses to her temple and eyelids as if he never wanted their connection to end.

He was so off-limits. Not supposed to be in her bed.

She pushed against his chest and turned her head when the crash of realization pierced her, bringing with it the black, suffocating guilt. "No."

She was the *worst sister ever.* Had betrayed Noelle in the most fundamental way.

Cale lazily raised his head and stared down at her, confusion in his green eyes. "What's wrong, baby?"

She sat up and pulled herself toward the headboard, away from him, feeling the stupid plastic Yoda jab into her back until she turned and leaned against the cold wall. She located her shirt and put it on in an attempt to feel less exposed. Blindly, she shook her head desperately from side to side.

"What is it, Rachel?" Cale asked, rolling onto his side at the edge of the bed. "That was…good. Wasn't it?"

God, it was world-shattering good. She nodded absently, sadly. "That's bad. Really, really bad."

He sat up, studying her, as if afraid to ask too many questions, afraid of this hot-and-cold basket case who'd just pretty much seduced him.

"You should go," she said in a rough voice. She leaned past him and fumbled around in the blankets for her shorts then pulled them on.

"I'll go after you talk to me. Let me help."

"You can't help me do anything. I…can't believe I did that."

He was quiet as he absorbed her words. "We. Pretty sure there were two people involved in that."

The regret closed in on her, squeezed the air from her lungs, blackened her vision around the edges. Her skin felt like someone else's, as though it didn't quite fit. She wanted to crawl out of it. She had to settle for scrambling off the bed and standing in the middle of the room, but that gave her no relief.

Cale stared at her almost fearfully as she ran her hands through her hair and pulled, wishing she could make this awful guilt go away simply by yanking every last strand of hair out of her scalp.

He put his shorts back on and then approached her, but she spun around, throwing her back toward him. Stopping a foot away from her, he said, "Rachel, it's okay. It's gonna be okay."

Not. Even. Close. It would never be okay.

Guilt was burning a hole in her chest and she yelled, a pained, frustrated sound, but she didn't care what he thought, what anyone thought. She was on the verge of being crushed by the awful feelings and only wanted relief. Even though she didn't deserve it.

"You need to leave, Cale. Please." She whirled around and dared to look him in the eye.

He sized her up, his eyes searching hers, and she stood strong, defiantly, not against him, but against her own self-loathing. If he saw that, he might stay and try to make her feel better—as if that were possible.

She so needed him gone, so she could fall apart—again—this time in private.

Cale swallowed and nodded once, the look in his eyes so sad—as if she'd let him down, too.

Rachel turned away again to try to get that look out of her mind. Behind her, she could hear him step toward the bed and pick up his shirt. Then he walked out of the room and down the stairs. She crossed her arms defensively over her chest just before she heard the kitchen door shut quietly behind him. Then she crumpled. Slid to the floor right where she was, not even waiting until she landed before the sobs came out, feeling as if they were wrenched from deep inside of her.

Thank God the air conditioner was on and all the windows were closed, because at this rate, the entire island would have been able to hear her.

She rolled onto her side, clutched at her middle, wished for something, *anything,* to lessen the all-encompassing pain. The relentless guilt.

She was the worst sister ever.

Rachel balled up her body and let the sobs rack clear through her, unsure that she would ever stop crying.

And that was exactly why she'd fought so hard for nineteen months not to start.

CHAPTER TWENTY-ONE

THE MESS CALE had avoided at his condo for months was going to take a hell of a lot longer to clean up than it had to make. Good thing he was in dire need of something to do—something physical and absorbing.

And then there was the "mess" he'd just gotten himself into with Rachel. That wasn't so easily taken care of.

What in the living hell had he been thinking?

He'd slept with his fiancée's sister.

It didn't matter that Noelle was dead—it was wrong. On so many levels.

He'd driven straight to his condo from Rachel's, moving on autopilot as his brain had been…numb. Now that the numbness was wearing off, he was heading straight for an emotional tailspin.

Best to focus on doing something constructive, he told himself.

The wall he'd attacked was a wreck. He'd gotten it more than halfway demolished his first go at it, but it had obviously been done in a rage. There was nothing professional about the job he'd done.

Time to fix it. He began pulling off the chunks of drywall that jutted every which way and throwing them into a pile in the corner.

He'd slept with Noelle's sister. Knowingly. She might have been in a sleepy daze, but he didn't even have that as an excuse.

He'd wanted Rachel.

What kind of a bastard did that make him?

He loved Noelle, to this day. When a person died, your love didn't just go away, he'd discovered. It lived on; it became stronger in some ways, more sacred. Cale had just basically taken a dump all over that sacredness for a twenty-minute roll in the hay.

But it hadn't been just a roll in the hay, and frankly, that made it worse. Had he picked up a girl at a bar, gone home with her and satisfied their mutual physical cravings, it would have been easier to accept. That would have been purely sex. Understandable for a guy who hadn't been with a woman for going on two years.

He couldn't begin to claim that Rachel was just sex. He cared about her. She'd turned him on in three seconds flat, no doubt, but before she'd even stirred, he'd been thinking about how content he was to wake up beside her. To be the one who was there when she finally let herself go, let the grief in. To be the one she turned to for…anything. He liked being that person for her.

But he loved Noelle.

Cale tossed another chunk of drywall to the pile that was beginning to amass on the floor and wiped the sweat off his forehead. He wandered through the dining area and the living room, shoved aside the vertical blinds and stared out the glass door at the rainy, gray gulf. He let his forehead rest against the window and swore at himself.

He knew Noelle wasn't here anymore, that she couldn't be hurt by his actions. God, did he know that after spending so many days and nights working to accept that. And yet…he was so damn ashamed that he'd been weak. So easily tempted by another woman. Just like that, he'd set aside his feelings for her when it was convenient.

Maybe someday the love he felt for Noelle would turn

into something only remembered in the distant past, allowing him to give himself to a woman but…not now. He'd planned to spend the rest of his life with Noelle, and those kinds of feelings couldn't just be laid aside when another woman happened along. Doubly so when that woman was Noelle's freaking twin sister.

God, what would other people think if they found out? That he was messed up? Trying to replace one sister with the other? Pretending they were one and the same? They'd no doubt be disgusted.

He disgusted himself.

Cale straightened and let the vertical blind fall back into place, blocking his ocean view. After standing there for several seconds, trying to calm his racing, guilt-ridden thoughts, he headed back toward the kitchen.

Thanks to his impulsiveness, Noelle wasn't the only one to consider. Judging by the way Rachel had kicked him out, she was having an even harder time than he was accepting what they'd let happen. And that was as much of a concern to him as how he'd desecrated Noelle's memory.

He went over to the outside wall of the dining room to the area he'd long ago set up as his "workbench" since he had no other available space. He searched among the tools and materials on the floor and finally located the saw he needed to destroy the studs. A little more searching yielded an extension cord. He plugged in the saw and tested it, then trudged back over to the former wall and went to work on it. It didn't take long for him to get into a rhythm with the power tool and his mind to return to his dilemma.

The bitch of it was that he cared for two women. One was no longer living, and logic said the thing to do would be to let that go. Let her go.

Shit. His throat clogged up with emotion at the mere thought. He couldn't let Noelle go.

Cale swore loudly as he forced a stubborn piece of drywall loose and scraped his arm on a nail sticking out of one of the studs in the process. He inspected the cut, decided it was nothing and kept working.

He couldn't let Noelle go, and that pretty much said it all. Until he could—if he ever could—he couldn't be with Rachel. Not that way.

He paused in his sawing and wiped some sawdust from his cut. Unfortunately, that conclusion didn't bring him any peace. He laid into the saw with a new determination, willing himself to concentrate only on the job, to get the women out of his mind.

An hour and a half later, the wall was gone and he'd vacuumed up the mess. The scraps were piled about three feet high in the corner by the kitchen. He surveyed the newly opened area, visualizing how the room would be once he carried out the rest of his plans—*their* plans.

Screw visualizing. His stomach rumbled so loudly the upstairs neighbors could probably hear it. He pulled out his phone and located the number for Chinese food delivery then stopped himself.

That was *their* restaurant. His and Noelle's. The one a block over from the condo. The one they'd ordered from countless times after he'd moved in here. Always pork lo mein, cashew chicken and a double order of dumplings. His first instinct was to try the sub place instead, or the brand-new Chinese place on Gulf that was a few blocks farther away. Everything he used to do with Noelle was harder now, ripe with memories, a blatant reminder of what he'd lost. But tonight…he needed that. Needed to feel closer to her. He pushed the call button, placed his order and hung up to wait for the first food he'd had since breakfast fourteen hours ago.

The silence in the condo after the scream of the saw for so long rang in his ears, and all at once, the physical labor caught up with him. The labor and the day with Rachel. He staggered to the living room and fell into the upholstered chair that faced back toward the dining and kitchen area. The missing wall gave this room a different feel to it, too.

He glanced around at the living room, wondering vaguely how it would best be arranged to open it up, as the oversize leather couch currently cut it off from the dining room. His eyes landed on a photo on the second shelf down of the bookcase along the opposite wall. Noelle. His favorite picture of her.

He summoned the energy to drag his butt out of the chair and walk over to it. Picking it up, he felt his eyes tear up for the second damn time today. But while it made him sad to stare at her pretty, too-young-to-die face, tonight it brought him comfort, as well. He felt so much relief with his earlier conclusion that he wasn't ready to let go of her yet. He carried the frame back to the chair with him and sat down, still staring at it, drinking in her every feature. It'd been a while since he'd allowed himself to do this, to linger over thoughts of her, and it felt right tonight.

He let the memories come. He opened himself to them, to Noelle, so much so that he could practically hear her voice, smell her sweet scent, feel her energy in the room with him. And as he looked into her eyes, those beautiful blue eyes that matched her sister's, he could imagine what she'd say to him if she were able to come back and have one more conversation with him. Once she got over the initial shock of what he'd done earlier today, she would no doubt threaten his life if he ever dared to hurt Rachel.

With or without an imagined decree from Noelle, he was certain of one thing—he never wanted to hurt Rachel. Directly or indirectly. And that meant one thing—he couldn't just try to shove what had happened under the rug and ignore it. Suck though it might, he was going to have to go back to Rachel and level with her about his intentions once she'd had time to work through some things. And then he was going to have to hold himself to the promise that he would never let things get physically out of hand between them again.

CHAPTER TWENTY-TWO

THERE WAS NO way to miss it when she turned down her street—Cale's orange Sport Trac stood out in the gloomy, overcast day like a bright red clown nose in an otherwise black-and-white photograph.

If her street hadn't been so short, therefore making it unlikely that he hadn't also noticed her car approaching, Rachel would have given serious thought to backing up and driving elsewhere. As it was, she pulled into her driveway and garage without glancing his way or giving him any indication that he was welcome.

Why in the world was he here? Hadn't she made her feelings known last night when she'd forced him to leave? It hadn't even been fifteen hours. Nothing had changed.

As she'd suspected, he didn't appear to care whether he was welcome or not. When she got out of her car, he was walking into the garage toward her, looking at her expectantly.

Rachel ignored the pang of longing brought on by a single glance at those green eyes. She turned away and went to the stairs without a word.

"Ignoring me isn't going to change anything," Cale said from the bottom of the stairs.

He wasn't scoring any points by speaking that truth. "Knock yourself out," she said flippantly as she unlocked the door at the top of the steps. "Come on up."

Cale clambered up the wooden steps and joined her in the kitchen as she took off her rain jacket.

"Not the best weather for kayaking," he said.

"How long have you been waiting for me?"

"Long enough to know you must be cold."

Freezing, but she wasn't going to admit it to him. She hadn't expected sunshine, but the precipitation on the weather forecast radar had been spotty enough that she'd hoped to stay mostly dry on her kayak outing. The mist that had shrouded the bay for the past two hours and the unseasonably cool temperature had penetrated her lightweight rain jacket within minutes of paddling away from Buck's dock.

"How'd you know I wasn't at work?"

"I went there and checked."

Rachel made a point of showing no reaction to his supposed dedication, but it took significant effort. "Talking about it isn't going to change anything, either, you know," she said, echoing his earlier declaration.

"I'm aware of that." His tone was somber, as if he, too, were experiencing some hard-core regrets over what had happened. "Do you want to change into dry clothes before we discuss this?"

She wanted to take a long, cleansing, hot shower and then curl up in bed for the rest of the day. Preferred never to discuss "this." "Give me five minutes," she said. "If I take too long, feel free to give up on me."

Not surprisingly, though she did take closer to ten minutes to change clothes and dry her hair, Cale proved he wasn't the type to just give up. In fact, he'd made himself at home in the living room and had thought to start the gas log fireplace. Either he was beyond considerate, or he was scheming to get her down there, knowing she wouldn't be able to ignore the warmth.

Unable to resist, she took the bait and stood in front of the fireplace with her back to him. She heard him lower himself to one of the chairs behind her, letting out a frustrated breath as he did.

"Rachel…"

She held her still-cold hands above the faux fire and waited.

"Obviously, last night was a mistake."

"Obviously," she mocked. His word choice had her hackles raised in a millisecond, and for a moment, she chose to defer the focus from her guilt to her lousy self-esteem. "Why else would someone be with the geeky sister?"

Before she could react, he was by her side, in her space, turning her toward him with gentle force.

"Geeky sister? Really? That's what you're going to come up with?" He stared into her eyes, his full of angry fire.

"I'm not 'coming up with' anything. It's ancient history, Cale. Just check the pictures if you need proof." She pointed to the yearly photos hanging on the wall above the stairs.

"Let's get a couple things straight, first off. I don't see you as geeky by any stretch of the imagination. You're smart as hell, yes. Damn good at saving lives. And pretty and sexy."

"I'm not—"

"Save it, Rachel. This is me. Not some guy who doesn't know you." His features softened from anger to a determined intensity. "I was with you because I like who you are. I care about you. You get to me like a woman is supposed to get to a man."

Rachel swallowed, unable to come up with a reply to that. Affected by his words even though she didn't want to be. She was such an easy mark where he was concerned.

With great effort, she sacrificed the glorious heat and stepped away from him, easily reminding herself of the bigger issue here.

"I care about you," he said in a voice that was barely there. "That never would have happened if I didn't. But it can't happen again."

Rachel gritted her teeth together and nodded. "Obviously."

He took a few steps in the opposite direction, chin raised, gaze pointed to the ceiling. "I still love Noelle. I probably always will. I don't know. I do know that what we did felt like betraying her."

That awful *B* word had been taunting her all night, and just like that, her control shattered again. Her eyes teared up, her throat closed and the physical ache in her chest nearly leveled her. "I know," she whispered, not looking at him.

"I'm sorry."

"No, *I'm* sorry," she managed to say before she was overcome by the awful, suffocating emotions. She bit her lower lip till it bled in an attempt not to cry yet again. The stupid tears fell anyway. God, she was so sick of tears. "It's my fault. Everything is my fault." She swallowed a sob and straightened. "She died because of me, Cale."

He frowned and narrowed his eyes at her, then tilted his head in question. "What are you talking about, Rachel?"

She wished with all her heart she hadn't said that last bit, and yet she needed to tell him. Needed to tell someone before the guilt burned her to nothing. And on some level, she knew telling him would make it easier for him to walk away from her.

Leveling a stare at him as she tried to get control of herself enough to speak coherently, she felt every amplified, accusing heartbeat in her temples. She lowered her gaze, swallowed down the taste of bile.

"When I tell you what I have to tell you, you won't be able to stand looking at me," she began, her voice coming out extraordinarily even, if hollow.

She dared a glance at him and saw he was staring at her intently. Doubtfully.

"Trust me," she assured him.

"Try me."

Rachel's heart raced as she pondered her options. Escape was the preferable one. God, if she could run away, she would never have to face this, face him.... But she'd still have to face herself.

She took three steps to the right to put space between them then turned and faced him. "The night Noelle died..."

He started to move toward her again and she gave a single insistent shake of her head to stop him.

"We fought," she said.

She saw him nod out of the corner of her eye. "Siblings do that."

"I was home for a few days because I'd gotten lucky on the residency schedule and finally succumbed to my mom's and sister's pleas to visit, but I had so much reading to catch up on, it was ridiculous. Typical, but ridiculous." She took a fortifying breath.

"I was sitting on the couch right here in the living room, my files spread out on the coffee table and beside me on the cushion, my laptop on my lap. I was my usual stressed-out self and Noelle came in and sat down hard on the chair. I could sense something was bugging her, but I wasn't in the mood. Didn't have the time." She blinked against tears. Damn never-ending tears. "She wanted to know why I didn't spend any time with the two of you. Why I didn't want to get to know her fiancé better. She accused me of not caring about you or her future or the family." She broke off as her voice cracked.

Pivoting forty-five degrees so she was no longer facing him, she noticed an empty nail hole in the wall, the paint scraped off around it, and she latched her gaze onto it. Stared at it intently as she forced herself to continue.

"All our lives, Noelle has been the pretty sister...."

"You're her identical twin, Rachel."

"The social sister. The popular one. The one with all the fashion sense and social grace. You know exactly what I mean, Cale. Don't pretend you don't." Rachel crossed her arms over her chest as if she could shield herself from age-old wounds. "She's always been the one with the boyfriend, the countless dates and guys calling her and asking her out. More than once, we liked the same guy, and I'll give you three guesses who won every single time. Here's a hint—it wasn't the shy, studious, geeky sister."

"I told you there's nothing geeky about you."

"You didn't know me in high school. None of this justifies anything that happened that night, but I'm just telling you how it was. How it's always been. Most times, I let her get away with it. The guy-stealing. Because let's face it, she couldn't really steal them from me if they were never mine to start with, right? I can't tell you how many times I told myself that."

"It must've been hard to handle, though," Cale said, his voice brimming with sympathy that made her stomach hurt.

"I loved her so much," Rachel said, her voice breaking.

"Don't think that I didn't. I would have done anything for my sister. And she felt the same about me—I know it."

"You're right, Rachel. Whenever she talked about you, it was obvious she felt the same way."

"It was just a fact—she was the social one and I was the brainy one. Most of the time, I liked it that way. But…I guess it was one time too many."

"What was?"

"When she accused me of avoiding you and making me sound like I was doing it because I was selfish, I lost it. I threw the truth at her. Listed all the guys she'd gone out with that, at one time or another, I had been interested in. Then I told her she was doing it again." She stopped, bit down on the inside of her lip because, damn, this was embarrassing and impossible to get out.

Cale waited quietly, the tension in the room becoming tangible.

"I met you first," Rachel said. "You probably barely noticed. Most likely pushed it right out of your mind that you and I talked outside before you ever ran into my sister."

"I remember. You were intimidated by the crowd and didn't know anyone but your sister. And she was surrounded by people all night."

Rachel nodded. "And then I watched when the two of you met. I knew within seconds what was going to happen."

"What are you trying to say, Rachel?"

"You know exactly what I'm saying. As I very bluntly explained to Noelle that night, I had feelings for you. From the very first night and the nights afterward when I was still at home on my visit and she came in gushing about you. When the three of us went to the beach together and I watched her flirt with you for all she was worth. Watched the two of you kiss and touch and…"

Keep your eyes on the nail hole and ignore the tears. Don't let the tears get you now.

"The night Noelle ran out of this house with nothing but her keys, she left because I made her feel like complete, utter crap for once again getting the guy. The guy that I wanted. You."

CHAPTER TWENTY-THREE

CALE BACKED UP to the chair and lowered himself heavily. To say he was stunned by Rachel's admission was the understatement of the decade.

His mind spun into overload as so many thoughts and emotions and God knew what else hit him at once that he couldn't get a grasp on any one thing. He ran his hand over his mouth, his fingers remaining on his lips as he tried to make sense of what Rachel had said.

He could imagine how upset Noelle must have been that night. Though she was carefree and rarely serious, she never wanted to hurt anyone, least of all her twin sister.

And Rachel... For her to lash out, it had obviously been a long time coming, resentments that had built up for years. To think she'd held all of it in until that moment.

He couldn't wrap his brain around his role in it, in between sisters. He'd never had any notion of Rachel's feelings in all that time. Nearly a year between when he and Noelle had met and the day she'd died. Nearly a year of Rachel suffering silently. Of Noelle being understandably oblivious.

Until that night.

That god-awful, horrible night.

And Rachel had been living with it ever since. No wonder she'd been fighting so hard to keep it all at bay.

Cale's eyes veered to her then, and he was stricken yet

again by the pain on her face. It was evident she stood there torturing herself. Still.

"You didn't do anything wrong, Rachel," he said, his voice sounding unfamiliar. "Being honest with someone isn't a bad thing."

She closed her eyes and tears overflowed at once, gushing down both her cheeks. He automatically went to her but her eyes popped open and she shook her head adamantly.

"Don't." The single word was full of so much torment and heartache, he flinched. "Just because she's not here, that doesn't make it okay for you to touch me."

"She's—" Cale broke off, bit down in frustration. He couldn't sort through everything he was feeling enough to argue with her. But there was one thing he was 100 percent certain of. "Noelle's death was not your fault. Do you hear me? Not. Your. Fault."

Rachel collapsed onto the couch and pulled her knees into her chest. After watching her for a couple of minutes, trying to figure out what to do for her, Cale sat next to her, put his hand on her leg.

"Rachel. Come here."

She shook her head.

He muttered a curse to himself out of frustration. "Baby, we're not going to let what happened last night happen again. Just let me hold you."

She didn't respond either way, which seemed like a step in the right direction.

"Do you think Noelle would ever want you to sit there feeling so horrible and alone?" He pulled her to him and she didn't fight it. "Would you ever want her to feel the way you do now?"

He was surprised when she relaxed into him, her forehead resting on his upper arm, her hand clutching his shirt at his waist as if her life depended on it.

They sat like that for some time. The only sound in the entire house was the sound of the rain, which had turned into steady, heavy drops, pounding on the roof and against the living-room window. Cale closed his eyes and tried to absorb what Rachel had revealed.

He'd always known she and Noelle had had a disagreement before Noelle had run out of the house that night. He'd not thought anything of it because, as he'd told Rachel, sisters argued. In the overall scheme of things, the topic of their argument wasn't important. If they'd fought about leaving the car windows open in a rainstorm, it would have had the same result.

But knowing the truth of what had happened, he tried now to imagine how Noelle must have felt that night. More than once, she'd confided in him about how much she wished for Rachel to find happiness with a guy. He remembered when he'd been with Noelle during one of her frequent phone calls with Rachel. Rachel had mentioned a guy, apparently, and Noelle had grilled her in her overenthusiastic, well-intentioned way about whether there was potential for this guy, whether they'd gone on any dates, and more.

For Noelle to find out the guy Rachel wanted to be happy with was *him*... That Noelle had unwittingly come between Rachel and other guys in the past…

It must have hit her like a wrecking ball.

All this time, he'd assumed Noelle had rushed off in anger, had imagined her spitting mad as she'd driven off the island and northward, out of town. But in light of Rachel's revelation, it had to have been much more complex.

Knowing the difference in Noelle's mindset that night didn't change a thing. Not in what had happened. Not in the loss he still felt. The only thing that changed was his understanding of Rachel.

Now he grasped it better, comprehended her on a different, deeper level. After learning the nature of their argument, he could understand—not agree with, by any means, but understand—how Rachel might feel such guilt. How she could convince herself she was responsible for her sister's death.

"I'm so weak," she said in a quiet, high-pitched voice. "I take full responsibility for what happened last night."

"Don't be ridiculous," he said roughly.

"I…started everything."

"I was right there for it to start," he said, remembering how he'd had to hold himself back from touching her. "*Right there.* And I continued it."

"I took my clothes off."

Just the memory made his pulse pick up inappropriately. "Rachel, there's no point in throwing around blame. We're attracted to each other. Things got out of hand."

"You're attracted to *her,* Cale, not me."

He sprung off the couch at that. "Oh, hell no, Rachel. We need to get one thing straight. Noelle was not there with us yesterday. I didn't mistake you for her. I wasn't imagining her. I wasn't even thinking about her."

She met his eyes defiantly, accusingly.

"No," he said again emphatically. "You can accuse me of a lot of things, but not that. It was you and me yesterday, Rachel. I don't want you to ever think otherwise."

Rachel averted her gaze. He went back to her side and sat, not about to let that one drop. "Are we clear?" he asked.

She blew out a breath. "If you say so." She didn't act altogether convinced, but Cale didn't know what else he could say to make her believe him.

"The rest of the world may see you two as identical but I never have. Not since the party when I met you both. Sure, you look damn similar on the surface, but you and Noelle..." He shook his head. "You've always been different to me. I could never look at either of you and *not* see your personalities coming through."

Rachel seemed to take that in, and after a while, she nodded once. Only a half nod, but he'd take it for now.

"You're not weak," he said, settling back into the cushions. "It must've been hard to live with Noelle at times. To watch her go out all the time, whether it was with the guy you liked or not."

She studied him as if assessing his sincerity on such a personal subject. "Yeah," she finally said. "Sometimes it was. Sometimes I convinced myself it was a more noble pursuit to get straight A's, to get into a good college. I don't know. It was easier that way. Easier to try to ignore it. Some people would call it being a doormat."

"I've never thought of you as a doormat."

Quite the opposite, in fact. She could be as stubborn and assertive as anyone when she needed to be. You didn't become an emergency-medicine doctor without having some cojones.

"Her social life was so much of who she was," Rachel said. "It somehow seemed more important to her. So..." She shrugged. "To keep the peace, I didn't make a big deal out of it."

She'd turned a blind eye to Noelle "winning the guy" to keep peace, yes, but also out of love. He'd seen firsthand the sisters' bond, directly and indirectly, and this was just further proof of that.

"When I was in high school, a Podunk rural school in Hill Country, my best friend at the time, Pete Loggins, knew I had a thing for Lexie Montague," Cale said. "Junior year, Lexie and Pete got assigned as lab partners in science. Before I knew what was going on, he moved in on her. Asked her out. They dated for half of junior year."

"And? What happened?"

"I haven't spoken to Pete since."

"It's different when it's your sister."

"It's different when you're a better person, as you are."

"Don't say that. Please." Her voice sounded pained. "A better person might have called her on it every time she did it. Then it wouldn't have blindsided her that night. Wouldn't have made her run away..."

He put his arm around her and drew her into his side again. "Shh. Rachel, you have to stop. Do you really think Noelle, who loved you just as much as you loved her, would want you to sit here blaming yourself? Imagine if you switched places. Would you want her to shoulder all this guilt?"

Rachel shook her head quickly. "But that doesn't make the guilt go away. Nothing does." She sat up and turned to face him directly. "And right now, being with you makes it worse."

"We're friends, Rachel."

"We crossed a line."

"We won't cross it again."

"You're right about that," she said hoarsely. "I need some space. Breathing room. When I'm with you, I want to touch you. I want to be with you like this." She motioned to how close they sat, to where her knees overlapped his thigh. "Can you give me a few days at least to sort everything out in my head?"

"Of course." He hated the thought of it, but he understood where she was coming from. He was struggling not to touch her, as well, and while that might have been "friendly" enough in the past, last night had changed things. “I’ll give you some time, and you let me know when you’re ready. Then we can put our mistake behind us.”

She tried to smile at him, but there was no joy in it, and that twisted something inside of him. He stood to leave before he could reach out for her again. Even though he understood her better, grasped a little bit of what she was going through, that didn’t make feeling helpless sit any better with him. Resisting the urge to hug her, he walked out of the Culver house.

CHAPTER TWENTY-FOUR

RACHEL HAD RUN dry on excuses at the very worst time.

She'd missed the past two publicity committee meetings as well as one of the large-group asthma-benefit-planning sessions using work, recovering from work and plain old forgetfulness as her excuses. It was tricky in the first place because of her mom's involvement—it curtailed any stretching of the truth Rachel might have been tempted to do.

And now, when she wanted—no, *needed*—to continue to avoid Cale, she hadn't been able to think of a way out. It'd been over a week since she'd seen him, and she still wasn't ready.

It didn't help that her mom had decided this week's meeting was a special beach picnic in celebration of the overall goal they'd hit in ticket sales a few days ago. Jackie was treating everyone to subs, chips, salad and cookies, and it was all being delivered directly to the beach at the site of the future benefit concert, on the Silver Sands Hotel property.

Rachel sat in her car in the hotel's parking lot for a few extra minutes gathering her nerve. The building blocked the view from here, so she had no way of knowing whether Cale had arrived yet. Having learned from experience, she'd insisted on driving separately from her mom this time and was undoubtedly doing what her mother called dragging her feet.

The days since she'd spoken to Cale—since the morning when she'd told him the horrible truth about her fight with Noelle—she'd done nothing but work and sleep. Or try to sleep, rather. She'd taken as many extra shifts as she could get, but even then, she'd been on alert in the E.R., expecting to run into Cale bringing a patient in. If he had, she'd missed it. Which was for the best.

Against her will, she'd replayed the embarrassing, gut-wrenching scenes—both seducing him and then leveling with him the next day—in her mind over and over like a movie that was stuck. Every time, the nausea still overwhelmed her as the humiliation and guilt bore down on her. And now it was time to face him again. If she didn't act right this minute and get it over with, she was either going to wretch right there in the parking lot or do something insane and inadvisable like drive her car right off the island and keep going.

Without a glance in the mirror—she knew damn well she looked awful with her sleep-deprived, haunted eyes and her pale skin—she opened the door, grabbed her bag and climbed out. Retrieving her beach chair from the trunk, she set off toward the sand.

She spotted the gathering as soon as she cleared the corner of the hotel. Heard her mom's laugh and saw Cale's light brown, shaggy hair right away. Her eyes zeroed in on him and nothing else, as if she had special radar. She forced her attention away from him, wanting to avoid eye contact at all costs. She slowed her pace and strategized as she took in the scene and the smaller groups that had formed. Cale was sitting on the far side near his sister and Eloise Painter, one of her mom's friends. Mrs. Lopez, an older woman who volunteered at the hospital, was on the fringes of the group on the near side, focused on her sandwich, looking as though she needed someone to hang out with as badly as Rachel did.

Avoiding another glance at Cale for fear of catching his attention, Rachel made a beeline for the friendly but shy older woman and set her chair up next to her, placing it sideways to him so she could keep tabs on him out of the corner of her eye without making direct eye contact.

CALE HAD SPOTTED Rachel as she'd walked across the sand toward the group. Not surprisingly, she was ignoring him. He blew off the disappointment when she kept to the opposite side of the group from him, reminding himself he'd fully expected her to keep her distance.

She was dealing with a crap-load of stuff, he knew. He himself was still kind of reeling from what they'd let happen. Rachel needed time and space as she'd said, and, though he missed her and had no intention of ignoring her altogether, he'd give her both until she gave him some kind of sign.

Without being obvious, he went for another roast beef sandwich at the makeshift buffet table, then sat on the other side of his sister for a better vantage point. He assessed Rachel's appearance from afar as she acted as if she and Mrs. Lopez went way back.

She hadn't been sleeping—he could tell it from here. Though she'd done her best putting herself together, dressing in denim shorts and a simple sleeveless shirt, her eyes looked hollowed out even from this distance. His mind flashed to waking up beside her last week, as a protective urge rippled through him. Uncomfortable with the direction of his thoughts, he turned to Trina Jankovich and Heather Alamillo, who'd both been close friends of Noelle, and struck up a conversation about nothing important.

The three were joking around when Cale's senses went on alert and he registered some kind of commotion up the beach a ways. A woman was screaming, but he couldn't immediately make out whether it was in fun or distress.

"Excuse me," he said to the two as he stood and walked in the direction of the ruckus as nonchalantly as possible, still unsure if there was cause for concern, but the back of his neck was prickling.

He'd closed half the distance between him and the distraught woman when he ascertained she was yelling for help. She'd gone into the waves up to her waist, then turned back and hollered some more. He realized she was speaking Spanish with an English word thrown in here and there, making it tough to understand her. *"Mis bebés! Ayúdame!"*

Without waiting to hear more, Cale kicked his beach shoes aside and took off in a run toward her. By the time he reached her, she was pointing, wading out farther and turning terrified eyes on him. She was crying hysterically as she tried to communicate with him.

"Mis nietas! Ayúdame por favor!"

He'd picked up enough Spanish living in southern Texas that he recognized the words for *granddaughters* and *help.* Before she could say more, he spied two dark heads way out where the waves seemed to form. He ran several steps as the water deepened then dived under toward them.

RACHEL HAD KEPT ONE eye on Cale since she'd sat down, and when he walked away from the group and eventually broke into a run, she dropped any pretense of not paying attention to him.

"I'll be back," she said to Mrs. Lopez over her shoulder as she took off in his direction, first walking and then, when he dived into the deeper water, she started running. A couple of other people were rushing to the distressed woman, as well, but Rachel kept her eyes on Cale. When she reached the water, another guy was heading out toward him, and a young woman, college age or so, stood next to the overwrought one, holding her arm and speaking to her in rapid Spanish.

"I'm a doctor," Rachel said. "What's going on?"

"Her thirteen-year-old granddaughter swam out too far and had some kind of problem. The girl was trying to get back to shore when the grandmother here spotted her," the bilingual girl explained, referring to the Spanish-speaking woman. "She sent her other granddaughter out to help because she herself can't swim."

Rachel saw the two dark heads near Cale then. "And the second one got into trouble, too?"

"Exactly. The first one grabbed on to the second one and they both went under. It looks like that guy out there has both of them." She spoke again in Spanish to the woman, who was covering most of her face with her hands, peeking around them as if she were scared to death to see what condition they were in.

The second rescuer reached Cale and took one of the girls, who appeared to be conscious. Rachel's adrenaline had long ago started pumping, and she zeroed in on the limp girl Cale was pulling back to shore. It seemed like an eternity before both men reached them.

"I think she's lost consciousness," Cale said as the bilingual woman and Rachel splashed forward to meet him and help get the girl to shore.

"I've got her," he said, breathing heavily.

Rachel was kneeling in front of the victim, assessing her condition practically before Cale had set her down. "She's not breathing. Weak pulse. Check the other girl," she told him as she tilted the girl's head back and began mouth-to-mouth.

She barely noticed the gathering crowd as she kept working, gently pleading with the unhearing girl to respond.

"Ambulance is on the way."

Rachel realized it was her mother who joined her on the sand as she bent forward for another round of rescue breathing. She was now more aware of the crowd, and she thought she heard Cale tell the grandmother the other girl was going to be okay.

"Come on," Rachel begged her victim.

As if hearing her, the girl sputtered and threw up a bunch of water, gagging and sputtering. Rachel gently turned her to her side. "Yes, that's it. Get it all out."

"Give her room, everyone," Rachel's mom said to the onlookers.

The girl was ashen and fear was evident in her eyes, but her breaths came easier, more evenly.

"It's okay," Rachel told her. "You're going to be okay." She hoped. Chances were a heck of a lot better now. "Try to relax." It appeared the girl understood English because she gave a half nod.

"Evie!" The girl's grandmother, who'd been hugging her other granddaughter, fell onto her knees on the sand and grasped Evie as Rachel did her best to keep her well to the side.

"Evie, you're doing great," Rachel said. "We're going to get you to the hospital so they can make sure there's no water in your lungs. Just keep breathing, sweetie. Just like that."

The grandmother gave Rachel a desperate, questioning look and Rachel nodded. "She's okay right now. Out of immediate danger. She needs to go to the hospital."

"Hospital?" the woman repeated in a heavy accent, renewed fear in her eyes.

Rachel looked to the bilingual woman to explain, and then the grandmother nodded.

The older Dr. Culver directed the gathered crowd out of the way to allow the arriving paramedics to get to the patient with the stretcher.

As Rachel updated them on the girl's condition, Cale came over with Evie's sister, who seemed okay on the outside, in his arms. "Hey, Paige, Rafe. Lili here needs to be transported, too. Can you guys get both girls and their grandmother in the ambulance?"

"Cale?" The female paramedic looked confused to see him there for a moment. "Shouldn't be a problem. Just the two of them are patients?"

Cale explained what had happened to Lili as they prepared Evie to be carried to the waiting ambulance. "I can follow behind," he said.

"No need for that," the paramedic apparently named Rafe said. "If you can bring her to the ambulance, we can take them from there. Go back to whatever you were doing."

Jackie again took crowd control into her hands and encouraged everyone to disperse. The paramedics carried Evie toward the lot where they had parked. Cale followed behind with Lili in his arms. Rachel hooked her arm supportively with the grandmother's as they trailed the others. Rachel had taken Spanish for several years, but the woman rambled on and on so quickly, recounting once again what had happened, as if she were still processing it herself, that it was difficult to pick words out. She hoped her reassuring pats on the woman's arm were helping to calm her down.

Minutes later, the ambulance set off from the parking

lot, leaving Rachel staring after it in the relative quiet and calmness.

Cale leaned down and spoke softly into her ear. “You’d make a damn good paramedic, you know that?”

Rachel smiled and felt some of the tension leave her body at the unexpected remark.

“I’m not sure I could handle the amount of training necessary for the job,” she joked.

Cale chuckled and tugged her backward, and she allowed herself to sag into him, relishing the uncommon moment of comfort after an emergency. He wrapped his arms loosely around her middle.

“I’m glad they’re both okay,” he said.

“Thanks to you.”

“And you.” They stood there coming down off their adrenaline rushes for several minutes as evening turned dusky and the light gradually faded. “Ready to go back?”

“I never wanted to come in the first place,” Rachel confessed.

“Don’t you hate it when a medical emergency forces you to speak to the one person you’re trying to avoid?”

Rachel couldn’t prevent a half grin. Then she scoffed good-naturedly, shaking her head. “Pretty much. You were doing a good job of avoiding me, too.”

“There’s a big difference between avoiding and giving someone space.”

“We still wouldn’t be talking if none of that had happened,” she said, waving toward the part of the beach where the girls had nearly drowned. If she had her way. She straightened and stepped away from him.

He grabbed her forearm, pulled her around and looked into her eyes. “Rachel, I’ve missed you. I want to go back to being friends.”

She cared about him so much that it hurt to stand

there with him, knowing she couldn't have him the way she wanted him. "It sounds good in theory, Cale, but…"

"But what?"

Rachel stared out at the distant waves. From here, they seemed quieter, less vicious than when she'd been standing in them watching two girls fight for their lives. "I don't know."

So many thoughts spun through her mind, dizzying her, making it hard to grasp any one thing.

She loved him. She was in love with him. Being friends was so damn hard, especially after what they'd done.

The very best thing for her to do would be to walk away from him forever, to tell him she couldn't handle *just* being friends. To remind him why she could never, ever allow herself to be more, even if he changed his mind and wanted some kind of romantic involvement. But she couldn't make the words come out. Any of them.

"Okay," Cale said, "how about this. The benefit is a week and a half away. Say you'll go to that with me and I won't bother you before then. Afterward, it's your call. You say what happens between us. I want you in my life, Rachel, but if you can't handle being friends then, I'll honor that."

She stared at him, his kind eyes and perfect lips making her ache with an inner torment she'd never expected. Even when Noelle had planned to marry him, though Rachel had kept her distance, there'd been a comfort knowing he'd always be around, be a part of her family. The lines had been so much clearer then, and the possibilities of anything besides a siblinglike relationship eliminated. That, she realized in this moment, had been simpler.

She became aware that she was nodding to the arrangement he offered. A week and a half. Ten days she

had to come to terms with the options: friendship or nothing. "I'll go to the benefit with you. We should be there together. For Noelle."

CHAPTER TWENTY-FIVE

"You look like hell," Rachel's mom said the next day when Rachel came into the kitchen to grab some dinner before heading to her night shift.

"Yellow must not be my color," Rachel said drily as she yanked at her scrub top. She rummaged through the fridge and emerged with a bag of soft tortillas and some smoked-turkey lunch meat.

"Pasta will be done in twenty minutes," Jackie said as she buttered slices of French bread and sprinkled garlic over them.

Rachel didn't respond, knowing her mom would be insulted by her plans to grab a wrap and call it good.

"Didn't sleep well?" her mom continued as she worked.

"Didn't sleep well."

"I would've thought you'd sleep like a baby after the unexpected adrenaline rush—and crash—on the beach last night."

"One would've thought." Instead of sleeping soundly, though, she'd been tormented by her waking thoughts as well as her dreams. All about Cale, naturally.

She wasn't sure what, exactly, he wanted from her. After she'd made an ass of herself on two different occasions, he still came back for more. More something. Friendship, he said. Rachel wasn't the kind of woman that men—or anyone, really—looked for in a friend. She

wasn't good at friendship. She'd always spent more time with books than people. So…what did he expect of her?

"You and Cale sure seemed close last night after the ambulance left," Jackie said, causing Rachel to jolt with guilt at her line of thought.

She racked her brain for how her mother could have seen them during the short time Cale had had his arms around her. They'd been alone. The rest of the benefit-planning group had returned to the picnic site. The layout of the area would have made it tough to see them unless someone had been looking for them specifically.

"Spying on me?" Rachel tried to keep her tone light, but with the lack of rest, she knew she'd probably failed.

"Is there something to spy?" Jackie's tone was light, too. Almost teasing. As if she suspected Rachel of shacking up with him on the sly. As if she knew.

A knot tightened in Rachel's gut.

"Someone nearly died, Mom. We were coming down from the stress. *Talking*."

Her mom popped the end of the bread loaf into her mouth and chewed. Then she said, "If I didn't know better, I might think you were overly defensive."

There it was. There was a distinct accusation in her voice, and that sent Rachel's blood pounding.

She set down her knife so hard it clattered on the counter and splattered mayonnaise all over. "Cale and I are *friends*. If you have something to say, an accusation to make, then put it out there. Quit hiding behind little jabs."

Her mom narrowed her eyes and tilted her head at Rachel, looking more confused and concerned than angry at Rachel's outburst.

"We've never minced words in the past. Just say whatever it is you need to say," Rachel continued as she manhandled her wrap, rolling it up so roughly that it started to break into pieces. She was too wound up to care, not to mention no longer hungry.

Her mom set her own butter knife down gently, and put her hand on her hip. “I was kidding around about Cale. I’m glad he was there for you last night, because I don’t care what kind of doctor a person is, a life-or-death emergency when you’re not even on duty takes a toll.” She opened the oven, pulled out the pasta to check it and pushed it back in.

“However,” she said heavily, turning back to Rachel, “I do have a few things to say. And since you asked—”

“Be my guest,” Rachel said, stuffing the wrap into a container to take with her to work because she now had zero desire to eat. “Like I said, don’t hold back.”

“You’re right that something’s changed between us, Rachel. And I hate it. You’re on edge all of the time. I know you’ve just started your job and that’s stressful. But you’ve always thrived with that kind of challenge.” Her mom shook her head.

“So all the tension in the house is my fault,” Rachel stated.

“I’m worried about you, sweetie. You seem…stuck.”

Some chopped vegetables would go nicely with her mangled wrap. Rachel removed the butcher knife from the knife block, set it on the counter by the mayo mess and took out a bag of raw celery and carrots from the refrigerator. She grabbed a cutting board from the lower cabinet, and, once she’d washed off a couple of giant carrots, she set about whacking them into snack-size sticks.

“This is the first time you’ve spent any real time at home since Noelle died.”

“You know I couldn’t just walk away from my residency, Mom—”

“Of course not. What I mean is that now you’ve been

forced back here, where it's hard to pretend it didn't happen."

"Pretend?" Rachel knew she'd miscalculated with the knife a full second before the pain in her finger registered. *Damn!* She closed her eyes, not in favor of the sight of her own blood, and reached for a paper towel. Wrapping the paper around her left index finger without inspecting the damage, she attempted to act as if nothing had happened.

"I didn't say that. You're twisting my words. Dammit, Rachel, I'm worried about you! You do nothing but work and read medical journals."

"*You're* taking me to task for working too much? Where do you think I learned that?"

"I don't think you're processing her death, honey. You're not coping with it. Not dealing with it. You're just...working. Overworking."

"I'm new at my job. I don't like being the peon. The only way I know how to change that is by working my butt off."

"As you said, I'm the ex-queen of workaholism, but I'm starting to become pretty damn convinced that your situation is more than that. Maybe it's by design, so that you can avoid the big, nasty truth. You're hiding out from everything, either at work or in your brother's room."

"I can look for a place to live."

"That's not what I mean, Rachel. You're being deliberately obtuse. I like the idea of you living here for as long as you want to or need to. But if you're going to stay, criminy, Rachel, get rid of the Yoda and the other teenage-boy decor! Is there nothing in your old room that you care enough about to go in there after? A flowered blanket? Some pillows? If not, go to the store and buy a couple things. Show me you're alive!"

"I've been in there," Rachel said in a low, crisp voice, finally daring to study the cut on her finger, only half seeing it. "When you were out of town. I started going through her stuff. Somebody had to. I sorted through her half-used makeup. Read the inscription on the book I gave her for what turned out to be her last birthday. Threw away her out-of-date magazine stash. How's that for pretending she's not dead?" She silently damned the tears that reliably sprang up in her eyes.

She could feel her mom's entire demeanor morph from self-righteous to sympathetic. Rachel didn't handle pity very well. Never had, never would. So when her mom tried to put her arm around her, she sidestepped and opened a drawer on the other side of the kitchen in search of a plastic bag for her veggies.

"I thought..." Her mom broke off. "It was your room, too, Rachel. I didn't think it was my place to barge in and go through her things."

"Right. That or you couldn't handle it?"

"All this anger is so unlike you, Rach." Her mom's voice had become a swell combo of pity and concern.

"You know what?" Rachel said, making eye contact. "I have to get to work. I'm out of here."

"Dammit, Rachel!"

As Rachel turned away, an ear-piercing crash stopped her. Her mom had shoved the pan with the bread on it across the surface of the stove into the back of the range. Bread lay scattered across the counter. "You're doing it again. Running away from it all."

Rage pumped through her, and she whirled around to face her mom again. "Me? What do you suggest I do instead? Take up baking and golf? Cut out of work early whenever possible? Is that the proper way to handle that my sister is dead?"

"Sweetie—"

"Don't 'sweetie' me."

"I've grieved for her every day of the nineteen and a half months since she died," her mom said, her voice cracking, which made Rachel soften a little toward her. "I had a lot of major regrets to work through. It took me a long time. I'm still working through them, I suppose. But I absolutely do not use my hobbies to block out the hard stuff, Rachel."

"Everybody is quick to tell me how screwed up I am, but you're not even the same person anymore."

"I am."

"The mom I used to know? She did not cook or play recreational sports in her spare time. She didn't *have* spare time. She was a lot like me—driven, dedicated to her career."

Her mom nodded pensively. "I suppose I do seem like I've had a lobotomy, huh?" She smiled sadly but Rachel didn't return it. Her mom leaned her backside against the counter. "When Noelle died, it did something to me. Did a lot of things to me, but what I'm talking about is the regrets. She'd been living here in this house for years, and yet I missed so much time with her. Because I was only focused on one thing."

"Work," Rachel guessed.

"You got it. Maybe it sounds clichéd, but it made me take a look at my life and decide what's most important to me."

"Healing people isn't important?"

"Of course it is. I still love my career."

Rachel narrowed her eyes at her.

"I do. I just love the other parts of my life, as well."

"Yeah, well, I don't have an established career to rest on. I have to fight for it."

"That's fine. Just…be sure you're working your butt off to achieve something as opposed to hiding from something." Her knowing look made Rachel squirm, and that renewed her irritation.

She'd gone in the damn bedroom. She'd started going through her sister's stuff. She was working on it. At her own pace.

"I have to go," she said, her jaw tight. "I guess I can only hope to someday be as enlightened as you."

Grabbing her to-go dinner, such as it was, Rachel stormed out of the house before her mom could try to straighten her out anymore.

CHAPTER TWENTY-SIX

SLEEPING MORE THAN two hours was apparently not in the cards for Rachel the next day. On the bright side, her mom was at work and would be for a few more hours. Rachel wasn't in a hurry to run into her after last night's let's-talk-about-how-screwed-up-Rachel-is session.

After twisting in her sheets for close to an hour, she climbed out of bed, irritated. The cause of her insomnia wasn't tough to figure out. Every second, she was still affected by the profound rawness of the emotions the past few days had brought to the surface. Even when she'd been working last night, when she'd been occupied by a patient or an emergency situation, the underlying heaviness was always there, weighing her down.

The thing was, she admitted to herself as she threw her hair into a ponytail, her mom was right. Sawyer was right. Everyone who suspected she'd avoided grieving for her sister was 100 percent correct. She'd had to, to protect herself, she supposed, though she wasn't sure she'd ever made a conscious decision to forego it. She'd just instinctively fought it. Every day for the past nineteen months plus.

So the question was, what the hell was she supposed to do about it? Feel like slow-moving, depressed crap for the rest of eternity? So holding it all in had been a mistake. Was she supposed to walk around blubbering now?

For all her education—in the medical field, no less—she didn't have a clue how to get through this.

Frankly, it pissed her off. She wasn't accustomed to not being able to puzzle through a problem.

Her mother's accusations echoing rampantly through her mind, Rachel stomped across the hall to her and Noelle's bedroom, determined to put a real dent in it. Show it who was boss and who was no longer going to be accused of hiding from the tough stuff.

As soon as she walked in, Noelle's diary caught her attention as if it had flashing neon lights where she'd left it on the rumpled bed.

"Nope, not going there today," she said out loud. "Not hiding. Need to make some visible progress so people quit accusing me of avoiding."

It sounded perfectly logical to her, even if there was an underlying nagging in her gut.

As she worked her way through Noelle's side of the closet, her back facing the bed, she felt it, though. Felt the diary sitting there on the bed as if it were a living, breathing being. Accusing. Taunting. Just like the door used to do.

She continued her sorting, making her pace deliberate and slow, as if to signal to the universe and that stupid book that she wasn't being intimidated, wasn't going to rush through the job just to get out of that room.

When she finished the closet, she stood and stretched, feeling stiff and about eighty years old from the lack of sleep and the overdose of emotions. Again, the book caught her eye.

Opening it would be brutal. Seeing her sister in every word, in every scrawled letter, would knock her on her newly grieving butt quicker than she could say *privacy issues*. Just reading the note in the front that Noelle had directed at her had sent her mind plummeting into momentary confusion. The warning was ages old, timeless. Familiar. The ongoing threat between sisters—particularly twin sisters. *Give me my space. Leave my innermost thoughts alone. Respect my boundaries.*

It said so much about the connection they'd had and made Rachel believe, if only for a second and only on some distant subconscious level, that her sister was still here. The next second was ruined with the yet-again realization that it was an illusion.

Traumatizing, to be sure.

And yet the diary begged to be opened. Rachel longed for that nanosecond of connection with her sister, in spite of understanding that it would, indeed, turn out to be false in the end.

No. She was still paying the price from her last run-in with the diary. Maybe in a few days she would be better able to handle it.

Swearing, she snatched up the book and slammed it down on the empty top shelf of the bookcase. The resounding smack wasn't satisfying, but she stopped herself from picking it up again and winging it against the wall. That would be *uncivilized.* And more importantly, it would reek of weakness.

Rachel bit her lip, burrowed both hands in her hair and pulled till her scalp burned. Catching her reflection in the mirror, she relaxed her grip and took a step toward the vanity, slightly horrified by her appearance. She was unusually pale. Her eyes looked like hollowed-out holes in her head, complete with heavy shadows beneath. Her hair was a scraggly, overgrown mess that, come to think of it, she hadn't done a thing with since she'd been back in town. Yes, she was busy, but that was no reason to scare patients in the E.R.—let alone herself when she looked in the mirror.

Feeling more in control than she had since the last time she'd forced herself into this bedroom, she marched out with purpose and went to find a current phone book. Unlike so many elements of her life, her hair was easily managed.

"I THINK YOU'RE GOING to adore this." Angel the peppy stylist's voice bubbled with excitement while Rachel's nerves stretched even more taut.

The salon chair swiveled around so Rachel could see her reflection in the mirror for the first time since the job was finished. Her eyes took in the short, jet-black hair then zoomed downward to locate the faded U2 concert shirt that Rachel knew she had worn today. Check.

Holy smokes.

"What do you think?" Again, the annoyingly perky Angel person's voice buzzed at her like a gnat.

What had she done?

"Umm." Rachel tried clearing her throat against the panic that was inexplicably welling up. "It's...different." Her eyes widened as she continued to stare without blinking.

"It'll take a couple days to get used to, huh?" Angel said, grinning widely.

"How...?" She didn't even know what she wanted to say. "Yeah," she finally responded. "Yeah."

She looked away. Noticed the seventy-ish woman across the room who was having the same curl put into her hair she'd probably had done for the past thirty years staring at her as if Rachel was a freak show.

Darting her own glance back to the mirror, she saw someone else sitting there. A decently attractive woman she'd never seen before. Someone with hair so black it looked almost blue in places. Hair that was cut into a pixie style so short the woman in the mirror would be hard-pressed to run her fingers through it. *She* would be hard-pressed to run her fingers through her new hair.

"Are you okay, hon?" Angel switched from admiring her client in the mirror to sticking her head in front of Rachel directly.

Rachel had come to this salon, to this stylist, because she was anonymous here. Unlike the hair salon where she, Noelle and their mother had gone practically since the twins' birth, no one knew her here. No one knew she had an identical twin sister. *Used to have one...*

"Want a mirror to see the back? God, you look good in that cut. Not many women can pull that off."

Rachel robotically took the hand mirror as Angel spun her around to see the back.

Yep. Killer short.

"Okay," she said, trying to breathe. "Yeah, nice job." She knew she didn't sound as if she meant it, but it wasn't every day a natural blonde with chin-length hair went pixie and jet-black. On a whim.

"I need to get that," Angel said, and Rachel belatedly registered a ringing phone in the background.

Being left in the wake of the ever-chattering hairstylist did nothing to lessen the churning in Rachel's stomach. Using her foot on the white-tiled floor, she pushed herself back around to stare at the front again. She immediately averted her gaze and located her purse on the floor next to the styling station. Grabbing it, she whipped open her wallet and counted out cash. Lots of it. Hopefully enough to cover the cut and color. She anchored the money below a heavy bottle of hair product on Angel's station and then, avoiding that mirror as if it could reach out and choke her, she walked out of the salon, attempting to look as nonchalant as possible…and likely failing miserably.

She'd thought when she'd woken up this morning that a radical change would be a good thing. A daring, bold move that showed she was in control.

What she hadn't taken into consideration, though, was that when she looked into the mirror, no matter how hard she squinted, she could no longer find Noelle.

CHAPTER TWENTY-SEVEN

"IT'S YOUR day, Mom," Cale said as he climbed into the driver's seat of his parents' conversion van. "Whatever you want to do tonight, we'll do it. You only turn sixty-seven once."

"She's probably too embarrassed to say, but she told me she wants to go to the gentlemen's club," Cale's dad said from his chair in the back.

"Oh, good heavens, Ted." She swiveled enough in the passenger seat to shoot her husband a scolding frown, which made him cackle. "I'd like to see your condo, Cale."

"You notice she didn't say your *home,*" Mariah said from the back, where she sat next to their dad.

"I'm getting there," Cale said. He knew his sister was kidding, but after the work he'd put in these past few days to try to finish it, the subject was a sore one. "Why do you want to see it, Mom? It's not done yet."

"You've owned it for, what, two years? And I've lived here for almost two months and you've never showed it to me once. I'm just curious to see the work you've done."

"We can stop by after dinner, then," Cale said.

"We're a block away," Mariah said. "Let's do it now. They can see it in daylight and then we can relax and enjoy dinner."

"That sounds perfect," Ronnie said.

"Dad?" Cale met his father's bushy-browed eyes in the rearview mirror. "You up for it?"

"Hell, if the women made up their minds, then that's what we do. I've been married for forty-eight years, son. You learn these things."

"Forty-nine," Ronnie said. "You've been married for forty-nine years, Ted."

"Forty-eight, forty-nine. When you have that much bliss, it's hard to keep track, my dear."

Cale pulled into his assigned parking spot outside of his condo. Getting his dad and his chair out took a while, and once again, Cale marveled that his mother had taken care of him by herself for so long, to say nothing of putting up with his blunt humor.

"Can I get in there?" his dad asked after rolling down the short ramp from the van.

"It's on the first floor." Lucky thing. His dad had still been mobile when he'd bought the place.

Cale unlocked the door and his dad waited for his mom to go in first. She gasped, first thing.

"It's beautiful, Cale. I love this tile floor."

"You remember Evan from the department? He helped me put it in on our day off. Then Clay helped me finish up the cabinets yesterday." He looked at the kitchen—which was fully in view now that the wall was down and the cabinets moved to their places along the outside walls—through his mother's eyes and realized she was right. It looked pretty damn good for a bunch of amateurs. It looked nice and new and contemporary, just like he and Noelle had discussed. Strangely, though, it didn't feel like home. Of course, living in his sister's apartment for so long, what did he know about home?

"Are these custom cabinets?" his mom, having moved into the kitchen proper, asked.

Cale followed her and his dad in. "Nope. Just refinished the old ones."

"The finish is gorgeous," Mariah said. "You know you can stay with me as long as you want, but I would think you'd be champing at the bit to get back here."

"Yeah," Cale said halfheartedly. He wondered at his own lack of enthusiasm but wrote it off to exhaustion. Anytime he'd been off-duty this past week, he'd been here slaving away, trying to make up for lost time.

"All this kitchen's missing is a woman," Ted said.

"Nice, Dad," Mariah said as she snooped in the fridge, no doubt finding it empty. "Do you try to come across as a caveman or is that just natural?"

"If he wants good food, he's either gonna have to marry or hire a cook."

"Hey!" Cale said good-naturedly. "I can hold my own in the kitchen. I make a mean scrambled egg."

"Let's go see the rest," his mom said. "I'm getting hungry, for something other than eggs."

Mariah carefully lowered herself to their dad's lap in his wheelchair.

"What in the name of Joseph are you doing?" he asked.

"I thought maybe you'd give me a ride." She gave him her infamous puppy-dog eyes and he switched the automatic chair on.

Cale and their mom followed them through the dining area to the living room. Ronnie walked directly to the sliding glass door and pulled back the vertical blinds. Again, she gasped in appreciation.

"Marvelous view."

"It's the same as yours, Mom."

"No. Mine is six stories up. This is better. The waves are…right *there*."

One of the reasons Noelle had been so excited about

living here, of course. Cale liked the gulf, too, but he did have concerns about being so close and on the bottom floor. The seawall outside their building, which you could barely see from this angle, wasn't very high. The one hurricane that had come through last year had veered off so the island didn't take a direct hit, but if it ever did, he could have problems.

"Bedrooms are this way. Master on the left with the view. Spare on the right."

His parents made their way through both of them, saving the master for last. He and Mariah, who'd disembarked from the wheelchair, waited in the living area for their mom and dad to rejoin them.

"The walk-in closets are bigger than our bathroom, and it's not small," his mom called from the master bedroom.

"It's very nice, son," his dad said as he steered back out from the hallway. Ronnie came out behind him. "You really do need to find a woman who would appreciate this so you can settle down."

"Ted." Ronnie sounded shocked. She gave her husband a look. The scolding look. "He's still trying to adjust to losing Noelle…." She cut herself off, choking up.

Cale noticed Mariah was studying him closely.

"Are you?" she asked, her voice heavy with meaning—some meaning he wasn't clear on. His gut was screeching with foreboding, though.

"Am I what?" he made the mistake of asking.

"Still adjusting or are you moving on?"

Moving on. The words made that foreboding harden into a knot. "What's that supposed to mean?"

Now his mom was watching him expectantly, as well.

"I don't know. I could have sworn there was…something…between you and Rachel."

"Rachel?" his mom uttered.

"Culver," Mariah said so damn helpfully.

"Rachel Culver? That's Noelle's—"

"Sister," Cale elaborated for his mom. "I'm not moving on. I still love Noelle." He said it quietly, not entirely comfortable talking about such personal things, even with his family.

"We understand, Cale," his mom said.

"Sorry," Mariah said. "I just thought…"

"Rachel and I are close but…" He shook his head, not knowing what else to say.

"Forgive me for being blunt here," his dad said, "but why would you choose to hold on to the girl who's no longer here with us, bless her heart, when you have this other girl?"

"I don't have this other girl," Cale snapped. He should've known if his dad actually apologized for his bluntness, the remark was going to be bad. Shit.

"Ted, you crossed a line," Ronnie said.

"I'm just being logical here."

"Dad." Mariah gestured for him to shut up and Cale headed toward the dining area.

He heard his mom quietly giving his dad hell as Cale flipped off the kitchen light.

"Hell, I'm sorry, Cale. I wasn't trying to be particularly insensitive."

"You just were," Mariah said with a sympathetic half grin.

"Forget about it." Cale knew his dad hadn't meant anything by it, even if he had about as much tact as a charging rhinoceros. But the words wouldn't let go of him. He pretended to check the workmanship on one of the cabinets in the kitchen, his back to the others.

"This is a really nice place," his mom said as the other

three neared the door. "You'll be happy here for a long time."

"Yeah," Cale said, the knot in his gut tightening even more. He straightened from where he'd been bent over the cabinets, then he shook his head. "No."

"No?"

"I think when I've got the work completely done I'm going to put this place on the market." The idea surprised him, as he hadn't given it any thought before the words came tumbling out.

"You're going to sell?" Mariah said in disbelief.

It also surprised him that he didn't hate the idea. In fact, on one level, it actually felt a little like…relief.

"Maybe. Just an idea." Doubt invaded as the three people closest to him looked at him in shock.

It was a little crazy. He'd just spent a bunch of hours and money fixing it up. Upgrading it from a decent place to, really, a showplace. It was on the beach. You didn't find an affordable place on the flipping beach every day.

"If that's what you want to do, then you should do it," his ever-supportive mother said as he opened the door.

Cale shrugged. "Let's go eat."

The two women went first, and then his dad motored toward the door but stopped when he got even with Cale. His old man stared him down.

"Elders first," Cale said, attempting a lightness he no longer felt.

His dad waved off the comment. "Was that brought on by my asshole comment, son?"

"What? Selling?"

His dad nodded, still examining Cale critically.

"No. I don't know what it was. Like I said, just a possibility. I'm not going to make any decisions tonight."

He already regretted saying he might sell. It'd been a

spontaneous thought. One that didn't take into account a major consideration: the condo was the last tangible piece he had left of Noelle.

CHAPTER TWENTY-EIGHT

THE HOUSE WAS a total loss from the blaze, no question about it.

Cale and the crew had been doing salvage and overhaul for what seemed like days, though in reality, it was only 9:30 p.m. The sun had set not too long ago, and the darkness had made the already tough job a little more difficult. The adrenaline from fighting the fire had long ago run out and now he and the others were just plain worn-out. The homeowners, though… He shook his head sadly.

His heart went out to the elderly couple whose single-story home had burned beyond recognition. They'd been at the site for hours, sitting on the curb across the street, watching. Crying. Comforting each other. Cale was struck by the way they supported each other—his eyes were drawn to them every time he came out of the former structure carrying equipment or debris. As he loaded up some tools on the truck, he glanced over at them yet again.

They had to be in their eighties. The man was tall and slim and a little hunched over. His wife was petite with the whitest head of straight, short hair. Someone had brought them lawn chairs for their vigil, and they'd parked them only a couple of inches apart on the grass near the sidewalk. Each leaned toward the other, and both of their hands were clasped together, resting on the woman's thighs. They'd lost damn near everything, and just looking at them from a distance, he'd bet there'd been a lot of years of memories in that house.

Once the tools were stowed, he headed back through what had been the front door to see what else needed to be done before they could return to the station. He'd give his left arm to be able to sleep before they got another alarm.

"Check this out," Derek said from the rubble to Cale's left.

Unsure whether Derek was addressing him, Cale walked toward him.

"Look at this thing." He shined a flashlight on what appeared to be an intricate, hand-carved cuckoo clock. "Still ticking."

Cale bent down to look at it. "Unbelievable. Where'd you find it?"

Derek pointed his light on the ground. "Right there. I think this was the dining room. It's the only place I've found anything intact. There are a couple pieces of pottery over there, maybe part of a collection, but if so, the only pieces left. A few pieces of broken china, as well, but none salvageable."

"I bet they'd like to see that," Cale said, gesturing to the clock. "They're still out there."

"Those poor people," Derek said, frowning sympathetically. "Take it out to them. Wish there was more we could give them but..." Derek shook his head, surveying the charred, wet remains of a lifetime.

Cale took the clock from Derek and shined his own flashlight on the pottery shards, discovering the two pieces that hadn't broken—one looked like a glass candy dish, and the other appeared to be a Native American piece. Both were charred in places, but Cale grabbed them anyway. The pottery had some kind of freaky ceramic figure extending from the top of it. Ugly. But possibly precious to these people at least for the fact that it hadn't been destroyed. Rummaging through the immediate area for any other pieces that had survived turned up nothing, so he took the three pieces and walked across the yard and the street to the man and the woman.

They looked expectantly at him when it became obvious he was heading toward them and not one of the rigs.

"I'm sorry to say we haven't found much so far that made it," he said gently. "Hopefully, a search in the daylight will turn up more, but we thought this might be important to you." He held out the clock for them to see by the light of the streetlamp.

"The clock Bernie gave us," the man said, his voice wavering with fatigue.

"Bernie's our son—" The woman broke off in a gasp. "Oh, my word, Harold. Look." She pointed at the ugly pottery Cale had in his left hand. "May I?"

"Of course," Cale said, holding both pieces out to her.

"Oh, Harold, there's not a crack in it. Not a new crack, at least." She took the creature-topped pot and held it reverently between her and her husband.

"Unbelievable," the old man said in a hushed voice. "Would you look at that, Bess." He nodded slowly, and Cale did a double take as the man's lips turned up in a tired smile.

The man, Harold, shifted his gaze from the pot—which Cale decided had a three-dimensional lizard on top—to his wife. Their eyes held each other's, and even from where Cale was standing, he was touched by the pure love between the two. He hated to break their moment, especially after they'd had such a harrowing day, so he stood there in respectful silence. The man bent toward his wife and pressed a loving kiss to her lips. Once again, Cale was affected when the woman smiled up at

Harold. After their day, for them to be able to smile said a boatload about them.

"This pot," Bess said to Cale, her neck craned upward so she looked him in the eye, "has a history. Many years ago, when our marriage was young, we had an argument, as married folks sometimes do. In my upset, I knocked this pot off its shelf and it cracked into two pieces." She held it up and pointed out the crack. Cale aimed his light at it.

"We'd bought it on our honeymoon in Santa Fe," Harold said, picking up the story where his wife had left off, as if they were of a single mind.

"It's from the Acoma Pueblo," Bess explained.

"The night it broke, we went to bed without speaking. Both of us were pretty ticked off," Harold continued. "When we got up the next morning, the first thing we did was apologize and glue this pot back together."

"Neither one of us had slept worth a darn." Bess was absently rubbing the side of the pot as they told the story. "That very day, we made a vow. We would never go to bed mad again."

Harold nodded emphatically. "And we never have since."

"Wow. That's impressive," Cale said, meaning it.

"God must've been watching over this pot the way he's watched over our marriage for sixty-three years now." Bess burrowed into her husband as he put his frail-looking arm around her. "We're very blessed in spite of this…." Her eyes watered as she nodded toward the ruins of their house.

"It's good that you have each other to get through the rough times," Cale said sympathetically.

"You bet your buttons, sir," Harold said. "Love isn't always easy but it's always worth it." He kissed his wife's temple. “Let’s take these items to our car. Thank goodness it was parked in the street.”

Cale handed the candy dish to Harold. “Do you two have a place lined up to stay tonight?”

“Our son, Bernie, is on his way from Austin. He insisted on coming and helping us take care of everything. We’ll get a hotel tonight and then stay with him until…”

“Until we have a place to go,” Harold said. “He’s a good kid.”

“Our sixty-two-year-old kid,” Bess added.

“Will he be here soon?” Cale asked. “We’ll be heading out in a few minutes and I hate to leave you two on the street by yourselves.”

“Should be here any minute, but thank you, son. You’re a good man.”

Bess handed the pot to her husband and stepped forward. “Thank you for all you do,” she said as she wrapped her arms around a flustered Cale.

As he always was when fire victims showed gratitude, Cale was humbled. Doubly so today, as they’d been unable to save these people’s home. “I’m sorry we couldn’t do more.”

“It was the candle in the kitchen,” Bess said matter-of-factly. “We lit it after Harold burned some popcorn. We were trying to alleviate the smell and forgot about it. We think the curtains must have caught and spread.”

“Did you tell the chief that?” Cale asked.

“He took notes on the whole story,” Bess said. “There’s Bernie.” She forgot Cale was there as she tottered off the curb toward a white sedan parking just up the block.

“Thank you for these,” Harold said, lifting the three recovered pieces. “I better go. She’s got a bad hip and I like to keep an eye on her.”

“I wish you the best.” Cale watched the two greet their

son. He met all kinds of people in his line of work, but he couldn't remember ever being as struck as he was by this couple. They made him long for what they had between them.

HOURS LATER, the truck and equipment were cleaned and restocked. It was a strangely quiet night for the department. After showering, Cale had closed himself in his cramped bunk room and tried for an eternity and a half to catch some z's.

Finally giving up, he pulled his clothes back on and headed to the common room. It was deserted and dark—not surprising since it was almost 2:00 a.m. Standing there in the center of the room, he felt closed-in and antsy. The air felt stale, confining.

Cale headed out to the patio on the beach and stared out at the dark water, his mind occupied by thoughts of Bess and Harold. He wondered where they'd wound up for the night.

Hell, who was he kidding? More than the couple's lodging for the night, he was stuck on their relationship. For him to even give it a second thought said a bunch. There was such a vibe of love between the two of them, it'd been almost tangible. He'd had the thought then and it wouldn't leave him alone now: he wanted that kind of bond for himself. And he wanted it with Rachel.

He wanted to be there when she woke up, as he had been the one day she'd slept in his arms. Wanted her to be with him for the tough times, as she had been that first time he'd gone back in the condo. He longed to bury all the painful stuff with happy things, good memories, laughter—and be the one by her side when the grief and sadness needed to surface.

His dad's blunt question about letting Rachel go because of a woman who was no longer alive, once the ticked-off feeling had dissipated, had taken root in his head. At first he'd fought the idea tooth and nail and refused to even acknowledge the thoughts that were raging in his head. The past few days, though, he'd found himself thinking about it more freely. Thinking about Rachel. Admitting to himself he didn't like not being able to see her or talk to her when he wanted to, which was several times a day.

And then Harold's words…

Love isn't always easy but it's always worth it.

To have love with Rachel, he'd have to finally "let go" of Noelle.

Shakily, he sucked in the sea-fresh, almost chilly night air at the thought. It wouldn't be easy. He had to do it whether Rachel was in the picture or not, for his own sake—because while he would always love Noelle on some level, if he held on to her as his fiancée, his future wife with whom he *had* no future, he was doomed to live his life in limbo. Without the love of another living, breathing woman, as his dad had pointed out.

Without Rachel.

She wasn't ready yet, he knew, but he had to do what he could to make her see she was not responsible for Noelle's death. That her feelings for him were not responsible. And if she still felt the same about him, he would spend the rest of his life showing her those feelings were reciprocated.

RACHEL HAD NO IDEA why she'd said yes when Cale's sister had asked her to meet for coffee. She had no clue what Mariah wanted from her.

Rachel wasn't an avid coffee drinker. She wasn't a social person. She and Mariah were friendly but not friends.

Her nerves jittered as she swished her grape-juice bottle around in circles in front of her.

From her spot in a large, rust-colored easy chair in the corner, Rachel watched for Mariah and sipped her juice. Mariah finally strode in and glanced around but didn't notice Rachel before getting into the coffee line. Of course, she was likely looking for a blonde. Rachel's uneasiness doubled.

When Mariah eventually came around the corner, still searching, Rachel shyly waved to get her attention. She could hear and see Mariah's gasp of shock when recognition dawned on her, even though Mariah was still halfway across the room.

"Wow!" Mariah rushed over to her. "Rachel, you look amazing."

Rachel tried to convince herself Mariah meant it and smiled nervously. "I don't know about *amazing,* but thanks."

"Still getting used to it?" Mariah nodded to Rachel's hair as she took the adjacent chair and set her coffee on the table in the corner between them.

Rachel nodded, her eyes wide with emphasis. "I'm not sure what I was thinking."

Mariah shook her head enthusiastically. "It looks really good. Really different but good. Has Cale seen it yet?"

Rachel shook her head quickly, probably too quickly. She was all too aware of the fact that Cale hadn't seen her new do. All too worried about what he would think. She'd spent too much time turning it over in her mind, recognizing that, though she hadn't intended it as a test for him, she was scared to death of the prospect that he might not be nearly as interested in her now that her resemblance to Noelle was not so obvious.

But the real question was, why had Mariah asked her

that? Not that Rachel was going to voice the question aloud….

An awkward silence fell between them as Mariah took a cautious sip of her steaming coffee.

"What did you want to meet about today?" Rachel finally blurted out. "The benefit?"

Mariah pulled her leg up into her own patterned easy chair. "Oh…no. Not at all. I just… I know we didn't get off to the greatest start, what with my 'great idea' that I threw at you at that very first meeting. And I thought it'd be nice if we just got acquainted a little better outside of the publicity committee. I feel like I knew Noelle so much better than I know you. Cale seems to care about you, though. Quite a bit."

Alarm shot through Rachel. "We're not—"

"Maybe not yet but you never know. Anyway, I've felt bad about the way I pressured you when it so obviously made you uncomfortable. I'm sorry about that."

"You're not going to try to talk me into it again today?" Rachel asked, forcing herself to smile in spite of the very real concern that that had been Mariah's motivation.

"No! I mean, don't get me wrong. I still think it would be really powerful, but I'm not going to try to persuade you."

"Thanks." Rachel breathed out and studied her juice. "I… It's been really hard coming back to the island," she said, her voice heavy with the sadness that seemed to be only a half layer below the surface lately. "I've had to face things I didn't want to face…." Her voice cracked and she fought for control over her frayed emotions.

"I understand." Mariah reached out and touched her arm. "Really."

Rachel filled her lungs with air and felt a little steadier. "How long of a speech did you have in mind?"

"*Speech* sounds so cold and impersonal…and long and intimidating," Mariah said warmly. "I was thinking just a couple of minutes. Nothing major as far as time goes, though I know it would be major in other ways."

"Understatement." Rachel bit her lip and again shook her head. "I walk around feeling like the littlest thing could set me off on a crying jag, you know? I'm not strong enough yet to think about talking about her in front of a large crowd."

"Fair enough. If you change your mind, though, it would require pretty much no advance notice to work you in. And it might, I don't know, help you in some way as you process everything and try to get your equilibrium back. To be able to do that. Just…keep that in mind, okay?"

Mariah's words weren't lost on Rachel. It would be a major step toward healing, to be able to do it. Rachel nodded, unable to commit.

"I'm sorry," Mariah said animatedly, sitting back in her chair. "I meant what I said…that isn't why I invited you here. So, moving on…no more sad talk. Have you seen how hot Tim Bowman is these days? It's become my goal in life to meet him before the concert."

Relieved at the subject change, Rachel laughed. "I'm thinking that shouldn't be too hard to coordinate. We've got connections, you know."

The next hour flew by faster than Rachel would have imagined, especially after the rough start. It was tough not to like Cale's sister…kind of like it was tough not to like Cale but without all the complications.

CHAPTER TWENTY-NINE

RACHEL FINALLY GOT IT. She finally understood the saying "drowning in sorrow." Thoroughly.

As she sorted through Noelle's DVDs in the living-room cabinet, the ones that had been untouched for so long they were coated with dust, her lungs had the sensation of being filled with something besides air. Her eyes…they were like a faucet that had been left on at a trickle for two weeks straight, and they were so red and swollen that blinking made them burn. And even though she'd done minimal physical activity for the past few weeks—kayaking was it—her body ached as if she'd been struggling against a riptide.

She took another DVD box out and wiped it off with a dust rag. It was one of the Nicholas Sparks movies—Noelle had owned just about all of them and watched them over and over. Rachel had sat through one of them with her sister and had wanted to poke out her own eyeballs. She set it on the library-donation pile on the floor.

Next, she hit Noelle's Hugh Grant collection in full. Some of the movies Rachel liked, but most of them she hadn't taken the time to watch. All of them were added to the donation pile because Noelle had been the only movie lover in the family. In fact, it would've been easier, both physically and emotionally, to just come in with a paper grocery sack and start stacking all of the movies in it without a glance, but Rachel was compelled to do this to herself, to face the memories. To show herself she could handle it.

When she heard her mom come in the back door, she hurriedly used the filthy dust rag to wipe her eyes then swore at the stupid move as her eyes burned even more.

"What's wrong?" her mom asked as she entered the dimly lit living room.

Rachel noticed her mom still looked taken aback and did a double take at her black hair even though she'd had days to get used to it. "Oooh." Her mom's concern turned to sympathy when she saw what Rachel was doing. "What made you decide to do that?"

Rachel systematically transferred movies from the shelf to the pile, no longer torturing herself with memories specific to each individual title. Without looking up, she said, "I finished the bedroom. Figured this was next. We can probably get rid of this entire cabinet once I get Sawyer to take these to the library."

"You're getting rid of all of them?"

Rachel paused with her hand on top of the growing stack to glare at her mother. "We don't watch movies, Mom. There's no sense in keeping them."

"Oh, I want that one," Jackie said, bending down to retrieve the chick flick on top. "Ah, and this." She grabbed the next DVD, as well. When she realized Rachel was still eyeing her, she shrugged. "I watch movies now. She had some good ones."

"You might as well have a seat and help me if there are others you want."

Her mom kicked off her shoes and sat cross-legged next to Rachel. "I didn't realize you'd finished your bedroom."

Rachel inspected the next three cases and handed them over. "Just her side."

"Just the hard part," her mom said. "I'm proud of you."

Rachel had nothing to say to that. Her mom probably wouldn't be so proud if she had seen the way the task had practically defeated Rachel each time she'd worked on it. And she sure as hell wouldn't be proud if she found out it'd resulted in her and Cale…

There it was yet again—or maybe it never really stopped, just ebbed and flowed. The swirling, toxic, black guilt rushed into her chest. She was getting better at handling this, though. Her eyes didn't even water anew. Of course, there was the distinct possibility that there was no moisture left in her tear ducts.

"Damn," her mom said as they continued to sort. When Rachel glanced up, Jackie was biting her lower lip and shaking her head morosely.

"What?"

Her mom seemed to fight for control for a few seconds. "I wish I'd taken the time then to watch some of these with her. So many nights, I came home from the office late and she'd be sitting there on the couch, wrapped up in a movie. And every time…" Her eyes closed and she pursed her lips together hard for several heartbeats. "Every time, she'd say, 'Wanna join me, Mom?' And every time, I'd say I was too tired, or too hungry, or had too much to do. So…damn…much…regret…" As she spoke, her voice went up in pitch till it was squeaky at the end of the sentence.

So much for Rachel hanging on to her own composure. She threw her head back, squeezing her eyes shut at the instant tears. Regret…*God.* She'd written the book on it.

They both sat there mourning, crying silently, separately, for some time. After a while, her mom breathed in air as if her lungs had been completely empty. The next moment, her arms were around Rachel, and that, more than anything, absolutely killed her. Sobs racked Rachel's shoulders. She was so absorbed in the pain it didn't even occur to her to try to hide it—for once.

"I can't even tell you how much the regret hurts," her mom said into her hair, and that made Rachel cry harder.

When she could form words, Rachel said, "You… don't…need…to." She recognized she was on the verge of hyperventilating again and focused on calming herself down, counting slow, measured breaths. "I…have you… beat," she eventually managed to say.

Her mom squeezed her harder. "Shh. It's okay, sweetie. It's okay."

Rachel shook her head, keeping her face buried. "It's not okay. It's my fault."

Jackie loosened her grip and tried to make Rachel meet her eyes. "What's your fault, Rachel?"

It was time. She'd told Cale, but her mom deserved to know the truth about how Noelle had died. *Why* she'd died.

Shit, shit, shit.

"Th-that night," she said, still breathing unevenly and fighting to get it under control. "Our f-fight."

"I know you and Noelle had a fight, sweetie. You told me that." Her mom rubbed her hand back and forth over Rachel's knee.

"Not what it was about. It was about…Cale."

At her mom's silence, Rachel dared to look at her. When she didn't see the shock she expected in her mom's eyes, she recited to her the main points of what had happened to send Noelle out of the house. And then she waited as her mother took it all in. Waited for an outburst, for the anger she deserved. Anticipated the blame.

Her mom bit her lower lip again and held out her arms to Rachel. "Come here."

"What?" Rachel started shaking uncontrollably, stunned and relieved and horrified and overcome with guilt all at once.

Jackie pulled her into a protective, loving mom-hug.

"Why are you hugging me?" Rachel asked.

"Ooh, sweetie." Her mom hugged her intensely, squeezing the air out of her. Nodding. "I knew. Or suspected."

Rachel's eyes popped open. "Suspected what?"

"You and Noelle were so opposite in so many ways, but you always liked the same boys."

"Not always," Rachel said defensively.

"A lot."

"How would you even know that?"

"I'm your mom."

"So?"

"A mother knows things about her daughters. I knew that boy Noelle went to senior prom with was someone you had a crush on. And Jimmy Vargas. You both had a thing for him and we know how that ended."

Noelle had dated him the whole summer after their senior year.

"Noelle never meant you any harm," her mom continued. "I don't think she was aware of it most of the time."

Rachel shook her head in agreement.

"And you've spent all this time feeling guilty for finally letting her know."

Understatement of the century.

"It *killed* her, Mom."

"No." The fierceness of her mother's reply startled her. It wasn't just insistent; it was angry. "I don't ever want to hear you say that again, Rachel. What killed your sister was her own damn carelessness. Her self-centeredness. She was forced to pull her head out of everything Noelle, to face up to the way she'd inadvertently hurt you,

and she couldn't handle it." Her mom stood, as if propelled by her outrage. "*She* ran away, Rachel. *She* left the house without the things that could have saved her life. *She* acted rashly, irresponsibly…"

"Stupidly. Selfishly," Rachel said, her mother's rage catching. She jumped up from the floor, too, gritted her teeth, raised her fist in front of her as if she wanted to settle the score. Fire ignited within her and her control blew. "If she'd just stopped and picked up her purse, she'd probably be here with us today!"

Her purse, which they'd later found, had contained both her inhaler and her cell phone. But Noelle had plucked only her keys off the table from where they'd sat right next to her purse.

"It was just like her to waltz out of the house so carelessly," Rachel said, venturing into angry-rant land. "I loved my sister with all my heart, but, *God,* why didn't she use her head for one damn night?"

Her mom stood staring at nothing, her arms crossed defiantly in front of her, the fingers of one hand pressed over her eyelids.

"You'd think she could have grabbed her purse so she'd at least have her beloved lipstick! And her phone… God forbid she was ever isolated from all her friends. How could she leave without it the one night she absolutely needed it?" Rachel wandered over to the last family picture they'd had taken some seven years ago, a large, portait-size print on the wall, and stared up at Noelle. "Gaaah! I swear if you were here right now, I'd strangle you!" she screamed.

She knew on some level she'd lost her damn mind, but she didn't care. She wanted to rant and yell and let it be known that *she was furious.*

She continued to pace the room and yell whatever

came to mind for a couple more minutes before her mom came up behind her and wrapped her arms around her from the side. "It's okay, sweetie. Get it out."

The semi-sane words in the face of Rachel's insanity penetrated her dense haze of anger and ultimately made her fall apart. She clung to her mom and let the emotions pour out through her eyes in big, burning tears. They continued to hold on to each other as the night stretched out, eventually landing on the couch, side by side.

"I wouldn't really strangle her," Rachel said at last in a hoarse whisper.

"I know you wouldn't. I know, Rachel."

"If I had had any idea she would get that upset, I never, ever would have said any of it, Mom. I'd do anything to have her back here."

"Me, too," her mom said. "Anything in the world."

Rachel sank more deeply into the cushion behind her, letting her head fall on top of it, every muscle in her body spent. And yet...she felt as if she'd expelled some toxic air from inside of her, as if she was lighter somehow. In addition, for the first time since she'd moved back home, she felt close to her mother. Closer than they'd ever been in the past, even when they were so much alike. Back then, one of their similarities had been an avoidance of talking about anything too personal. Their conversations had centered on things like medical advances and test scores and her mother's more challenging patients.

Curling on her side to face her mom, Rachel leaned her head on her mom's shoulder and clasped her upper arm. "I think I needed to do that, maybe."

"Needed to do what?"

"Go on a psych-ward-worthy, crazy tirade."

"You've needed to do a lot of things, sweetie. And you're doing them. Finally."

"I hate it. Hate. It."

Nodding in the near-dark, her mom said, "Pretty much sucks. We get so bowled over by grief and sadness, we forget to celebrate the wonderful, fun-loving girl Noelle was."

"That's true." Rachel had vague memories of talk at the meal after the funeral services about celebrating Noelle's life, but she'd been so beyond comprehending the concept that day—and so set on avoiding thoughts of it ever since—that she'd never really considered what it would mean. "We should honor her somehow."

Jackie took Rachel's hand in hers and squeezed. "I like that. Got any ideas?"

"Actually…yeah. Something very Noelle. Come on."

Without a thought of her train-wreck appearance or what she was wearing, she led her mom out of the house and into the car.

CHAPTER THIRTY

THE PUBLIC BEACH parking lot was deserted. Not surprising since it was after midnight. Even though it was a Friday night, beach traffic dwindled and tourists turned their attention to the bars and clubs after dark. Rachel pulled the car up in the space closest to the beach and hopped out.

Her mom was slow to follow. By the time Jackie got out of the car, Rachel had impulsively grabbed the three oversize, mostly dry beach towels from her trunk. She had a bad habit of leaving them there after she went out in her kayak, but tonight they would come in handy.

"What are we doing?" her mom asked, her light brown hair blowing in her face.

"She loved the beach."

Her mom crossed her arms and looked out toward the water. "She adored the drama of the waves starting when you two were itty-bitty. I could barely keep her out of them from the time she could walk." A bittersweet smile tugged at her lips. "I remember the first time your dad took you two to the beach alone one weekend when I had to work. He came home and swore he'd never do that again. Trying to keep track of Noelle aged him five years in an afternoon."

"I think I remember that. Either that or I've heard the story before. Come on."

With a questioning look, her mom followed her onto the sand. The wind on the shore was fierce tonight, making the waves wilder than usual. The moon was nearly full. Clouds periodically blew over it, for the most part, but every few minutes, it peeked out and lit up the sand and the water. Like Rachel and her mom, Mother Nature was having a dramatic night. Apparently, she'd scared the tourists inside—there was no one in sight up or down the beach.

"What are we doing, Rachel?"

Rachel dropped the towels in a pile several feet from the wet sand, thinking. What would Noelle do? No-brainer. "Night swimming."

Her mom laughed halfheartedly. "I didn't bring a suit."

"That would never stop Noelle." Rachel unsnapped her shorts and shed them without hesitation.

"What?" Jackie said, sounding scandalized but smiling. "You are not..."

"I am." She lifted her T-shirt over her head and threw it in the sand next to her shorts then stood there in her bra and underwear. "We used to do this all the time. Well," she amended, "Noelle did. She dragged me out late at night after you'd gone to sleep—"

"She did *what?*"

"I made her swear to always take me with her, even though I never got in," Rachel continued. "The thought of her swimming at night all alone..." It still made her shudder.

"So you'd come out here and do what?" her mom asked.

"I sat with a book and a flashlight. She did this." Rachel ran toward the water and splashed in. The drama of the crashing waves flowed through her, enlivened her. It was scary and invigorating at once. "Get out here, Mom!" she yelled, unsure whether her mother could hear her over the roar of the waves.

Rachel went deeper, diving into a wave and coming out drenched on the other side. Splashing as she regained her footing. Laughing.

"This is crazy!" her mom said, suddenly six feet away and soaked, as well.

"You wanted to honor your younger daughter!" Rachel said, scooping the water with both arms and flinging it toward the sky.

Her mom looked thoughtful for a few seconds, and then she nodded once emphatically and flung herself into the next wave as it overtook them.

The two women played in the waves until they were exhausted, laughing and carrying on as if they had no worries in the world. Something strange came over Rachel, an exhilaration she couldn't describe or explain. She suspected there were tears involved—she couldn't tell for sure with so much salt water from the gulf pouring down her face—but they didn't feel so devastatingly sad the way they had for the past two weeks.

Anyone watching them would've thought they'd either lost their minds or were a couple of twelve-year-olds having the time of their lives. Without conferring, they slowly made their way toward shore in their underwear and bras. The air temperature was lower than the water temp, and Rachel shivered, rubbing her hands over her upper arms. Once they were fully on land, fat raindrops began to fall, though it took them a few seconds to realize it. They looked at each other and laughed.

"Good thing we're already soaked," her mom said.

"Here." Rachel threw the top towel to her and wrapped the second one around her own shoulders. Spreading the third one out on the sand, she flopped down onto it.

Her mom followed suit. "Noelle would watch the storm come in, too."

"Yes, she would."

Lightning zigzagged down to the horizon way out over the gulf. It took several seconds, but the crash of thunder finally reached their ears. The hairs on the back of Rachel's neck stood on end as she watched the show. Her mom sat next to her, pulling the large towel up over her head and grasping it tightly at her neck. "This is crazy."

"Exactly."

They'd managed to capture the spontaneous, life-loving spirit of Noelle. To live it themselves for a few amazing, carefree minutes. If Noelle were here, she would've loved every second of it. Rachel refused to let in any wish that she would have opened up and done this when her sister was still alive.

As the rain let up just as suddenly as it'd started, Rachel realized this was the first time she'd thought about her sister without being dragged under by sadness and tears. "We absolutely have to do this again sometime."

Her mom nodded thoughtfully. "I like that idea."

Being able to think about Noelle like this, focusing on the wildly alive version of her instead of as a distant, painful memory, emboldened Rachel. An idea occurred to her and she tried to push it away, but it persisted as they sat there with the roar of the waves and the wind enveloping them. "Do you think...?" she began, then stalled.

"Do I think what?"

Rachel pursed her lips before speaking, giving herself every opportunity to *not* say what was on her mind. "A while back, Mariah Jackson suggested I say a few words about Noelle at the benefit concert...."

Her mom's hand snaked out from under the towel and clasped Rachel's.

"I said no initially—repeatedly, actually—but I think I'm going to do it after all," Rachel said. "I'm not sure what I'll say yet. Just a few lines. A minute or two, no more. It's a rock concert, after all."

"I love the idea, Rachel. We'll make it happen. You can do it right before I introduce Tim Bowman."

Just like that, Rachel sobered, wondering what she'd gotten herself into but knowing she couldn't change her mind. It scared the daylights out of her, but she felt compelled to do it. A simple public tribute to the amazing woman who was her sister—it was long overdue.

THE MORNING OF the benefit concert, the air was so thick with humidity you could slice it like heavy pound cake.

By the time Cale stood on the beach, watching Tim Bowman's crew assemble the stage, the midmorning sun had broken through, clearing the overnight rainstorm, and gave hope they'd have clear weather by the 8:00 p.m. start time.

Today marked twenty months since Noelle's death. That seemed significant in light of all that was running through his head. Twenty months. Six hundred-some days. He wasn't sure when it had happened, or even whether there had been a specific moment or if it had been a gradual thing, but he finally felt as if he could breathe. As if he could stand the thought of having a future.

Rattling his keys in the pocket of his cargo shorts, he left the concert site and walked north in the sand. He had things to take care of—big things—before he went home to steal a few hours of sleep after work. Last night had kept him and the rest of the crew on duty busy enough he'd only snoozed for a couple of interrupted hours. Tonight had the potential to be draining, and he'd promised to come back late this afternoon to help with last-minute preparations.

When he'd walked out of work this morning, he'd had an unexpected moment of clarity regarding the condo. As he hiked closer to it now, that clarity was gone, and he wondered if he'd just been sleep-deprived and delirious instead. Maybe the alarms last night—a garage fire, a domestic altercation that had turned into the man trying to set his house on fire and a vehicle extrication—had been too stressful and had knocked him all the way off his rocker.

As he passed the Shell Shack bar, he looked for Derek's wife, Macey, out on the patio or inside the thatched-roof building before remembering she'd given birth—a month earlier than she and Derek had expected—only a week or so ago. He kept walking, as tempting as it was to stop in for a burger. Procrastinating wouldn't make anything easier.

A few minutes later, his building was just up ahead, on the other side of a small, older motel. The condo building jutted out a few feet beyond the motel and towered four stories higher than it. His eyes automatically sought out his door, and he was taken back to another time, another walk up to it from the beach. The first time he'd taken Noelle to see the place, he'd purposely taken her by this route, the scenic route. The selling Realtor at the time had left the beachside door open for them. Cale kept a security bar in the sliding glass door now, so he had to go around to the main door to enter.

When he did, he waited for the familiar pang—the sting of interrupted plans and jackknifed futures—to hit him in the gut as it always did. He cautiously shut the door and looked left toward the kitchen and then right toward the living room.

Nothing.

Furrowing his brow, he flipped on the light switch suspiciously, as if searching for a live enemy.

The pang was still missing. As he narrowed his eyes, it hit him why: there was very little about the remodeled place that was familiar now. This was no longer the home he'd planned to share with Noelle. He'd gone with more masculine, muted colors and materials than anything they'd ever seriously looked at in the home-improvement store. The light fixtures were steel and glass, something she never would have gone for. Between them and the sleek, black blinds he'd installed in all the windows, the condo had the feel of an upscale bachelor pad.

It hit him now that his subconscious had been hard at work. Though he hadn't realized what he was doing at the time, on some level, it'd been deliberate. He'd been preparing himself to walk away, gradually letting go of what he and Noelle had envisioned without really realizing it.

He strode to the spotless, unused kitchen. Nope. He could no longer imagine Noelle cooking in here. It was gray, black and white, and the stove he'd wound up buying wasn't her dream appliance with five burners. There was no clutter or traces of crumbs on the counters, as there always had been if Noelle had been making something. Relief began seeping into his veins as he headed toward the bedrooms.

She wasn't back here, either. Though Cale hadn't done any structural work to the bedrooms or bathrooms, the blinds and a different comforter changed the vibe. He could look at the bed now and not see her sprawled across it with her blond hair spread across the pillow, sound asleep when he came home from work.

Cale went to the window and opened the blinds to let in the sunlight, then did the same to the rest of the windows and the vertical blind at the sliding glass door. The bright light brought the place back to life like it hadn't been in months. It made the condo look appealing, homey.

But not for him.

The set of keys felt heavy in his hand, still buried in his pocket as he jingled them. He gave the living room a critical perusal, searching for anything out of place. The *Sports Illustrated* was long gone, tossed into the Dumpster he'd had to rent to dispose of all the remodeling debris. He'd packed away the pictures and stowed them in a box in the top of the closet. It looked like a picture-perfect layout that would appear in a home magazine.

The Realtor would love it.

He took the keys out of his pocket and removed the one to the condo. Clenching the single key in one hand, he held up the keychain in his other, a gold letter *J* for *Jackson* on a black background that Noelle had given him when he'd closed on this place.

The key would go, the condo would be sold, but that didn't mean he was "getting rid" of Noelle.

Certain now that his moment of clarity had been accurate, Cale walked out of the condo one last time and headed to the real-estate office one block over, next door to the Chinese restaurant.

No matter what happened in his future—if Rachel gave him a chance, if he one day had a family of his own—he'd always have the keychain, and he'd always have Noelle in his memory and in his heart.

CHAPTER THIRTY-ONE

CALE HAD LOOKED everywhere for Rachel and was beginning to wonder if she was standing him up—or at least avoiding him.

Instead of letting him pick her up, she'd insisted on riding to the concert with her mother and meeting him here on the patio of the Silver Sands Hotel, at the preparty they'd organized for all the volunteers. As he stood on the threshold between the lobby and the patio, he scanned the crowded area for her familiar blond head. Unfortunately, as short as she was, his chances of seeing her from afar were not good. He began a meandering path toward the long buffet table that was covered with finger foods and desserts, keeping an eye out for Rachel.

"Hey, Cale."

He turned to see Captain Joe Mendoza, who slapped him heartily on the back.

"It's the big night, huh?" Joe said.

"Long time coming," Cale responded. "Figured you'd be home with that new baby. How'd you get out of the house?"

Joe whipped out his phone and showed Cale a photo of his wife, Faith; their two-week-old daughter; Derek's wife, Macey; and their tiny baby girl. The two women sat side by side on a couch and held up the infants as if they could smile for the picture.

"I made sure she's got sympathetic company tonight," Joe said. "Derek's on duty, so it worked out well."

"Look at them," Cale said, grinning. "Yours has her mama's eyes, doesn't she?" Her eyes were open and alert, while the Severson baby snoozed on.

"Yep. Amaya is one beautiful little girl. Gonna be a knockout someday," Joe said, pride dripping from his voice. "I'm completely unbiased, of course."

"When she hits the knockout stage, you're gonna have your hands full."

"Oh, she'll be locked in the house till she's thirty."

The two men laughed and Cale excused himself to search for Rachel. He made it to the buffet table without a glimpse of her, so he picked up an appetizer plate and filled it with mini sandwiches, nuts and butter mints. As he glanced back in the direction he'd come from, still searching, really starting to wonder if Rachel was okay, he became aware of someone to his left, near the make-shift bar, staring at him. He turned his head and saw a woman with coal-black hair watching him from ten feet away. His eyes collided with her familiar turquoise ones and he dropped his paper plate, scattering everything he'd just loaded onto it. He ignored the mess and stared, his jaw likely sagging to his chest.

"Rachel?"

She made her way to him, attempting to smile but managing to look only nervous. "Hey," she said when she reached his side.

"Hey? What the…? You… Your hair… I didn't recognize you."

She touched the very short do and laughed, but it wasn't her usual laugh. "It's different. Way different. I know. I'm not sure what I was thinking."

"It looks good," he said, narrowing his eyes in an attempt to see her more objectively. It was true. She looked hot. He'd never seen her in a skirt before, but she wore a short denim skirt and the same shirt as him—the Noelle Culver memorial concert shirt they'd had designed specially for tonight—hers in bright green, his in navy blue. She looked one thousand percent different from the Rachel he knew and loved, but hot.

Yep, *loved.* The thought didn't make him so much as flinch. God, it was good to see her. It'd taken some serious willpower to honor her need for time away from him. So many times throughout the days, he'd had things he wanted to tell her, thoughts he'd wanted to share.

He pulled her into his arms and kissed her on the lips.

"Really good," he said again when he pulled back enough to look at her.

"Thank you," she said shyly, increasing the space between them. "I decided to speak tonight. Onstage. About Noelle."

Cale looked down at her in surprise, easily remembering her response weeks ago when Mariah had suggested it. "You did?"

"It's been a rough couple of weeks. Lots going on, lots to process, but I think I need to do this."

He nodded slowly, letting the idea sink in. "That's great, Rachel. I think you should. Do you know what you're going to say?"

"I wrote it all down." She pulled a small stack of notecards from her back pocket and waved them around.

Looking at the quantity, he said, "Did you notify them the concert will start an hour late?"

"I wrote big," she said earnestly. "I'm scared to death I'll lose my place or that I'll cry like a baby. And then I wouldn't be able to see what I wrote, so not only would

I embarrass myself by blubbering, but also by not knowing what I was going to say."

Cale grinned and put his arm around her, pulling her in to his side. It was just like her to not leave anything to chance, even a potential, understandable emotional outburst.

"There are worse things than crying, you know."

"In public? On a stage? Not really."

"I'll be as close as I can get, Rach, waiting for you if you want."

"I want."

"Did you eat anything?" he asked, finally bending down to clean up the food he'd spilled.

"A little. I think I need a drink. Just one to calm my nerves."

That she was doing this, getting up onstage to honor Noelle, in spite of all her worries… It made her all the more lovable. He wished he could take away all her fears and worries, even though he didn't have a single doubt she'd face them and do fine. More than fine.

Cale put his arm around her and led her to the bar, tossing his plate and food into a trash can on the way. "You're sure about this? My guess is your tolerance for alcohol is that of a toddler's, unless you have a habit I don't know about."

"Your guess is pretty right-on. I'll have some wine. Only a little bit."

"Red or white?" he asked as they stepped up to order.

Rachel shrugged.

"Give her a glass of Riesling, please," he said to the bartender.

The woman, dressed in black pants, a formal white shirt and a bow tie, set a wineglass on the bar, picked up an open bottle of Riesling and poured it. Cale handed her cash and ushered Rachel away to the outer edge of the crowd, near the planters that separated the patio from the sand.

"I didn't intend for you to pay for it."

"I'm your date, remember?"

He spoke the words lightly, but Rachel looked up at him intently, a half smile on her face. "How could I ever forget? I've waited a long time." Her tone was a mix of flirtation and shyness.

Cale stared at her, again taken aback by the difference in her appearance, until he homed in on her beautiful, remarkable eyes and tempting lips.

"Hey, you two." Sawyer came up to them, followed closely by the older Dr. Culver. Rachel's brother shook Cale's hand and kissed the top of Rachel's head. "Heard you're going up onstage, Rachel." He eyed her glass of wine and then raised his brows at Cale.

"I'm monitoring her intake," Cale said, laughing.

"I've had three sips, overprotective men." Rachel held her glass up, took another swallow and amended, "Four."

"We should head toward the stage," Rachel's mom said, checking her watch.

Rachel hurriedly took another drink—a large gulp—and shuddered from it.

"I'll hold that for you," Cale told her. "You can have one more swallow before you go out onstage, but that's all. In addition to your other fears, falling on your face would be less than desirable."

The four of them headed from the patio to the back side of the stage. Cale wasn't sure if Rachel even realized she'd taken his hand, but her mom noticed it and gave him a puzzling secret smile. He'd wondered how Jackie would react if she found out he and Rachel were involved. He'd actually been concerned about it, but maybe he didn't need to be, after all.

"What do you think of shorty's rebellion—er, I mean, do?" Sawyer asked as they walked.

"Nice," Rachel said. "If you're going to dish about my hair, wait till I'm not around."

"I already told her I like it," Cale said, looking again, because no matter how good it looked on her, it was a huge change and he wasn't used to it yet.

Rachel studied him as if she didn't believe him, and then they arrived at their destination, a kind of holding area behind and under the stage. It was small and packed full, and Rachel's mom was the only reason they got past the security guards. Cale spotted Bowman and a couple of his band members over to the side, surrounded by local TV and radio personalities and a flock of overeager women…including his sister.

A few minutes later, a man with headphones on gestured to Rachel. Her grip on Cale's hand tightened, and then she let go. Before she could rush off, he grabbed her arm, turned her toward him and pressed a quick, intense kiss to her lips. "Noelle would be proud of you," he said directly into her ear.

She didn't respond, just looked as if she wanted to throw up as she took a deep breath, closed her eyes for a moment and followed the guy to the stairs.

Cale watched her every determined, brave step, his feelings for her overwhelming him. He'd been thinking that tonight would be the wrong time to tell her how he felt, but as they'd both found out, time was precious. He no longer wanted to waste another minute.

OVERWHELMING.

That was the word that kept running through Rachel's

mind as she stood just offstage. It was all too much. The crowd, the band, the support of Noelle and the drive for funds for asthma research. *Cale.*

When she'd first spotted him tonight, an involuntary calmness had come over her, as if having him there made everything okay, soothed her nerves. The next second, when he'd spotted her and taken in her new hairstyle, she'd gotten caught up worrying about his reaction. In typical Cale style, though, he'd said the right things about it. He made her believe it really made no difference to him what her hair looked like. Made it easy to lean on him, rely on him, pretend it was okay.

She tried to ignore the nagging deep in her gut. Not now. Blocking out her doubts was vital right now, when she was crazy-nervous and so on the edge emotionally.

The next thing she knew, her name was announced. She squeezed her notecards so tightly they bent as she made her way out to the microphone. As she took the mic from Heather Alamillo, the committee member who'd been tasked with entertaining the crowd from time to time before the show started, Rachel happened to catch a glimpse of navy blue on the ground at the corner of the stage, on this side of the barricades holding the throngs of concert-goers back. Cale's navy blue concert shirt. He'd staked out a spot where she could see him, feel his support. The smile she gave the audience was genuine, if scared spitless.

"Good evening," she said tentatively into the mic.

The crowd was restless and not exactly silent until she said, "My name is Rachel Culver. Noelle was my sister."

She inadvertently noticed one of the Jumbotrons to the side of the stage at an angle. There was a giant blowup of the photo of Noelle that Trina had taped to her planning folder so many weeks ago. It threw Rachel off for a second that felt like an hour. She swallowed hard and glanced at Cale. He winked at her and smiled…that smile. She could do just about anything when that smile was aimed at her.

"My *twin* sister," she continued. "Identical, believe it or not, but I recently flipped out a little bit and now I look like this."

There was a respectful din of laughter and several hoots and hollers from a section of guys close to the stage.

"Thank you," she said to the guys, smiling, trying to lighten her own mood. "Do you have an extra ticket for me?"

They answered by throwing both hands up helplessly, as if to say she had the better seat already.

"So," Rachel said, glancing down at her notecards, her heart racing. She looked back out at the crowd and abruptly shoved the cards back into her pocket, deciding to ad-lib it instead, because there was no way she could have prepared for what she saw, what she was feeling. "Wow. This is unbelievable. I came up here with the intention of thanking you for buying tickets to tonight's show, as all the profits are going to research the disease that killed my sister when she was only twenty-nine years old. You can see on the big screens how much was generated already just through ticket sales. That's huge, people. Thank you."

The audience erupted in cheers, and as it died down, someone yelled out, "We love you, Noelle!"

Rachel had been about to speak again, but that comment got to her. She lowered the microphone and took in a few deep breaths, staving off the mix of emotions. When she thought she could speak without losing it again, she lifted the mic. "I was also going to plead with you to buy a T-shirt to support the cause, but…" She indicated her own shirt and shook her head in disbelief as she gazed out at the multitudes. “It looks like seventy-five percent of you already did! As I look out, I see a rainbow of Noelle shirts. It's...” She shook her head again, momentarily speechless. “This is amazing. In fact, don't mind me. I want a picture.” From her other back pocket, she removed her cell phone, pushed the button for the camera, held it up and clicked. She had to cover the audience a strip at a time because it was too big to fit in one photo, and each time she moved the camera, the new section went wild.

When she'd covered the whole place, she stuck her phone back in her pocket and continued her impromptu speech. “Anyway, the only thing I wanted to say besides ‘thank you’ is this. My sister was a free spirit. The kind of person who enjoys pretty much every moment. I was always the serious twin, and her carefree ways sometimes used to drive me a little crazy, but now I admire her so much for that ability to go with the flow....” Her throat swelled painfully and her temples throbbed, but she was determined to get this out. “So tonight, I hope you'll let loose and love your life, love the moment especially for Noelle, since she isn't here. She would have loved this concert so much. Thank you.” She rushed the end bit out before she was overcome completely.

She'd never been so glad to see her mother, who came out as planned to introduce Tim Bowman and his band. After a quick hug, Rachel hurried off the stage...and straight into Cale's arms. He held her there without saying anything, for several minutes—as the band was introduced, as the guys rushed past them toward the stage, as the first song started. He just held her. And she let herself be held, soaking up every second of it. Loving it. Savoring him. And when the emotion from her time onstage had passed, she still didn't immediately move. She just…was. For once, she took the advice she'd given to the crowd and went with the flow.

CHAPTER THIRTY-TWO

GOING WITH THE FLOW, it turned out, made for an amazing night when you were by the man you loved, listening to excellent live music, on the beach under the stars.

Though Rachel hadn't had any more of her wine, she was riding a serious high an hour into the concert. She and Cale had found a place to stand on the far right side, only a few feet from the stage. The people in the area apparently recognized Rachel and were happy to let them squeeze in closer.

Rachel held on to Cale's arm and leaned her head on his biceps as the guitarist started into the next song, a mellow, plaintive melody. After the exhilaration of the day and having her emotions all over the map the past several weeks, her fatigue hit hard.

"We're gonna slow things down a bit for a few," Tim said into the mic. "This song is kind of a surprise just for you guys."

The crowd cheered and the singer waited for them to calm down.

"We wrote this song just for tonight. In memory of Noelle Culver." Again, he paused for cheers. "I never knew her personally, but being a couple years younger than her, I remember her well. You didn't go to school at San Amaro High and not at least know of Noelle Culver."

Rachel nodded, recognizing the truth in what he said. Noelle had commanded attention without trying.

"I want to thank Trina Jankovich, one of Noelle's friends, for helping us out. She put together a little show especially for those of you who knew Noelle that you'll see on the video screens while we play our song."

The shot from earlier, from Trina's folder, reappeared larger than life on the twin screens that flanked the stage. As the other band members joined the guitarist in playing a beautiful, haunting song about a girl whose spirit was larger than life, Noelle's life flashed in front of them in a string of images. Trina had managed to find photos as far back as kindergarten to include.

Rachel's chest tightened as she watched her sister on screen, with friends, with the family, with her pet box turtle, homecoming dates and more. Cale's arm slipped around Rachel and pulled her tightly against him, as if he knew she needed the reinforcement. And maybe he needed hers, too. She breathed in Cale's scent and drew strength from his warmth that encircled her in the night air as she watched the images through blurred vision. The pictures became more recent, and there were a lot Rachel hadn't seen before, most of them probably taken when Rachel was in med school.

And then there was Cale, up on the big screen, holding Noelle, both of them laughing as if they didn't even know there was a camera pointed at them, and Rachel's whole world crashed around her.

This was not her life.

Cale wasn't her boyfriend or her fiancé or her future. He was the man who had loved her sister. He was her sister's man.

Rachel ducked out from under his arm, hurried through the crush of people and ran away.

RACHEL HAD BEEN gone for a full five minutes before Cale decided he was an idiot for assuming she'd just needed a bathroom break. Not when she'd left during *that* song. Not when she hadn't taken the time to mention where she was going.

He felt like a salmon swimming upstream as he headed away from the concert. Tim Bowman and his band had just started playing one of their biggest hits, and that drew every last fan who had wandered to the concession stand or the Porta Potti line back into the stage area. The concert had been excellent so far, but with Rachel MIA, Cale couldn't care less about missing the rest of the show.

He scanned the row of mostly vacant portable toilets as he walked by, and then he went through the hotel lobby and asked a random woman coming out of the women's restroom there to check for his escapee date. She reported the indoor restroom was deserted, though. No surprise.

Cussing himself out yet again for not following her right away, Cale headed for his truck, which was parked fairly close thanks to the fact that he'd shown up at 4:00 p.m. to help with preparations on the beach.

The idea that Rachel might be heading to her house would be too easy, but he drove by there first anyway. All the windows in the place were dark and her car was in the driveway, but that was expected since she'd ridden with her mom to the hotel. Just in case, he hopped out, leaving his engine running, and went to the door. Knocking three times produced no response, and when he tried the knob, the door was locked. He jogged back down the flight of stairs and briefly pondered his next move. It was a no-brainer. He knew exactly where she went when she was upset.

OLD HABITS GOT a person caught every time.

Caught was the last thing Rachel wanted right now, so when she heard a car pull up in the parking lot on the other side of the boathouse and subsequent footsteps on the gravelly ground behind her, she silently called herself a slew of not-so-nice names.

Why hadn't she gone…anywhere else besides the boathouse on the bay? Because she hadn't been thinking straight, of course. She'd been going on instinct. The walk from the beach to here was short, as the island was only about a half mile across at that point, and she hadn't given a second thought to heading for the quiet of the deserted boathouse.

When she'd gotten to Buck's, which she'd known was closed for the night, she'd at least had the foresight to go around to the back side and find a place in the shadows to sit by the placid water. But she was in plain sight if anyone really wanted to find her.

Obviously, Cale wanted to find her.

"There you are."

The smooth, low timbre of his voice breaking into the quiet made her want to weep. She drew her knees to her chest and buried her face in her arms.

"I'm surprised Buck hasn't given you your own set of keys," he said, not taking the hint that she didn't want to see him.

She so wasn't capable of mindless chatter or heart-to-hearts and didn't want any kind of company whatsoever. She said nothing and prayed he would give up easily and go away, even as she knew full well he wouldn't. That wasn't the kind of man Cale was. He was the good kind, the persistent, caring, get-to-the-heart-of-the-problem kind of man.

He sat down next to her on the man-made embankment. "You didn't think you should tell me you were leaving the concert?"

Rachel sucked in a leveling breath, steeling herself,

and dared to look at him. She intended to reply but found she had no answer that would make sense. She merely shook her head, her heart breaking all over again at the sight of his concern and confusion.

"That song was rough." Cale's fingers trailed lightly through the coarse sand between them, back and forth, digging a minivalley. "It was perfect for her. So perfect it hurt. And the photos..."

He thought she was upset merely from Tim's song? A month ago, it would have been her undoing, but tonight, though it had made her chest ache from the moment Tim had said he'd written it about Noelle, Rachel could finally handle that kind of reminder of her sister. In a way, she almost embraced it. However, letting Cale believe the music was the root of the problem was easiest. She nodded halfheartedly.

"Did you know they were planning to do that?" Cale persisted, and again, Rachel responded with only a head signal, this time in the negative.

"Come here," he said, holding his arm out for her to burrow into.

Except she couldn't.

He stared at her expectantly and then slowly dropped his arm. Not easily swayed, he scooted close to her side, until their thighs brushed together. When he put his arm around her, she couldn't stand it. Couldn't sit there and act as if everything between them was status quo when it wasn't. When it could never be. She jumped up to her feet and put some space between them, walking away from the water, her back to him.

"Cale." His name got caught in her throat and she dug deep for the right words.

He was standing behind her, his hands on her shoulders, before she even realized he'd stood.

"Rachel."

She felt his breath at her ear and shook her head.

"Baby, let me in. We can get through this together."

"No." She stepped away, shaking her head. "I can't do this, Cale. Once and for all. No."

"Whoa. Rachel, what's going on here? I think I missed something."

She kept her back to him and it took every ounce of her will to not start crying. But she didn't. She held strong. The only problem was that she couldn't speak a word.

"Are you gonna talk to me?" he asked.

Rachel could only shake her head.

He swore under his breath, obviously frustrated. "Okay, then. I'm gonna talk. I have some things to say. Are you at least going to turn around and face me?"

Rachel squeezed her eyes shut. God, she wanted to disappear, not listen to another round of how she still wasn't handling Noelle's death right. Curling up in a fetal position would be a close second, but only in the privacy of her room. Gritting her teeth in determination, she slowly pivoted, her eyes locked on the ground.

"Rachel, I love you."

Her eyes veered upward to look at him before she could rein in her response, and the intensity in his gaze nearly did her in. That. That was what she'd longed for for all her life. The right guy saying *that* and looking like *that.* Cale was the right guy. Had been since the night she'd met him. But she wasn't the right girl, and there wasn't a right time. Not for them.

At her lack of response, he touched her cheek, pressed his forehead to hers, and all she could do was stand there stock-still as her heart pulsed with searing pain. Cale wrapped his arms around her and said it again.

"I love you."

"You can't," she choked out. "You loved Noelle."

"I did. Past tense. She's not here anymore, so I can't love her in the same way." He ran his fingers through her hair, his chin resting on her head. "I fought loving you, Rachel. I rationalized with myself that you two are so different it didn't make sense. But I love you. I love your freaky-smart brain and the way you set goals and go all out for them and the way you are so sure about who you are. Watching you handle everything you've had to deal with since being back… You're one of the bravest people I know. So determined. Strong. You make me stronger somehow."

She shook her head emphatically.

"Shh. Let me finish. At the same time, you've got this soft spot that you only let certain people see, and it makes me want to hold on to you forever, so nothing ever hurts you again. You've hurt too much. I want to make a future of good stuff with you."

She wanted to die.

She wanted so much to be able to throw her arms around him and say *okay.*

"I thought when I didn't look like her anymore, you would get it, Cale. That I'm not her and you don't want me."

"I've never thought you were her. I take it back. The first moment I saw you in the E.R., I did a double take, but that's because it was from a distance. There's never been any confusion in my mind. When Noelle would have laughed and done something spontaneous, you bite your lip and think so hard I can practically see smoke coming out your ears. But I stopped comparing you two long ago." He took a step back. "You're beautiful with black hair. You're beautiful with blond hair. I don't care if you dye it bright purple. Shave it off. Try me."

He was saying everything right. If she'd been subconsciously testing him by changing her appearance, he'd passed with flying colors. Set the curve for every other man on the planet. Dammit, he was turning out to be the perfect man for her.

When she studied that face she loved, though, she couldn't get Noelle out of her mind. How could they build a future when she'd stolen it from her sister? How would she ever be able to live with herself?

"I can't," she whispered. "I'm sorry. I'm so damn sorry, Cale, but I can't get over the guilt."

The pain in his eyes cut into her and she struggled to breathe.

"I love you," she said, her voice stronger. "You're so easy to love. But I don't feel right about it. I wish I did."

He stared at her with imploring, heartbreaking eyes for a long moment. "We could work through it. You can do whatever you put your mind to—"

"Don't you think if I could I would have already? You're what I've wanted. But she got you first. And last." She shut up before she lost it.

Cale looked as though he was going to reach out for her and then ran his hands through his hair instead. He turned away, toward the water. The calm, beautiful bay water that didn't make anything okay tonight.

"This is stupid, Rachel!" He spun around, and the pain in his eyes was gone. Now they flared with anger. With his voice more in control, he said, "You're telling me that we love each other and yet we can't make this work?"

"Yes. Why can't you understand that there's a loyalty to my twin sister? We shared a womb, Cale. I knew her before I knew how to breathe."

"You've worked through so much. But you're just going to give up now? This isn't worth fighting for?"

"It's not a fight I can win," she said quietly. "I wish I could."

Cale swore crudely and squatted down as if the pain had knocked him over. He stayed that way, his head bowed, eyes closed, looking every bit as miserable as she felt.

Rachel needed to get out of there before she broke in two inside. "I'm gonna go. There's a bus due in..." She glanced at her watch, as if she had a clue what the bus schedule was. "Any minute," she lied, fully intending to walk home but knowing he would insist on driving her if he knew. "Goodbye, Cale."

As her sadness threatened to swallow her up whole, she turned and walked away.

CALE KEPT HIS HEAD down, fighting the need to watch her walk away. He didn't want that image burned in his mind.

Shit-fire, he'd never felt so powerless in his life. So close and yet so completely denied what he wanted, what was *right,* dammit. The sense of loss, yeah, he knew that like an age-old enemy, but his helplessness to convince Rachel she had nothing to feel guilty about...that was going to eat him alive.

The torment in her eyes would haunt him for the rest of his life.

That was when it hit him—she would never get on a city bus or any other kind of public transportation looking and feeling like she did. She was intensely private and would avoid it at all costs. When he finally looked up and squinted into the darkness in the direction of the nearest bus stop, which was two blocks straight over, she was nowhere. He was sure she was walking home alone in the dark even though the Culver house was a good distance southeast of here, probably close to two miles.

Leaving his truck, he jogged a block to the east. When he got to the corner, he looked to his right. Sure enough, a couple hundred yards away, Rachel headed along the sidewalk toward home and not the bus stop. He followed her, sticking to the opposite side of the street and keeping the same distance between them. There was nothing else he could say to her to change her mind, but he could at least ensure that she got home safely.

Then, after that, he could fall apart.

CHAPTER THIRTY-THREE

MAYBE RACHEL HAD finally done it.

Sawyer, who'd been hanging around more than usual the past two weeks, ever since the concert and the last time she'd seen Cale, come to think of it, swore she was going to work herself to delirium. As she stirred from her postwork nap, she wondered if she'd succeeded at last—and if so, what was so bad about it.

The dream about Noelle had been so realistic that if she believed in spirits and visits from the dead, she'd suspect her sister had been in the room with her. However, practical, levelheaded girl that she was, Rachel knew better.

The fact that she'd moved back into her room was likely the cause, but not because Noelle's spirit was visiting it, simply because she was surrounded by so many memories of her sister in spite of the changes she'd made to the room.

After the concert, after walking away from Cale, Rachel had been determined to move forward with her life. It felt as if the months she'd been home had been spent either spinning her wheels and getting nowhere or churning over the past. Necessary steps, she realized, but she couldn't stay there forever. So her first action had been to have a discussion with her supervisor, once again, to plead with him to let her work more shifts. During the weeks before the benefit concert, he'd gradually tapered her number of shifts down to what he considered "normal," and she'd been so wrapped up in handling her grief she'd barely noticed. He'd agreed to give her the maximum amount of hours each week, but it had taken no small sales job on her part.

The second step she'd taken was to change up the bedroom she and Noelle had shared enough to make it possible to walk in without being bombarded by the past. She and Sawyer had gotten rid of Noelle's bed and her vanity, and then Rachel had rearranged the remaining furniture to make the room look like a new place entirely. The walls were now a dusky purple color, also thanks to her brother, who was proving to be a rock of support in so many ways. The only thing remaining of Noelle's was the bookcase and a handful of her belongings that Rachel hadn't yet decided what to do with.

Still mired in the drowsiness of an uncharacteristically deep sleep, the sensations from her dream lingered. She kept her eyes closed and rolled to her side, curling into the feeling she'd had an actual conversation with Noelle. It had been on an inconsequential topic—she couldn't even put her finger on what it'd been about—but Rachel longed to continue it.

Her eyes popped open and she sat up on the edge of her bed, driven suddenly by that need to connect with her twin. Rubbing the sleep from her eyes, she went to the half bookshelf on the other side of the room and plucked out the item that drew her out of bed, that had been beckoning her for days. She hadn't been ready to tackle it until now.

Noelle's diary.

When she had the journal in her hands, there was a second's twinge of guilt left over from when they were teenagers. Noelle would scream if she knew Rachel was reading her most private thoughts.

Rachel shook it off. Noelle would never scream again. The woman who had had the thoughts contained in this thin, bright blue and green volume no longer had any thoughts at all. It was merely a link to the past. The connection to her sister she was yearning for.

Skipping over the warning specifically to her on the inside cover, Rachel opened the book as she padded back to her bed and slipped under the covers.

At first, she flipped open to a random page and practically inhaled the words in the familiar scrawl, her chest expanding with love and her heart breaking with loss at the same time. After a couple of entries, Rachel thumbed back to the beginning to read every single page, intent on spending the day with her beloved, beautiful sister.

Noelle had kept a journal since they were in grade school. Rachel remembered the Christmas they'd both received coordinating, girlie diaries, hers pastel blue with dragonflies on it and Noelle's apple-green with flowers. Rachel had used hers to play "school" with her plush animals, but Noelle had begun a lifelong semiregular habit. She'd not been the type to write every day; sometimes weeks passed between entries. She'd said she wrote when she had something to say, otherwise, what was the point? Rambling about nothing on paper was a waste of time to Noelle.

One thing Noelle did faithfully was note the date every single time she wrote—month, day and year. This particular volume began several years ago when Rachel was starting med school. There was the Christmas that Rachel almost hadn't made it home due to a snowstorm back in Iowa. She was touched by Noelle's worry that Rachel would end up all alone for the holiday and Christmas wouldn't be the same, and also her hope that she'd get to watch Rachel open the velvet-soft lavender-and-white-striped winter scarf Noelle had knitted for her. Rachel had ended up getting into the Brownsville airport after midnight on Christmas Eve, but she'd made it. And she adored the scarf to this day, having worn it every single winter-weather day when she'd lived in the north. The scarf had become like a toddler's security blanket to her, keeping her close to her twin even when she was so far away physically.

There was the long-distance argument they'd had over what to get their mom for Christmas four years ago, the time Noelle and Sawyer had visited Rachel at med school and the periodic mentions of some of Noelle's men over the years, though only the few she'd dated for more than a couple of months made the journal. A fight with their mother over whether a twenty-six-year-old woman should have a curfew even if she was living at home. Her sister's outrage made Rachel smile sadly because she remembered listening to Noelle rant about the same topic on the phone at the time.

And then she got to Cale. The date of the first entry that mentioned him was two months after they'd met. Rachel froze, her pulse pounding in her throat.

She couldn't handle this. Not now.

Sliding the book under her pillow, she threw the blankets back and rushed out of the room to take a shower, aching for distraction.

As she let the hot water rain down on her, she hated herself for being jealous. Hated that she could be remotely upset by Noelle's writings about the man she loved, when Noelle was gone now. Of course she'd written about the man who'd asked her to marry him. Why wouldn't she? Rachel had known Cale would be in the pages, but she'd managed to put it out of her mind as she'd relived the years through Noelle's eyes. By the time Rachel had reached the words *Cale Jackson is the most amazing man ever,* her guard had been down.

It occurred to her, as the hot water ran out due to her cowardly record-long shower, that she needed to read to the end.

Maybe experiencing Noelle's love for Cale by reading her innermost thoughts and feelings about him would help Rachel to let go of him. It could serve to further cement it in her head that, no matter how much she loved Cale and missed him, he'd been her sister's guy. She needed all the help she could get, because some nights, lying alone in her bed, the loneliness made it almost impossible not to call him or track him down just to say *hi.* Maybe reading Noelle's entries about him would help Rachel make peace with her decision not to give in to the temptation to take what he'd offered her.

It would hurt like hell, but then, so did her lingering thoughts of him, her periodic musings about what could have been.

With renewed determination, she dried herself off, dressed and went back to the journal.

Feeling less cozy and more guarded, she opted to sit on her desk chair to tackle the rest of the pages instead of lounging in bed.

She found herself nodding in agreement, her heart in her throat, as she read the first four entries about Cale. About his patience, his gentlemanly ways, her awe at what he did for a living, his tenderness. How he went out of his way for others, how he supported her no matter what.

And then she got to the fifth entry about Cale, which

started with *I called Rachel tonight to tell her Cale asked me to marry him.*

Rachel lifted her feet to the desk chair and wrapped one arm around her legs as she held the journal with the other. She closed her eyes for a moment, bracing herself to read all about the life-changing evening her sister had told her about back then. The entry, she gradually realized, though, was about Rachel, not Cale.

I love that girl so much. I wish she was here in person. Of course, I always wish that. When I told her Cale proposed, she was so happy for me it just made the best moment in my life all the more special. Not that I expected anything different from Rach. She's the most supportive sister a girl could ever ask for.

She said something along the lines of "every girl should be lucky enough to find her own Cale" and those words have stuck with me. I told her at the time my greatest wish was exactly that: that she find and fall in love with a man as wonderful as Cale. She deserves it so much. Crap, I'm tearing up just writing this. My only sadness in life right now is that my sister hasn't yet found her soul mate, the man who makes her get out of bed with a smile every morning in anticipation of seeing him. The man who gets her through the hard times and makes the good times ten times happier. The man who treats her like the amazing woman she is. And I hope she can set aside work and her ambitions and everything else she regularly lets get in the way of her most basic needs so that she can embrace love with the right man completely. That right there is my wish for my sis.

Rachel read the page five times, then skimmed the rest of the book through tear-blurred eyes, finding only two more entries came after it, neither of which mentioned her or Cale. She shut the book hard and dried her eyes.

She went back to the shelf and picked up the framed picture of her and Noelle—a photo they had taken of themselves on the beach the last time her sister had convinced her to make the trek with her so Noelle could do her night-swimming thing. It was one of four or five they'd taken and this one had always been Rachel's favorite of the bunch. In the others, they'd both been looking at the camera, but in this one, Noelle had turned her head slightly toward Rachel. The look in Noelle's eyes was so full of love it filled Rachel with warmth every time she saw it. Up until last week, when she'd finally "moved in" by unpacking the rest of her belongings and reclaiming this bedroom, she'd had it tucked away in a box because it had been too painful to handle. Now Rachel hugged it to her chest, the warmth flowing through her.

Rachel had found the man who made her smile, who got her through the tough times and made the good times better. She'd found her soul mate.

And her sister's diary entry felt almost like a push from the other side. Like permission for Rachel to have a future with him. To *let* herself have a future with him.

CHAPTER THIRTY-FOUR

SOMETHING CAUGHT CALE'S eye as he came out of Mariah's second-story apartment in a rush to avoid being late. A woman paced the sidewalk next to the parking lot, her head down, arms crossed, fist pressed to her lips as if she were absorbed in deep thought.

Was that…Rachel?

He couldn't help but think at first that he was hallucinating what he wanted to see, but he watched her as he descended the steps, and by the time he was on the ground level, he was certain it was her.

"Rachel?" He jogged to her, concerned that something was terribly wrong. Had something happened to her mother? Someone else?

She spun to face him, and the next thing he knew, she was running at him and throwing her arms around his neck, clinging to him.

"What's wrong, baby?" he asked, feeling panicked as he hugged her to him, bowled over by the feeling of having her in his arms again, whatever the cause.

Her shoulders began shaking and his concern grew. She buried her face in his shoulder, her sobs soundless, so he did the only thing he could do—held on for all he was worth and waited.

The next ninety seconds were eternal, but finally, she loosened her hold on him enough to wipe her eyes. "I'm so sorry," she said after gasping for air.

"What is it? Tell me what's wrong, Rachel."

Again, her shoulders shook, but now he could see her face and…she was laughing?

"Are you crying or laughing?"

"I don't know," she said, covering her mouth and nose with both hands and shaking her head. "Both. Oh, my God, I got ahead of myself. It feels so good to see you." She took another deep breath and sobered. "Sorry. Nothing's wrong. Yet. I need to talk to you."

Relief started to seep in at the announcement that nothing was wrong, but the way she was acting was truly bizarre. She was…giddy. He wondered if she was drunk, but he didn't smell alcohol.

"Okay. Where?" he asked. "Here?"

She glanced around just as one of his neighbors got out of his car, slammed the door and strode past them, nodding at Cale.

"Not here."

"My sister's upstairs but we can go inside if you want."

"Over there," she said, pointing at the playground equipment fenced in on three sides on a corner of the apartment property. Before he knew it, she was climbing the equipment to the top level.

He followed her, if for no other reason than to try again to find a hint of the smell of alcohol.

When she got to the highest tower, where the spiral slide originated, she stood, holding on to one of the bright red support rails and looking out toward the gulf. "Not a bad view here for the six-year-olds," she said.

Cale was surprised to catch a sliver of a glimpse of the beach between two buildings. "It's a better view than we have from the apartment, considering we have none. Rachel," he said, curiosity and a tinge of alarm making him impatient. "What do you want to talk to me about?"

She turned to face him, looked up at him with the eyes that got him every time and said, "Cale? I love you."

His heart stuttered and he narrowed his eyes, so caught off guard was he by the simple, to-the-point confession.

"I think I kind of started loving you the night we met, when you were my hero for introducing me to that other med student and trying to help me fit in."

His pulse thundered and he stood there speechless, waiting for the catch, or the *but* or…where she was going with this. He didn't dare hope. Did he?

She wove their fingers together and he kept his gaze on hers, trying to read her. "Rachel?"

"Yeah?"

"When you were pacing on the sidewalk over there, when I came outside… You were trying to plan out what you were going to say to me, weren't you?"

She laughed. "Maybe."

"What else you got?"

"I love you. You love me. We…should be together, don't you think?"

"Uh, yeah," he said slowly. "Last time I tried to make that point you ditched me." Unable to stop himself, he drew her closer, until their bodies touched, chest-to-chest, thigh-to-thigh. "And then I spent half the night following you home to make sure you made it safely, since that bus idea of yours didn't work out so well."

"Crap. Busted. You followed me? In your truck?"

"On foot. And once I saw your light go on in your house, I walked back to get my truck."

"Why in the…?"

"That love thing you mentioned. I knew you wouldn't get on a bus."

"I was fine walking by myself."

"I know. I saw." He smiled, his heart hammering and

his head feeling light and airy. "Could we get back to the matter at hand? You said you couldn't be with me. What changed in the past two weeks?"

She let his hand go and reached into her back pocket, producing a folded-up, ripped-out page. She held it out to him.

"A love letter?" he said with a goofy grin.

"Read it."

He unfolded the paper and recognized Noelle's feminine handwriting.

"I ripped that out of her journal," Rachel said, watching his face expectantly as he read.

He read about when Noelle had called Rachel with news of their engagement. A couple sentences in, he paused. "That must have been a tough phone call to handle."

She shrugged, never breaking eye contact. "In a way. You have to believe I was thrilled for her more than I can say…."

"I believe it completely. I got a sense of the bond between you two just from the way she talked about you. She would have been just as excited for you had the tables been turned."

"Read the rest."

He did and nodded the whole time, not surprised at all but yet again affected by the depth of the sisters' love for each other. When he finished, he handed it back to her. "Yeah."

"Yeah?" Rachel folded the paper and put it back in her pocket. "That's all?"

He pulled her into a tight hug and lifted her off the ground for a second, closing his eyes and inhaling the no-nonsense clean scent of her and feeling his chest expand with so much love. "She said the same things to me on more than one occasion. She loved you so much, Rachel. Wanted nothing more than for you to fall in love and be over-the-moon, crazy happy."

Rachel stared at him, her eyes crinkling with the broadest smile he'd ever seen on her. "I am. Over-the-moon, crazy happy. Or I will be."

"Will be?"

"I'm waiting for you to tell me we're okay. That we can have what she wanted me to have. What I've always dreamed of having." She thumped his chest lightly. "You're cruel."

He laughed and leaned down to kiss her, pouring all of his love into it and then some. "How's that for cruel?" he said minutes later when he finally broke the contact.

She took a second to catch her breath. "Your 'cruel' is definitely a start."

"Only a start?"

"I'm kind of wondering where we go from here."

There was no question in his mind about where they went. "So I'm late for an appointment," he said, conversationally.

Rachel narrowed her eyes and tilted her head in confusion, making him laugh.

"It's relevant, I promise."

"Where's your appointment?"

"My Realtor called me a couple of hours ago. There's a home right on the bay that's about to be listed. She's giving me an early heads-up because she made a killing on the sale of my beachside condo."

"Yeah?" she said, running her hand over his chest, goose bumps of excitement breaking out on her arms.

"Not many homes on the bay," he said.

"And they never come up for sale."

"Almost never. But the best part? Apparently this one

has its own little boathouse, just the right size for a couple of kayaks."

Rachel laughed and kissed him again. "It sounds perfect."

"Good. Because the mortgage payment's a little steep. I was thinking it'd be best if I had a roommate."

"A roommate?"

"There are three bedrooms, two baths. Not that big of a kitchen, so I'm looking for someone who doesn't love to cook."

She grinned.

"Plenty of room, though, in case that roommate were ever to be crazy enough to, say, marry me and make babies."

Her eyes sparkled, reflecting the joy he felt in every cell. "You might have a deal with the marriage thing," she said slowly, "but the babies… I would have to work up to that. It would require practice. Lots of it. And the other thing? I'm not about to get into this home thing sight unseen." Her tone was teasing now.

"Hold up. Was that a yes to marriage?"

"Was that a real proposal?"

"Yes."

"Then yes."

"If we hurry, we could probably catch the sun setting over the bay from the very-soon-to-be-ours deck."

"Sunsets are pretty good…if you have the right person to enjoy them with."

Cale stared into her eyes, all kidding aside. "It's taken me a while, but I definitely have the right person."

EPILOGUE

RACHEL SUDDENLY APPEARED in the back doorway of their home that led to the small yard between the house and the bay itself. Dressed chest-to-ankles in white. Looking…stupendously gorgeous.

Cale's eyes teared up and he wouldn't have been able to utter a word at that moment if he'd had to. She stood twenty feet away from him, with forty-some people between them, but when she lifted her chin at last and met his gaze with her beautiful blue one, the rest of the world faded away. Her strapless dress showed off her narrow shoulders and muscular arms. It hugged her breasts—revealing a hint of her luscious cleavage—gathered beneath, then billowed down in a fitted but not tight cut that showed off her curves and suited her more than a ruffly, flowy number ever could. The simple, silky material reflected the bright, midday sun. It would probably be difficult to look at it for long, but Cale wasn't proof of that because he couldn't take his eyes from her face.

Her once-again blond hair, which had grown out to her chin, was pulled back from her face. Her lips glistened with light pink gloss, and he couldn't wait to taste them, to seal the promise they were about to make to each other.

She was the perfect woman for him. She made her way down the white carpet with slow, sure steps in time with the tempo of the music. He knew how nervous she was at the prospect of being the center of attention, but, not surprisingly, she showed nothing of it on the outside. In fact, she couldn't seem to keep the smile off her face. For that matter, neither could he.

Sawyer, his best man, nudged him with his elbow and said, "You're a lucky man. And if you ever hurt her, you'll be an unlucky man…." Both men chuckled, having had the friendly discussion of what Sawyer would do to him if Cale ever let his sister down.

Rachel had almost reached him when Cale belatedly noticed Buck at her side. The old geezer had been beside himself when they'd asked him to give Rachel away, and he looked proud as a father now. When Cale stepped up beside Rachel to have Buck hand her over, so to speak, Buck's eyes sparkled, and he held on to her an extra two seconds, just to mess with Cale. Everyone who had gathered to share their moment laughed, and Cale pointed his finger at Buck as if to say he'd get him back. Then, as Rachel handed her bouquet to Mariah, the maid of honor, and entwined her arm with his, Cale's attention zeroed in on the woman he loved, and he lost all awareness of anything around them.

RACHEL HAD WAITED for about as long as she could—she couldn't stand it anymore.

"You," she said, pulling on Cale's hand. "Husband of mine."

The most amazing man in the world bent down and kissed her in reply, which started yet another round of howling from the raucous group of firefighters and spouses, all of whom had become so important to them both.

"Get a room!" Evan hollered when Rachel turned to face Cale full-on and put both her arms around him.

"It's not a bad idea, you know," Cale said privately to

her with the biggest, most boyish grin on his face. "It's what married people do."

Rachel laughed, feeling her cheeks warm under the bright sun. "True, but it's two in the afternoon. You'll have to wait."

He nipped at her nose and squeezed her side affectionately. "For you, I'll wait. But only for a few hours."

Now was the time, at last. "Come with me," she said, dragging him toward the table with the cake, which they and their guests had already devoured, past Evan and Selena; Derek, Macey and their nine-month-old daughter; past Clay, Andie and their daughter, Payton; and Faith and Joe, who was lavishing his own nine-month-old with love. As they went by her mom and Sawyer, who were sitting with Mariah, Buck and Cale's parents, her mother caught her eye and winked conspiratorially. When they walked by Scott, Mercedes, Charlie, Penn—who was an arson investigator and tended to socialize with their group, as well—and Penn's girlfriend, Nadia, the five guests held out their hands and Cale slapped each one in sequence, as if he'd just hit a home run.

Rachel picked up the mic, turned it on and tested it.

"So…I know a lot of times the bride and groom exchange gifts privately, but with my love of the spotlight and all, ha-ha, I wanted to do this in front of all of you. Because, thanks to this guy, all of you have come to mean so much to me. As a former loner, I really don't know what to do with so many friends except to say thank you. So thanks for being here to share our big day."

Several of the guys called out comments in fun as Rachel swallowed down the surge of emotion she hadn't expected.

"Anyway—" she turned to face Cale "—this dear, understanding, patient man has been so, so good to me and has put up with my insane work schedule for months without complaining. Much."

Laughter filtered throughout the group.

"And I'll admit, I pushed him by insisting on taking so many extra shifts, and yet he loves me, workaholism and all."

Cale gazed down at her and nodded helplessly, his love shining in his eyes, making her heart soar yet again.

"Because of my job and the fact that I haven't been there for quite a year yet, we weren't able to plan a honeymoon, and yet you never complained once."

Several of the women in the group said "Aww" in unison.

"The thing is, though…I haven't been completely honest with you."

Cale's smile faded slightly and he tilted his head. Raised his brows in question.

"We're leaving in—" she checked the dainty silver bracelet watch around her wrist "—approximately ninety minutes for our weeklong trip to New York City, where neither of us will be allowed to think for a second about work…except for the day I take you to the Fire Museum."

"Really?" Cale said, his face-splitting grin back. "You're mine for an entire week?"

"I'm yours for an entire lifetime."

"But I, uh, I'm scheduled to work three shifts."

"That schedule was a fake!" Joe, the captain and the one in charge of making the schedule, called out.

Cale looked at Joe in disbelief then back at Rachel. "Really? We're going on a honeymoon?"

"Your sister packed your bags. And all of our guests will now be understanding when we leave our own reception early."

"Wow." Cale pulled her to him and squeezed her so

tightly she became airborne. "I don't know what to say." He glanced at Joe again. "Thanks, Joe, for starters. And you…my beautiful, sneaky wife…" He shook his head and she could swear she saw moisture in the corners of his eyes.

"There's one last little thing," Rachel said when she was able to breathe. She no longer used the mic, figuring this was more personal, and probably everyone could hear her anyway, if they wanted to. "My work schedule? The double shifts? The extra days? I figured out a while ago that's not the way I want to live long-term, thanks, in part, to my mom and her sometimes-annoying wisdom. I did it these past few months with the sole purpose of saving up for our honeymoon, but…when we come back, I'll be working no more than four shifts a week. Like a normal person. I know you'll still have twenty-fours, but hopefully we'll have lots of time for *us.* More than we're used to."

"That," Cale said, as he reached down and grabbed her in a cradle hold before she knew what he was doing, "is the very best gift you could ever give me, Dr. Rachel Jackson."

* * * * *

COMING NEXT MONTH FROM

HARLEQUIN®

super romance®

Available July 1, 2013

#1860 BETTING ON THE COWBOY

The Sisters of Bell River Ranch • by Kathleen O'Brien

Brianna Wright has ventured to the Bell River Ranch to make peace with her sister. She's *not* here to be romanced by Grayson Harper—no matter how good-looking he is. But working together on the ranch proves he's more determined than she guessed, and he just might win...her!

#1861 A TEXAS HERO • *Willow Creek, Texas*

by Linda Warren

Abby Bauman has found her ultimate hero. Detective Ethan James brought her through a terrifying kidnapping, but will he be there for her in the days that follow—when she needs him most?

#1862 ONE-NIGHT ALIBI • *Project Justice*

by Kara Lennox

A disgraced cop. An heiress. A night of passion and a murder. Now top suspects Hudson Vale and Elizabeth Downey must fight their attraction *and* work together to prove their innocence by finding the real killer.

#1863 OUT OF HIS LEAGUE

by Cathryn Parry

Professional athlete Jon Farell is the nurturing type, and there's no one he'd rather have lean on him than Dr. Elizabeth LaValley. Though she seems to enjoy their kisses, she wants her well-ordered life back. Well, Jon will just have to show her how much fun a little chaos can be!

#1864 THE RANCH SOLUTION

by Julianna Morris

Mariah Weston keeps her distance from the city dwellers who visit her working ranch. Then she meets single dad Jacob O'Donnell and his troubled teenage daughter. Try as she might, Mariah can't get Jacob out of her thoughts, no matter how wrong for her he might be....

#1865 NAVY ORDERS • *Whidbey Island*

by Geri Krotow

Chief warrant officer Miles Mikowski fell for lieutenant commander Roanna Brandywine the first time he met her—but she's repeatedly turned him down. Now a sailor's unexplained death draws them both into an undercover investigation. And that means working together. *Closely* together...

YOU CAN FIND MORE INFORMATION ON UPCOMING HARLEQUIN® TITLES, FREE EXCERPTS AND MORE AT WWW.HARLEQUIN.COM.

HSRCNM0613

Navy Orders

By Geri Krotow

On sale July 2013

Chief Warrant Officer Miles Mikowski fell for Lieutenant Commander Roanna Brandywine the day he rescued her mother's cat. Too bad she's always turned him down. But now they're working together investigating a sailor's death and the attraction is growing. Then, one night to avoid detection, Miles kisses Ro...
Read on for an exciting sneak preview!

"That was a surprise." Ro's voice was soft but Miles heard steel in its tone.

He traced her cheek with his fingers. "I'm not sorry I had to kiss you."

"You did it to keep the wing staff from seeing us, didn't you?"

"Yes."

"Is this how you usually run an explosive ordinance op, Warrant?"

"Out in the field, the guys and I don't do much kissing." He saw her lips twitch but no way in hell would she let him see her grin. Ro was so damned strong. He knew it killed her to

HSREXP0613

let go of her professional demeanor, even in civvies.

"No wonder, because it would prove way too distracting. I hope you don't plan a repeat maneuver like that, Warrant."

"I do whatever duty calls for, ma'am."

She glared at him. She didn't usually show this kind of heat, and it took all his control not to haul her onto the bike and take off for his place.

"What we're doing will not call for that kind of tactic again, get it?"

"Got it," he replied. She'd enjoyed it as much as he had, he was sure of it. But this discussion was for another occasion, if at all. "It's time to get to work, Commander."

Will this *really* be the last time for that kind of tactic? Or will circumstances keep pulling Miles and Ro together? Find out in NAVY ORDERS by Geri Krotow, available July 2013 from Harlequin® Superromance®. And be sure to look for other books in Geri's WHIDBEY ISLAND series.

HSREXP0613